THE SHOALS

T.S. Markham

Published in the United States
Copyright © 2024 Timothy Tuttle
The Shoals
First Edition, November 2024

ISBN: 979-8-9914147-2-2

Dedication

I dedicate this book to the memory of my late wife. She was my muse and reason for being. Without her love, support, and guidance this novel would not have been possible. Thank you to my family both past and present and friends who have been there to encourage me along the way.

A special thanks to my editor, Liane Larocque of Mystic Canyon Publishing, who has inspired me to go above and beyond this book.

Prologue

Benjamin Blake had never experienced such excruciating pain. His right arm broke. It had snapped like a dry twig when he landed hard on the deck of the boat. His hand, which now dangled at his side, was separated at the wrist. He had been picked up and carried by the most massive man he had ever seen and then thrown onto the deck of his boat as if he were a rag doll. The man who had carried him sneered at Benjamin as he heard the sound of his arm breaking.

"Benjamin, you've got to excuse my friend Tank. He doesn't have a 'take it easy' button. Soon, the pain in your arm won't even matter."

Tank looked at Benjamin Blake, crossed his arms, and stared at him with hollow eyes that were as black as night and devoid of emotion.

"Benjamin, you are a gullible old cuss. Thankfully for us, you are. I have got to tell you, Benjamin, I was astonished when you bought this old wreck. You did an amazing job getting it back in shape."

Benjamin looked at the man he only knew as Mr. Jensen from the FBI and wondered who the hell he was.

"Don't worry, Benjamin. I have been following you for quite a long time. It was surprisingly easy to get a spare set of keys made. You really should be more careful about leaving things around."

He bent over and patted Benjamin Blake on the side of his face before pulling the set of keys out of his pocket and starting the motors. Within seconds, they were humming like a finely tuned instrument. Benjamin worried about what would become of the boat which he had spent almost every waking hour restoring. He'd spent two years rebuilding it. Refinishing the mahogany decks was the most challenging part of the restoration. He remembered how it felt after a year and a half into the rebuild when he turned the engines over for the first time. It was almost like the birth of a child. He had done what he set out to do—brought a run-down relic back to life.

Tears were now welling up in the corner of his eyes. He was thinking of his only child, who had been killed by a hit-and-run driver while riding her bicycle. She was beautiful, vibrant, headstrong and took direct aim at managing her own life. She had lived just twenty-eight short years. She was engaged to be married and had a promising career ahead of her. Her death seemed like such a waste to him. He had warned her repeatedly about riding after dark. Nevertheless, what child ever really listened to their parent? She thought she knew everything and wanted to conquer the world on her terms. So much like her mother, he felt.

As they backed away from the dock, he looked up at the night sky. Stars were shining as far as he could see. The Aurora Borealis was just beginning to be active. He tried to find the North Star, but the pain in his shattered right arm made focusing on anything challenging. He accepted the fact that he would soon be dead. He said a prayer for everlasting life with his wife and daughter, and that someone would discover what he had done and bring the people responsible for his death to justice.

The boat was slapping hard against the waves. Every time it sliced across one, Benjamin Blake's broken body bounced against the deck. He wanted to scream out in pain but could not. They had injected him with a drug, that made it impossible for him to move or speak. He thought back to when he got involved. The money they'd offered him was too much to refuse. He let his thoughts trail off to something his father had once told him when he was young: if it seemed too good to be true, then it most likely was. *Why didn't you heed your father's words?* he thought to himself.

The boat was slowing. Benjamin could see the Alki Lighthouse. Based on the stars and the light from the beacon, he knew they were near the shoals. Often, Benjamin would shut off the engines and drift just taking in the scenery. He never got bored or tired of it. Using the money was the only bright spot in the affair that would now cost him his life. The end of his life was near, and he knew it. The boat came to a complete stop.

"It's time to go for you, Benjamin. Unfortunately, you won't live to tell anybody about our little excursion. It seems such a shame we had to push you over the edge to get you to help us. Your daughter was quite a beautiful woman. Trust me, she never knew what hit her."

He wanted to scream, yell, and curse but couldn't. He wondered if they would leave his body on the boat. His answer came quickly. He was pulled up to a standing position like he weighed absolutely nothing at all. His captors moved him close to the rail of the boat, jammed a gun underneath his chin, and wrapped his right hand around it. His very last thought was, dear God, I am sorry for what I've done. I know I'm not worthy, so please accept a sinner into your house.

Chapter 1

The Rusted Harpoon

Detective Ken Fisher was so focused on the voicemail he had received before leaving work that he almost missed his turn. He spun the steering wheel as hard as he could to turn left into the Idle Brook Marina. The speed at which he was going was higher than the posted limit. The rear end of his red Chevy Camaro slid hard to the right on the pavement, barely missing a concrete planter that held the Marina sign and cascading layers of flowers. The force of the turn threw a shower of loose stone and gravel into and over the sign for the marina. He overcorrected the slide of his car, sending the rear end in the opposite direction, almost losing control of it. He turned to the right and shot down the aisle toward a parking spot at the end of the lot in front of a locked gate, which led to where his boat, the Salt Life, was moored. The car lurched to a stop and rocked back and forth for a few seconds. Getting out, Ken scanned the western sky. The clouds were turning dark and gray, and the wind was beginning to pick up.

Fisher's mood was as angry as the sky. He grabbed an overnight bag, slammed the door, and headed toward the locked gate. He quickly punched in a code and heard the pop of the electronic lock as it released. He passed through the gate, turned around, and shut it, making sure that it locked behind him. His boat was a Sea Ray Sundancer 450, a cabin cruiser which was moored in slip nine. It looked as sleek moored at the dock as it did at sea. Within a couple of minutes, Ken tossed his overnight bag over the boat's rail, climbed over, and jumped down, almost losing his balance on one of the many empty beer bottles that were everywhere on the deck. He took two steps toward the cabin and felt one of the many empty beer bottles shatter under his feet.

Looking at the mess that had been made on his boat, his mood became bitter and angry. He kicked empty beer bottles and cans out of the way, clearing a path to walk as he made his way to the door of the main cabin. He swung the door open and let out a loud groan seeing empty bottles and cans everywhere. The sink was piled high with dirty plates and glasses.

"John, what the hell did you do to my boat?"

Ken pushed his way further into the bowels of the boat. The door to the stateroom had been left wide open. His anger turned to rage when he saw the mess. He threw the overnight bag toward the headboard. Its impact shook the entire bed. Running his hand through his hair, he looked over at the carnage that just a few days ago had been a neat and tidy room. Blankets and sheets were piled on the floor at the base of the bed, and clothes were strewn all over the floor. He bent over and started picking up the clothes, carrying them to the closet.

There was a note taped to the full-length mirror on the closet door. Ken opened the door, threw the clothes in, and slammed the door. He reached over and flicked on the light so he could read the note better. It read:

Dear Ken,

I'm sorry that I left you a mess. I intended to clean it up but just ran out of time. I know that I told you that I would be the only one on the boat. At the last moment, some of my friends asked if they could come along. I just thought it would be easier to ask for forgiveness than get your permission. I promise that I will do my best to make it up to you.

John

Ken slammed his fist into the center of the note. The mirror behind it shattered from the impact. Shards of glass fell at his feet. He looked down and saw drops of blood forming on the carpet. He had cut his hand. Uttering a long string of curses, he rushed into the bathroom, looking for some bandages. Not finding any, he grabbed a small hand towel and a roll of duct tape and made a makeshift bandage.

"Shit!" Ken yelled as he bent over and picked up the note, which had fallen free. He wadded it up, threw the crumpled note as hard as he could, and then finished his tirade.

"John, the next time I see you, I'm going to make sure that I tell you that even though you're my brother, I think that you're just another asshole who likes to take advantage of people!"

Leaving his bag on the bed, he stormed out of the cabin and onto the deck and climbed over the rail. He headed back up the dock toward the Rusted Harpoon, which sat on the far-right side of the marina and commanded a view of the boats and the bay that led out into Puget Sound. A light, icy rain had started to fall and was stinging Fisher's face and neck. He turned the collar of his coat up to protect his neck and closed it at the points to cover as much of his face as possible. The walk to the Rusted Harpoon took longer than usual as the wind had strengthened considerably, slowing his pace.

Ken finally passed through the side door of the restaurant and surveyed the bar's surroundings. The Rusted Harpoon was always busy with patrons on Mondays because of Monday Night Football. Tonight, the crowd was lighter than usual due to the downturn in the weather. Pictures of sailing ships, mounted fish, harpoons, and nets hung on the walls. The one exception to the nautical décor was one oversized calendar emblazoned with the Seattle Seahawks Logo. Ken looked for a place to sit. He sat on the fifth bar stool and smiled at the girl behind the bar. She was about 5'5" in height, had a round, cherubic face, and sported glasses that hung around her neck by a chain.

"I like what you've done to your hair, Shannon."

"Why, Fish, I thought you would never notice."

"I'm a detective, Shannon; I notice everything."

"You notice everything Fish. Are you sure about that?"

"I'm sure, without a doubt, Shannon."

"Well, now I know why I've been losing sleep, Fish. You see, I cut my hair for the first time in ten years about five weeks ago. Some detective you are."

"You know, Shannon, women are all alike."

Shannon shook her head in disgust at Fish and walked away as Ken watched.

"Shannon, are you mad at me?"

"I'm not mad, Fish. I'm just disappointed."

"What do you have to be disappointed about?"

"I'm disappointed in the fact that most men don't know that women's real beauty is above the shoulders and not below."

"If it matters, I apologize that I haven't noticed."

"I'm not interested in your apology, so I guess you're just going to have to grovel a little."

"Can I have a menu while I practice groveling?"

Fisher looked at Shannon intently, studying her face for a moment, which turned quickly from a frown to a smile. Ken was counting the piercings she had in her ears, which tallied twenty-one in all.

"Now, this is a real breakthrough, Fish."

"What breakthrough would that be, Shannon?"

"That you noticed what I have above the shoulders. Can I get you a drink while you look over the menu?"

"I'm not drinking today."

"Are you sick, Fish?"

Fish didn't reply. He sat on the bar stool for the longest time, staring off into space. Shannon stood on the other side of the bar, waiting for him to say something.

"Earth to Fish, hey big guy, are you sure you're okay?"

Shannon bit her lip slightly and looked at the walls of the bar. Her eyes stopped and locked in on the oversized calendar.

"Oh, shit, Fish, I'm sorry. I didn't realize today was the 21st. What's it been four years?"

Fish tried to fight back the tears.

"Five. It's been five years since the fire. I still can't believe that my sister and brother-in-law are gone and that I can't find any trace of my niece. Why did this one have to be the one that I can't solve?"

"Well, Fish, maybe some things are meant to remain a mystery."

"This isn't going to remain a mystery, Shannon. It's not a closed case, not now, not ever."

"If it's any reconciliation besides being her uncle, from what I've heard, she has the best detective in Seattle working on her case."

"If I'm the best, this case would be solved, wouldn't it?"

"I can't answer that for you, Fish. It's just one of the demons you're going to have to handle. So, give me a shout when you're ready to order."

Fisher felt a hand slap him on his right shoulder. He spun around and grabbed the wrist of the man now standing in front of him. The man yelped in obvious pain.

"Are you trying to break my wrist?"

"Not at this moment."

"Is your hand okay? It wasn't like that earlier today. I hope I didn't cause that."

"You didn't, Mark. I owe this to my brother."

"If that's because of family, I sure as hell don't want to see what you do to your enemies."

"No, you wouldn't, Mark. What the hell do you want?"

"Look, Fish, I just wanted to buy you a beer."

Fisher let go of the man's wrist and turned around.

"My name is Fisher, Detective Ken Fisher. Only my friends call me Fish."

"I didn't mean to piss you off, Detective Fisher. Besides, I thought we were friends."

Fisher turned around and looked hard and long at the man standing in front of him, who looked like he had just stepped off the cover of the latest issue of Gentlemen's Quarterly.

"Mark, let's get one thing clear: you and I will never be friends."

"That hurts, Detective Fisher. I mean, after everything we've been through, I just thought..."

Ken cut Mark Brandt off mid-speech.

"Look, Mark, I will be the first to admit that you helped solve a case. But it wasn't from any great investigative journalism, and it wasn't from anything that deserved to win an award."

"Is that what you're pissed about, Ken? Is it the fact that I won an award, and you didn't even get as much as a commendation? You can rest assured that I didn't ask for an award."

"Mark, I could give a shit about the award. If you want to know why I'm mad, it's because you broke the story early. I asked you to wait one more day, and you wouldn't. You put my life and the life of my partner at risk. It will be a cold day in hell before I work with you again."

"That's too bad, Detective Fisher. I thought we made a good team."

"You and I will never make a good team, Mark. You're here because of my niece, aren't you?"

"Look, Detective, is it against the law for us to be in the same place at the same time?"

"No, Mark, it's not against the law. It's just that I come in here frequently, and I've never once run into you here. If you're here to ask me questions about my niece, I'll put my foot so far up your ass, I'll be tickling your tonsils with it. What is it you're here for, Mark?"

"Detective Fisher, I was supposed to meet this girl here. She's a no-show, so I thought maybe we could talk."

"Mark, I'm not surprised that she's a no-show. You have a reputation that precedes you."

Mark Brandt frowned at Detective Fisher's comment and then stood silent for a moment as if he was deep in thought.

"Detective Fisher, I want you to know I'm going to run a column tomorrow about your missing niece and the fire out at Hidden Shores. Maybe someone will read it who can shed some new light on what happened."

Fisher began thinking about his sister. He remembered when she called to tell him that she was pregnant with her first child. She couldn't wait for motherhood. It was as if it had been expressly created for her. Things started to change when her husband, Charles, started his own company. Contact with his sister began dwindling by leaps and bounds. He was heartbroken to find out that his beloved sister had perished in a fire in their new house.

"Get out of my face now, Mark. Go while the getting's good."

"Is that a threat, Detective? I would hate to report to your superiors that you threatened a law-abiding citizen with bodily harm."

Fisher's face turned beet red, and the veins in his neck started bulging as he clenched his right fist.

"Don't blow a gasket, big guy. I would hate to lose someone I consider my friend."

Fisher stepped closer to Mark Brandt until they were almost touching nose to nose. "Get out of my face now, Mark. Consider this your last warning."

"Alright already. I'm going. If you change your mind, I'll be in the booth over in the corner near the bandstand."

"Mark, it will be a cold day in hell before I change my mind. So, please go."

Mark threw his hands up in the air.

"Well, at least I tried to be nice, Detective Fisher."

Fisher glared at Mark, turned around, and sat down as Mark walked away.

"Hey, Fish, who the hell was the guy getting you all wound up?"

"That, Shannon, was Mark Brandt, the reporter."

Chapter 2

Connor Darke

Newer homes surrounded the Victorian-style house. Built at the turn of the twentieth century, its once-proud facade had been allowed to fall into disarray. Its grandeur was gone, carried away by years of biting wind and intense rainstorms. The snow, which had been falling with a vengeance, had all but stopped. The wind had picked up, causing a loose shutter to bang against the side of the house with a cadence that made Connor think of a waltz. *One, two, three*, he thought to himself as he listened to the wind whipping the shutter against the house.

Connor Darke rolled over and buried his body deep underneath the covers to ward off the cold and drown out the noise from the banging shutter, which matched his throbbing headache. The cell phone on his nightstand started buzzing incessantly. The vibrating of the phone caused it to fall to the floor. Connor reached down and picked it up, looking at the number displayed on the cell phone. Thinking to himself, *it's too early, Mother; you need to leave me alone.*

Connor's thoughts turned to the last conversation he'd had with his mother. He knew there wouldn't be much that happened in his life that his mother wouldn't know. There was one thing he hadn't shared with his therapist. He hadn't told him about the random voices that drove him to be a marriage psychologist. It had helped his insights into what was at the heart of the matter between married couples and had become voices with visions. Trying to come to grips with the images in his head had driven him to drink heavily. Admitting himself to a clinic to dry out was the hardest thing he had done in his life. The visions had subsided while he was in the clinic, but ever since he moved into his grandmother's house, they had come back with a vengeance. Connor started running again because he was able to clear his mind and shut the door to the visions. He looked at the clock on the wall; it was 11 a.m. He turned his cell phone back on and called his mother.

"Connor, are you still in bed?"

"I am if it matters, Mother."

"Well, of course, it matters. Connor, are you drinking again?"

"What makes you think that, Mother?" Connor almost didn't want to hear what he knew his mother would say.

"Because you have a history, Connor, and I'm your mother, and I care."

"History, that's it, Mother? No long list of reasons? No twenty-minute dissertation on my failings and shortcomings? Why the sudden change in tactic, Mother?"

"Connor, John thinks that I may be part of your problem."

"Mom, John is still my therapist, so I am going. I don't want to regurgitate the conversation we had last night."

"But, Connor, there is so much that I want to talk to you about."

"Mom, I am getting up to go for a run, so I am letting you go, goodbye."

Connor ended the phone call with his mother, stood up, hurried to his dresser, and got socks to wear. He grabbed his sweatsuit and put it on, and he donned a ski cap and gloves to keep warm. Walking out the front door, he picked up the newspaper, which was lying at his feet, and turned to put it inside the house. Glancing at the front page, he noticed a picture on the bottom of the page. It was a picture of a young girl. The same girl that had been haunting his dreams. He felt confused and conflicted. He read the first few lines of the newspaper article quickly which stated that Charles Surly, the owner of Gentec, a genetics company, and his wife died when they couldn't escape a fire that consumed their new home. The Surly's daughter Cassie is still missing, and if you have seen the girl in the photo, please call the 800 number at the end of the article.

He started running. His thoughts centered on the call with his mother. He felt hurt that his mother hid her relationship with his therapist. The air was brisk and cold, but he hardly noticed as he pushed himself harder than he ever had before. He headed down the hill toward Colvin Ave. and Manley Field House. On his way down, his eyes fixed on a girl who had left her dormitory and was heading toward the university bus stop. Immediately, the vision of the young girl who was on the front page of the morning newspaper and had been haunting his sleep roared into his brain like a freight train.

As soon as the vision appeared, it went away. It was replaced immediately by the image of another girl, then another, and another. All in all, he mentally counted the images of thirty-four different girls. Over and over again, the visions appeared in his head like a spinning top that wouldn't stop.

Connor pushed to quicken the pace of his running, hoping it would stop the endless stream of images. After a few minutes, he became acutely aware of his heartbeat pounding in his ears and mentally started counting the beats of his heart. Quickly as they came, the images of the girls were gone. Sucking in the cold icy air, Connor pressed on running with a clear head. He looked around and realized that he had run farther than he had initially intended, which always happened. He turned around and headed home, running hard.

Connor started to question the reason for the visions when a new image became clear and focused in his mind's eye. He saw a tall man whose hair was dirty and stringy. There was a long, jagged scar running down his face. The man in Connor's mind turned and looked at him as if he were searching the depths of Connor's soul. His long icy, stare was emotionless and utterly devoid of life. The vision disappeared within a few minutes. Connor rounded the turn for his house and noticed a black car parked in his driveway. He looked at his watch but didn't stop in front of his house. He continued to walk to the end of his block, turned around, and walked back. The windows on the car were tinted dark, making it hard to tell if anyone was inside. He stopped to unlock the front door to his house and heard a door on the car open. He turned around to see a man he did not recognize standing there. Connor sized up the man quickly. The man was about 6' with a medium build and wore round, wire-rimmed glasses that made him look studious and nerdy. His mustache and goatee were neatly trimmed.

"Judging by the look on your face, Mr. Darke, the answer to what you're thinking is a resounding no," the man spoke in impeccable Queens English.

"You seem to have me at a loss. You know who I am, but I have no clue as to your identity."

"My apologies, Mr. Darke. I am Hamilton Gardner, Mrs. Gertrude Lane's aide."

"You said that the answer to what I was thinking was no. Are you sure you know what I was thinking?"

"As I approached the house, you were sizing me up, Mr. Darke, trying to determine if you could triumph over me if needed. I assure you, it would have gone badly. I am here to bring you to Mrs. Lane's estate for lunch in one piece. It is exactly what I intend to do."

"To whose estate am I going?"

"Didn't you read the invitation sent to you, Mr. Darke?"

"I'm sorry. I haven't opened any mail in the last few days."

"Had you read the invitation, you would have already known Mrs. Gertrude Lane has invited you to her estate on Cazenovia Lake. Your run was impressive, by the way."

"In what way did you find my run impressive, Mr. Gardner?"

"Well, based on the fact you just finished the length of a marathon in almost record time for your age group, I would say it was most impressive of you, old chap.”

“So, how did you know I ran twenty-six miles?”

“Mr. Darke, I am paid to know these kinds of things. You have a daily routine of running. Because you are a creature of habit and always start your run at noon unless it’s raining, it was easy for me to know when you would return to your domicile.”

“But I don’t always run the same distance.”

“As I said, you’re a creature of habit. On odd days, you run ten miles and perform wind sprints. On even days, you run twenty-six miles. Today you ran it quicker than you have in the past.

“Mr. Gardner, you’ve been keeping tabs on me?”

“Yes, I have, at the request of Mrs. Lane.”

“What is Mrs. Lane’s interest in me?”

“Mr. Darke, if I told you, it would spoil all the fun. You wouldn’t want me to do that, would you?”

“No, I guess not, even if it is at my expense.”

“I assure you, Mr. Darke, you will be returned later this evening in a perfectly safe condition.”

“In any case, I need time to take a shower, so I guess I’ll drive myself there.”

“You can if you wish, but Mrs. Lane wanted you to be able to enjoy this glorious day. We rarely see the sun. Since I am supposed to drive, why don’t you take advantage of the situation?”

“Fine, but you will have to wait a few minutes as I desperately need to shower and change into some suitable clothes. Why don’t you come inside and wait while I do?”

Once inside, the man removed his hat, revealing he was completely bald. He also had a short-upturned nose. Connor softly chuckled to himself as he seemed to be a cross between Mr. Clean, an owl, and one of the three little pigs. Therefore, he decided Hamilton would be the most appropriate nickname for him.

"Mr. Gardner, you can wait in the Hall of the Dead while I get myself cleaned up."

"Why on earth do you call a room the Hall of the Dead, Mr. Darke?"

"All the people in the portraits in there have been dead an extremely long time."

Connor opened the two French doors that shut the room off from the rest of the house. Hamilton Gardner stepped into the room and exclaimed.

"My isn't this room quaint."

"Mr. Gardner, would you like me to prepare some tea before I go upstairs."

"That won't be necessary. I'll be just fine waiting here."

Thirty minutes later, Connor was standing at the entrance of the Hall of the Dead, wearing blue jeans with a white shirt with alternating blue stripes and holding a winter jacket. His wavy black hair was short and parted in the middle.

"I am ready if you are, Mr. Gardner."

"Good, Mr. Darke, let's get going. Mrs. Lane is anxiously awaiting your presence."

Connor got into the passenger side of the Tesla S series. "What a nice car, Mr. Gardner."

"This is one of Mrs. Lane's many cars. She wanted me to drive this one so you would be comfortable. From what I know, you have a nice collection yourself, Mr. Darke."

"I own a few different cars. I collect them for their looks."

"Mr. Darke, of the automobiles you own, what is your favorite?"

"My favorite car is my 2011 Morgan Super Arrow Eight."

"Morgan's are nice automobiles, aren't they? I own a 1942 Morgan Roadster myself. It's not nearly as nice as the Super Arrow, but it's just as fun to drive."

"I know Mrs. Lane is a noted philanthropist, but I'm not sure what she would want from me."

"As I said before, Mr. Darke, you just have to wait and see."

"Mr. Gardner, what part of Britain are you from?"

"I am from Tudberry, in Essex. I was an assistant to Mrs. Lane's husband. I promised him before he died that I would stay on with his wife."

"Do you like living in the States?"

"We Brits refer to it as the colonies. I find living here positively smashing. While I was waiting for you to get ready, I took a stroll around your first level. The new woodwork is beautiful. Did you do it?"

"The detail in the woodwork belongs to my uncle, JC."

"Ah, that would be your Uncle John Carleton, who goes by JC because his passion is the Bible. I've been to some of his Bible study sessions. His knowledge of the Bible is amazing."

"What else do you know about me?"

"I know practically everything there is to know about you."

"I'm quite sure you don't know everything there is to me."

"Try me if you don't believe me."

"Okay, what was the name of my fifth-grade teacher?"

"Mr. John Sanders, who has been married to his wife Jane for forty-one years. He retired eight years ago. I can give you his address if you'd like."

"That won't be necessary. What was the name of my first girlfriend?"

"Alice Haynes."

"My first dog, what kind of dog was it?

"You got your first dog in 1988. He was a Husky and Collie mix you named Skippy. If you want to keep asking me questions, Mr. Darke, I can keep answering them until you get tired of asking them."

"I think it would be fruitless, Mr. Gardner, don't you?"

"Mr. Darke, I do, but you are welcome to go on asking."

"I find all of this a little unnerving, Mr. Gardner."

"I am sorry if I've made you uneasy, Mr. Darke."

"Uneasy isn't quite how I would put it, Mr. Gardner. You aren't some crazed person who got pissed off over one of my books, are you?"

"My word, heavens no. I know about your books, but I've never read them."

Hamilton Gardner pressed a button on the steering wheel. The interior of the car filled with the sound of "Hymn of Hope" by Secret Garden.

"I suppose that I shouldn't be surprised that you know my favorite performing artist. Should I?"

"Mr. Darke, I know everything there is to know about you."

The remainder of the ride out to the Lane estate, which was on a bluff on the east side of Cazenovia overlooking the lake, was without incident and serene.

As they arrived, two massive iron gates that had a giant monogrammed "L" in the middle swung open. The car began a slow winding climb up to the Lane manor house.

Connor wondered if calling the palatial estate spread out before him a house was the right term for it. He could see a lot of smaller outbuildings off to the right and behind the expansive mansion. *Quite impressive,* he thought.

The car pulled up in front. Hamilton quickly jumped out, opened the car door, and led Connor into the Estate House. The massive set of walnut doors opened into a vestibule that led into a long hallway with a marble floor that had a red rose with pink tips set in it. There was an incredibly ornate rack with the face of an angel carved at its peak for placing umbrellas, coats, and hats immediately to the left. Hamilton led Connor into a library with a vaulted ceiling covered with the paintings of angels. There was a double set of French doors that opened to a veranda with a sweeping view of the lake.

Hamilton looked at Connor and stated, "I must leave you as I have other duties to do. Mrs. Lane will be with you shortly, so please make yourself comfortable."

Connor decided to peruse the impressive collection of books in the library. He slowly chuckled to himself as he came across multiple copies of his book on marital help he had written. Connor worked his way over to a brass telescope resting on a tripod. He bent over and peered through the eyepiece. The telescope was adjusted so someone could watch the various activities out on the lake. It was a bright day, and the sun rays reflected off of the icy surface of the lake that danced, glistened, and sparkled in an almost iridescent fashion.

Chapter 3

The Seattle Police Department

Ken Fisher could tell the weather had worsened. His boat was being battered hard at its mooring. He rolled over in bed and picked up his cell phone to look at the time. It was 4:30 in the morning. He groaned twice and decided to head to work early. It was the fifth anniversary of the loss of his sister and brother-in-law. He had already planned on spending the day going through the cold case file, looking for any small detail or scrap of evidence that he might have overlooked. He doubted he would find anything new but had to try. Looking for some evidence that might lead him to locate his niece was the least he could do to honor the memory of his sister.

Ken got dressed and headed up the dock to the parking area. His car was underneath one of the lights that illuminated the parking area. He could see that a thin sheet of ice was covering the windows. Getting to work would take longer than usual. Due to the inclement weather, the traffic on the ride in from the marina was lighter than usual. When Ken arrived, there were no other cars in the parking lot. *Thank God,* Ken thought to himself as he punched in his entrance access code. *I'll be able to work in quiet for an hour or more.*

Ken's office was on the cold side. The heating systems would start the warm-up of the building around six-thirty. Ken hung up his jacket, removed a sweater from the hangar next to it, and put it on. His first course of action was to head to the cold case file room in the basement. He bounded down the stairs, taking two steps at a time as he went down. He flicked on the hall light switch and walked to the storage room. Stopping at the entrance, he punched in the access code and opened the door. Looking into the room, he let out a loud gasp as he scanned the room. File boxes were piled all over the floor. Finding his sister's case file might take a while. Luckily, whoever had removed the boxes from the shelves had not done much to disturb their order. Within fifteen minutes, Ken had the contents of his sister's case file arranged in neat and tidy piles on the table in the main floor conference room. There were separate piles for his sister, brother-in-law, and niece, one for eyewitness reports and another for the arson investigator. He knew the contents of all the documents like he knew the back of his hand, but he had to go through them again for his sister's sake. *She would do the same for me,* he thought to himself. *She would kick over every rock multiple times until there was nothing left.* Today would be his turn to kick rocks. He picked up a bag containing a small teddy bear pin and sighed, wondering if his niece had left it behind on purpose.

He was deeply engrossed in reading the coroner's report when he heard a familiar voice.

"Morning, sunshine."

"What the hell are you doing here so early, Hawk?" Ken looked up and stared at his partner, Eric

Steinbrenner, standing in the doorway of the conference room.

Eric stood 5'10" and was 185 pounds of lean, trim muscle with curly blonde hair. He had a three-inch purplish scar on his left cheek that he'd received from an assailant while saving a woman from an attempted rape. His nose looked like an Olympic ski jump. To say his nose was a big beak was a massive understatement. It was guarded, however, by two of the keenest emerald-green eyes alive. Steinbrenner, or Hawk as his friends called him, never missed any details, no matter how small.

"Look, Fish, I knew you would be in early, working on your niece's case. I thought I would come in and give you a hand."

"Thanks, Hawk, I appreciate it."

"Any time, Fish. It's the least I can do. Do you want some coffee?"

"I would have to be dead to drink a cup of coffee. Some tea would be great."

"So, what did you do to your hand?"

"You know how I told you yesterday that my brother sent me a text message apologizing for the way he left my boat?"

Yeah, you went out of here like a bat out of hell. You didn't hit your brother, did you?"

"I would have liked to, Hawk, but he was long gone. I took my frustration out on a mirror in the stateroom."

"I guess those sessions on controlling your emotions aren't working very well, are they?"

Ignoring his partner's comment, Ken stood, walked out of the conference room, and went over to the counter where the coffee was brewing. He grabbed a mug, put a tea bag in it, and filled it with hot water, dunking his teabag on the way over to the window overlooking the street. He watched the traffic move slowly from one intersection to the next. The rain had begun to bead up on the window.

"Why do I have to live in one of the rainiest places on God's green earth?" he muttered. "Hawk, did you get it finished?"

Hawk was walking toward Fish. "Did I get what finished?"

"The stupid car you took the last two weeks off to finish."

"First of all, Fish, it's not a stupid car. It's a 1938 Cadillac Roadster, and yes, I did. If you look below to your right, you can see it."

Fish peered out.

"From what I can see from here, it looks great."

Fisher's cell phone began to ring. He pulled it out of his pocket as he walked back into the conference room.

"Who the hell is calling me this early? Shit!" Exclaimed Detective Fisher.

Detective Steinbrenner looked at his partner.

"It's my favorite reporter. I might as well answer, or he won't leave me the hell alone."

"Detective Ken Fisher, how can I help you?"

Listening intently for a moment, he asked. "What the hell do you want, Mark?"

Mark Brandt's voice had a nervous tone to it.

"I need to meet with you ASAP, Detective Fisher."

"You know it's early, Mark. I am technically not even on the clock yet. So, you want to meet, for God's sake, why?"

"I'm sorry, I just can't talk about it over the phone, Detective Fisher."

"You don't want to talk about it over the phone, When do you want to meet?"

"As soon as we possibly can, Detective."

"What's the urgency?"

"Look, Detective Fisher, you'll understand once I get there."

"Fine, how about we meet here at the office? So, help me, if you are coming here to talk about my niece's case, I will put my foot so far up your ass you will wish you had never been born."

Hawk looked over at his partner and best friend and said, "Does someone need a refresher course on phone etiquette?"

"Damn it, Hawk, you get on my nerves sometimes."

"I'm sorry, Fish. I was just trying to lighten the situation a little."

Looking at his partner, Fish quickly flipped him off.

"What was that for?" asked his partner.

"I'm sorry, it's just that damn Mark Brandt from the *Seattle Times* gets to me. I ran into him last night at the Rusted Harpoon."

"Was he there to gloat about yesterday's award ceremony?"

"He said that he was there to meet someone. He also told me that he is going to run the story about the death of my sister and her husband again. It's been five years, and he runs an article in the Seattle Times every year on the anniversary of the fire. He burns my ass, no pun intended.”

“You shouldn’t let him get to you, big guy.”

“I know, Hawk, I shouldn’t. But he thinks we dropped the ball on the investigation. The guy gets lucky and strings together some good investigative reporting, wins an award for it, and suddenly everybody and their brother thinks he’s the damn ‘Shell Answer Man.’ Somehow, he can get information nobody else in law enforcement can. My niece’s disappearance is still not solved, and Mark Brandt thinks we screwed up. I, for one, am not so sure that we didn’t.”

“Well, Fish, I think for the most part the guy is a bloody idiot and hinders police investigations more than he helps them. Look, we’ve done all that we could.”

“Have we? I’m not so sure.”

“I think we’ve done our best.”

“Hawk, maybe this time our best just isn’t good enough.”

“I don’t know what we could have done differently. We’ve spent over two years investigating the case.”

“Maybe two years wasn’t enough.”

“Fish, we’ve looked in every nook and cranny. There isn’t a lead we didn’t chase until we exhausted it or a rock we didn’t kick over. All roads have led us to the same point—she is simply missing. Case closed.”

Fish’s face was beet red, and the veins in his neck were bulging out. He slammed his fist down on the desk.

"Look, Hawk, she's my niece, and until I find some trace of her, this investigation will never, ever be over."

"Take it easy. I know how important this case is to you. I plan on staying the course until we find her. It's been a while since we circulated an updated image showing what she would like today. Why don't we get Jan to update her picture and get it circulated?"

"That's a great idea—let's do it."

The words excuse me came from a man standing in the doorway of the conference room. Fish and Hawk turned their heads toward the door simultaneously.

"Mark, how did you get here so fast?"

"I was already in the lobby when I called you, Detective Fisher," Mark answered, stepping into the conference room.

"What the hell happened to you, Mark? That's not what you looked like when I saw you at the Rusted Harpoon last night."

Mark Brandt's face was a mass of black and purple bruises. There were stitches on his left eyebrow, his right eye was almost swollen shut, and his lips were puffy.

"Well, Detective Fisher, you should have stayed around for the show. I did my best impression of a punching bag."

"I hope you pressed charges."

"I decided not to, and I prefer to leave it at that for the moment. I need to tell you what happened at work yesterday."

Fish pointed to his partner. "Eric and I are all ears. The floor is all yours."

"Yesterday, I was sitting at my desk, writing my daily column, when Greta, our receptionist, called to tell me I had a visitor in the lobby. I went downstairs to see the most beautiful woman I have ever seen standing in the lobby." Mark opened his briefcase, removed an 8" by 10" picture, and slid it across the table.

"Wow, she is stunning," Hawk said.

"As I started to tell you, the woman in this photograph was standing in the lobby of the newspaper yesterday. She introduced herself as Samantha Blake. We exchanged some idle chit-chat as I gave her the once, maybe two or three times look over. She then proceeded to tell me that she was not interested in being one of my many conquests."

"Based on your reputation, it must have made you feel a little putout."

"No, it didn't bother me. Besides, you can't win all the women, if you know what I mean."

"What was she after?"

"She told me that she knew I was a good investigative reporter and wanted me to investigate the murder of her father."

Detective Fisher let out a loud, guttural laugh.

"What's so funny, Detective?"

"Nothing. Did she tell you who her father was?"

"She said, Benjamin Blake."

"Did she say when and where it happened?"

"No, she didn't, Detective. I told her it was a matter for the police to investigate."

"What was her reply?"

"She said she couldn't trust the police and asked if I would please help her. I told her I was on my way to an appointment, so she asked if I could meet her at the *Rusted Harpoon* at 6:00 pm. She thanked me for listening to her and said she would be there. Right before I left work, I checked the internet to see if there were any reports of a person named Benjamin Blake being murdered recently in the Seattle area. I found no reports at all. I waited at The Rusted Harpoon until seven-thirty for her to show up. That's when my face got used as a punching bag."

"Did the thought occur to you that maybe this woman showed up in the lobby because her job was to lure you there?"

"I can't tell you what I don't know, Detective."

"What can you tell us?"

"I came here to tell you what happened this morning. When I got to work this morning, I decided to do an internet search on Samantha Blake. If you have a computer in here, I can show you what I found."

Fisher opened a large closet door. There was an array of electronics inside door, including a computer. Flipping a switch, a large panel in the wall slid open to reveal a huge monitor. He typed the name Samantha Blake into the search bar. After a few seconds, it returned a hit. Fish clicked on the first listing. The same picture Mark Brandt had brought with him popped up. Next to it was an article about Samantha Blake.

"Holy shit! What the hell is going on here, Mark? Did you concoct this bullshit story for the fun of it?"

"I know what you're thinking. I swear to you, as I stand here living and breathing, I talked with this woman yesterday. God as my witness, she was in the lobby of the Times. Tom Davis, our sports editor, also saw her. Greta, our receptionist, called me to tell me she was in the lobby. Please feel free to talk to them. I'm sure they will corroborate what I'm telling you."

"We might do that."

"Hell, Tom Davis even asked me for her phone number."

"Mark, you're standing here telling us yesterday you talked with someone who was supposedly killed in a hit-and-run vehicle accident."

"Yes, that's what I'm telling you."

"Maybe the woman you saw yesterday just looked a lot like her, or maybe she was a close relative like a cousin or sister who closely resembled her. You know, I've heard that almost everyone has a body double. Maybe someone found Samantha Blake's body double and sent her your way."

Mark Brandt became agitated.

"Look, guys, I know what I saw and what two other people saw. I saw Samantha Blake yesterday."

"Maybe she isn't dead."

"Hey, Fish, maybe, just maybe, she faked her death," Detective Steinbrenner offered.

Mark opened his briefcase, extracted a DVD, and handed it to Fisher.

"What's on this?"

"This is a copy of the surveillance video from the Times taken yesterday. It is a composite video from six different camera locations in the lobby. There are no places to avoid being captured on film."

"Why is this important?" Hawk asked,

"It's important because she is not in the video."

"What do you mean she's not in the video?"

"Look, I know what I saw, Detective, and I also know that she's not in the video. Other people will also swear to what they saw yesterday. If it had been someone who looked like her, she would be in the video, and she is not. I am going to stick with my original theory somehow, someway, I talked with the ghost of a dead person yesterday."

"Gee, Fish, maybe we should have Mark talk with that guy you're always talking about."

"Just who would that be, Hawk?"

"Come on, Fish, you know as well as I do that Mark should talk with the one, the only 'Love Doctor.' He might be able to help Mark in more ways than we can."

"Look, guys, when you have finished picking on me, I want to say that I saw a woman who is dead, and no one can convince me that I didn't."

"Maybe you should have called Ghost Busters Mark. I bet they could help you better than we can," chuckled Hawk.

"Look, Detectives, I saw Samantha Blake yesterday."

"Relax Mark. It's just that I don't quite understand what it is you would like us to do for you."

"Well, Detective Fisher, I was hoping maybe you could have this disk analyzed."

"Analyzed for what? We don't have any ghost detection software."

"Can you have someone look at it to see if someone altered it?"

"I suppose we could."

"If it hasn't, I have no clue as to what to do."

Fisher pressed one of the buttons on the phone. A female voice answered.

"This is Fergie."

"Hey, Fergie, this is Ken Fisher. Would you please come up to the main conference room. I need you to examine something."

"I'll be there in a couple of minutes, Ken."

"Mark, we can take a look at this and let you know if we find anything. Unless we turn up a body, then I don't think we will be able to help you."

Three minutes later, a female voice came from the doorway. "What have you got for me, Ken?"

"Fergie, this is Mark Brandt from the Seattle Times. Mark this Sarah Ferguson, our technical specialist."

"You wouldn't happen to be love 'em and leave 'em Mark Brandt, Seattle's most eligible bachelor, would you?"

"Yes, I am," Mark admitted, giving Ferguson the once over.

"I know what you're thinking, Mark. I am not interested in becoming another of your conquests."

"Now, Fish, what is it you would like me to do for you?"

"Fergie, I need you to examine this surveillance video from the Seattle Times," Fisher explained.

"What are you looking for?"

"Just look at it and see if you think there was any way it might have been altered."

"No problem. I can probably have an answer sometime later today, but by tomorrow for sure, if it's okay?"

"That would be great." Picking up the disk, she quickly exited the room.

"Mark, we will let you know what we find. Can we call you at the office?"

"Here's my business card. My cell phone number is on the bottom. I prefer you to use it to contact me if you don't mind."

"No problem. Detective Steinbrenner will see you out."

"You know, Fish, maybe this would be an excellent opportunity for you to bond with the Love Doctor. If he is a psychic, maybe his dead people can talk with Mark Brandt's dead people," Hawk said, letting out a resounding laugh.

Hawk stopped in the doorway, turned, looked back at his partner without saying anything, and stared.

"Hawk, were you expecting me to say something? If so, don't hold your breath waiting."

"No, Fish, I guess I wasn't."

Chapter 4

The Coast Guard

The phone at the conference room table rang. Fish answered.

"Hello, this is Fish."

"Fish, is Hawk with you?"

"Not at the moment, Caleb, but he should be right back."

"Good. I need to see the two of you immediately."

"We'll be there in a couple of minutes."

In less than five minutes, Fish and Hawk were standing in the doorway of their boss Caleb Clarke's office on the 8th floor.

"I want you two to head over to the Coastguard station. The base commander called and said one of the patrols is bringing in a boat they found stuck on the shoals near the Alki lighthouse with no one on board. They are concerned about what they found and have asked for our assistance. I want you guys to get your butts over there and find out what's going on. You're to ask for a Captain Danny Stevenson."

Both detectives stood at the same time and exclaimed, "We're on our way, Boss."

"Let me know what you find when you get there."

"It's too bad it's raining, Hawk. We could walk over to the coast guard base. It's only a mile away."

"I thought we could take my car."

"Are you sure that I'm worthy since it's an antique?"

"The way I look at it, you'll look good in it since you're almost as old as it."

"Be careful, Hawk. I'm still capable of giving you a run for your money."

US Coast Guard Base Sector Seattle

It took longer to get to Hawk's car than it did to get onto the Coast Guard base. They stopped at the main gate. Hawk rolled down his window, the sentry leaned over and spoke.

"Nice car, gentlemen. Please state the nature of your business."

"Detectives Steinbrenner and Fisher with the Seattle Police Department. We are here to see Captain Stevenson," Hawk answered, presenting their badges.

The guard wrote down the badge and license plate numbers. "You gentlemen can proceed to the second stop sign and turn left. At the next intersection, turn right and go to the end of the building, where you will find parking spots. Captain Stevenson is on the Coast Guard Cutter Albemarle, which just tied up at pier 52. It will be right in front of you when you get out of your car."

It took about ten minutes to find a parking spot. The Cutter Albemarle was precisely where the guard said it would be. The Albemarle was sleeker than its counterparts—it was the newest boat assigned to Coast Guard Sector Seattle.

"It's quite an impressive-looking boat, isn't it, Fish?"

"It sure is, Hawk. Shall we get to it?"

A member of the crew stopped them from walking up the gangplank.

"Can I help you, gentlemen?"

"I am Detective Fisher, and this is my partner, Detective Steinbrenner. We are here to see Captain Danny Stevenson," Fish said as the detectives presented their badges.

"If you gentlemen will wait here, I will get Captain Stevenson for you."

Before long, a brunette about 5'8" with her hair in a braid that ran down to the middle of her back appeared in the doorway of the main cabin. She was wearing a neatly pressed uniform, which had a captain's insignia on it, approached the two detectives.

"Good day, gentlemen. I'm Captain Stevenson." Noticing the surprise on their faces, "You were expecting someone else?"

"Our boss sent us here to see Captain Danny Stevenson. We're surprised to meet a woman."

"Don't worry, boys. You're talking with the right person. I am Captain Danni Stevenson. My name has an "I" at the end rather than a y. My father was expecting a boy and named me after his older brother, who died in Vietnam."

Once again, the detectives presented their badges and introduced themselves to Captain Stevenson.

"I am Detective Ken Fisher, and this is my partner, Eric Steinbrenner."

"Would you happen to be the same Ken Fisher who finished second in the City Tennis Tournament this weekend?" she asked, pointing to Fisher.

"One in the same, Captain. Were you there?"

"No, I wasn't. I was on duty all weekend."

"Do you follow tennis, Captain?"

"Only to the extent that my brother was your opening opponent."

"Sterling Dix is your brother?"

"He is my stepbrother. He called me and told me that he didn't even remember seeing most of your serves."

"You can tell him for me, Captain Stevenson, that my game isn't always that good and not to give up or give in."

"I will make sure I tell him. Do all detectives dress alike, or do you guys discuss what you are going to wear the next day before you go home?"

"We just happened to dress alike today by chance," Fish answered

"I bet your favorite movies are the Men in Black Series," she quipped, trying her hand at a little levity

The two detectives stared at the captain.

"You need to lighten up a little, boys."

"I am sorry, Captain Stevenson, but code 34-16A of the Seattle Police Department handbook expressly forbids any laughter while on duty. So, can we cut to the chase about why our presence was requested?" Hawk retorted.

"While we were on routine patrol this morning, we came across the yacht Il Dono di Maria. She was run aground on the shoals near the Alki Lighthouse. There wasn't anyone on board."

"Have you checked the registry of the boat?"

"We have. It's registered to a Benjamin Blake of 1755 Bluff Point Road."

"Excuse me, Captain, did you just say the boat belongs to a Benjamin Blake?"

"I did, why?"

"There was an earlier discussion in our conference room about a Benjamin Blake."

"What was the discussion about, Detective Fisher, or are you not at liberty to tell me?"

"Do you know Mark Brandt of the Seattle Times?"

"Everybody in Seattle knows Mark Brandt. Why?"

"He was in our conference room yesterday, claiming that he spoke with a young woman who wanted him to investigate the murder of Benjamin Blake."

"I think you're going to want to get your crime scene technicians down here to go over the boat."

"Captain, are your guy's performing both an aerial and water rescue search?"

"At the moment, we don't think an air search is necessary."

"Why is that?"

"We only do an aerial search when we are looking for survivors."

"You don't think he is alive?"

"Based on a note left in the main cabin and blood splatter next to the port rail, we believe the owner is most likely a floater. We plan on going back out to search after we get done examining the boat."

Detective Fisher flipped open his cell phone, dialed a number, and waited.

"Caleb, this is Fish. I need a forensics team down here to catalog evidence on a boat the Coast Guard brought in. How soon can you have a team over here?"

"I'll get a team over there in thirty to forty-five minutes."

"Good. Caleb, please tell them we will be waiting for them dockside at the Cutter Albemarle."

"In the meantime, I am going to talk with my commander about helping with this end of the investigation, at least until we find Benjamin Blakes's body," the captain announced.

"I'm sure we can handle the investigation, Captain."

"Until we release the boat, it's under the jurisdiction of the Coast Guard, Detective Fisher."

"Then, you can come along as the Coast Guard Liaison, Captain Stevenson."

"I have extensive training in crime scene investigation, Detective Fisher."

"Our team does this on an almost daily basis. Do you?"

"No, I can't say we do."

"I guess it's settled then. You're welcome to come along, but our people will lead. I would appreciate it if no one else goes on the boat until our crime scene unit has a chance to look it over. We'll review the findings of our investigation with you as soon as they are available."

"That's fair enough, Detective Fisher."

"Is there somewhere we can get a warm cup of coffee and get out of this damn misty rain while we wait for our team to get here?"

"There is a small canteen in the Operations building. If you don't mind a short walk, Detective Steinbrenner, we can get you something hot to drink."

"Great, lead the way, Captain."

Within fifteen minutes, the group approached a two-story building that seemed very out of place compared to the rest of the buildings on the station. Matte black carbon fiber panels covered the building. No doors or windows were evident in the structure. Two panels slid open as they approached to expose an entrance to the interior of the building. Stepping inside, Captain Stevenson pressed her thumb on a biometric lock, and a door unlocked with a loud click. They passed into the bowels of the building, following Captain Stevenson. After a short walk, they were in the center of the building, which had a center court that opened to a glass dome. A café was on the west side. Several tables were occupied.

"This is quite a building, Captain."

"The design of this building was a joint venture between MIT and Georgia Tech. Its design is environmentally and ecologically friendly and supplies about seventy percent of its utilities."

After grabbing a cup of coffee, they sat down at a table in the center court.

"Captain, were there any other boats in the vicinity when you found the yacht on the shoals?"

"Nothing was on our radar, Detective Fisher."

"How long do you think it was on the shoals?"

"Not more than twenty-four hours. We patrol out there at least once a day, sometimes more often."

"If Benjamin Blake was in the water, in which direction would he float?"

"That would depend on the wind currents, tide, and where he may have gone into the water. The boat may have drifted by itself before running aground on the shoals."

"What you're saying is that if there is a body floating in the water, it's anybody's guess as to where it might show up."

"We also found a lot of cash hidden onboard."

"Approximately how much did you guys find?"

"We haven't counted it, but there are two bags of it."

Within an hour, the forensics team arrived.

"What have you two got for us?"

"This is Captain Stevenson. Her patrol brought in a boat we need to go over."

"It's nice to meet you, Captain. I'm James Randall," he introduced himself, shaking her hand.

"I'm Adam Carter, Captain Stevenson."

"The boat is all yours, gentlemen."

"We're ready, let's go."

The Il Dono di Maria was fifty-five feet in length. Its hull was deep blue with white pinstripes. Her decks were mahogany. The handrails were highly polished brass.

"Wow, a 1960's vintage Chris Craft Constellation series yacht. It has two Detroit Diesel engines. It has been impeccably kept up or restored," Carter exclaimed as they approached the boat, Adam Carter exclaimed,

"Are you into boats, Carter?"

"Just the wooden ones, Hawk. My grandfather had an eighteen-foot Chris Craft when I was growing up. These old boats are a lot of work to upkeep, but they are sure are pretty," he shared, passing out rubber gloves.

"I've brought along everything I need, so if you guys don't mind carrying one of the bags on board, we'll get started."

"There is blood in the center of the main cabin, but the worst is near the port rail," Captain Stevenson shared.

James Randall grabbed the camera and went to work taking pictures while Adam Carter started collecting a blood sample.

"Where did you find the suicide note, Captain?"

"It was on the table in the main cabin, Detective Fisher."

Entering the main cabin, Fish picked the note up and began to read.

"To whom it may concern:

I have learned today about the death of my beloved wife of 52 years. My only daughter is gone, and now so is my wife. My dear Maggie, I am old and tired. I am ready to leave these earthly bounds to join them. Please forgive me for what I have done. I intended to hurt no one.

Benjamin Blake

"I can see why this guy might have been distraught enough to kill himself," Fish said, pausing to think. "I have to wonder what he is asking forgiveness for?"

"Detective, maybe he's Catholic."

"What does it have to do with anything?"

"It's a sin for a Catholic to commit suicide."

"Oh."

Hawk entered the cabin carrying two large duffle bags. "Hey, Fish, Captain Stevenson was right. There has got to be at least a quarter of a million in these two bags."

"I wonder what the hell this guy was into?"

"It's hard to tell. I'm not quite sure this was a suicide, Fish."

"Why's that?"

"The controls in the engine compartment have been smashed."

"So, the boat is inoperable?"

"Look, Fish, there is no way anyone could have gotten this boat restarted. I highly doubt someone would have taken the time to disable a boat in such a way before he killed himself."

"It could have been a drug deal gone bad."

"If that's the case, Fish, don't they always take the money with them?

"You're probably right. I think that this has just become a murder investigation. We need to talk with Caleb and fill him in on what we've found."

"Adam, and I will stay here and look for evidence. We'll head back to the office as soon as we finish."

"Give me a call if you or Adam find anything unusual."

"Will do."

"I'll keep a guard posted here until your guys finish with the boat."

"Thanks, Captain Stevenson."

"Not a problem. In the meantime, I think we'll head back out toward the shoals to see if we can find a body."

"You've got my card, Captain. Call me if you find anything out there."

"Gladly."

Chapter 5

Mrs. Gertrude Lane

Connor Darke peered through a telescope set up to observe the activity on the ice. He could see a large group of sailboats designed for sailing on ice, racing toward him. There was a group of people playing hockey in a small cove on the east side of the lake.

Without much warning, a voice Connor had not heard for quite some time but was quite familiar to him asked, "Do you see anything that interests you out there, Mr. Darke?"

Stunned, he did a quick about-face and stood like a statue, unable to speak.

"What's wrong, dear boy? You look like you've just seen a ghost."

Connor stared at the woman standing before him and finally spoke.

"Gert, it's so good to see you. I need to apologize to you. I didn't make the connection. I'm not sure my grandmother ever introduced you by your last name."

"No apologies needed. Won't you hug an old friend?" she asked.

Connor responded by giving her a gigantic hug.

"This is quite the place you have here."

"I inherited this place from my father. It's as much a part of me as I am of it."

"It's been a long time, Gert. It's nice to see you again."

"I think the last time that I saw you was about ten years ago when you helped your grandmother and I serve Thanksgiving dinner to the poor."

"That is a memory I will carry with me the rest of my life, Gert. The simple look of gratitude on the faces of the people we served dinner to spoke volumes to me."

"I am so sorry you weren't able to pay your final respects to your grandmother. She was an exceptional soul all unto herself."

"She was, wasn't she?"

"We have much to talk about, so I have taken the liberty of having some food prepared for us."

"Sounds great, I'm starved," which, after his long run, was the truth.

"Connor dear, what would you like to drink?"

"A glass of ice water, please."

"Ice water it is. I'll have a pitcher brought in."

They sat down at a table in the library, where lunch was waiting. Connor carefully studied Gert's features. Her hair was as white as the driven snow. She had lost considerable weight since he had seen her last, which made the skin on her arms hang loosely. Her shoulders drooped a little more than the last time he had seen her. Her eyes and cheeks were more sunken than he remembered, but her emerald-green eyes still sparkled with a vitality that was younger than her years.

"Gert, you look a little too thin. You've lost a lot of weight since I saw you last. Are you feeling all right?"

"I felt very depressed and moody after the passing of your grandmother. Her passing was a huge loss to me, but I've come to accept it. Before she passed, I made a promise to her that I would do a better job of taking care of myself. Since I would no longer have her to cajole me into eating healthy. She was a regular mother hen when it came to my health. It just took me a while to get over her death. It seemed like I had lost a part of me."

"I know how you feel sometimes. I felt closer to my grandmother than I do to my mother. I'm sure we both miss her dearly."

"Now, I dedicate every day to her memory. Weather permitting, I walk a couple of miles every day, and I also swim fifteen laps in my pool. But enough about me. I've asked you here so I could hear about you."

"Before I begin, I would like to ask you a question," Connor said.

"Go ahead, I'm all ears, so ask away."

"What's with your aide?"

"Nothing, why do you ask?"

"He seems to be wound a little too tight."

"Hamilton is overly cautious about people. He feels he must protect me."

"What he knows about me is scary, Gert."

"Trust me, he means well."

"How come you have multiple copies of my books?"

"Well, first of all, I think your grandmother and I were your biggest fans, and secondly, I do volunteer work at a family center for the poor. So, whenever I have a young couple having marital issues, I always give them one of your books. I believe it helps them."

"So, I've been told by others. It just seems ironic I was able to help others through their marital strife but was unable to recognize that my marriage was falling apart at the seams."

"Dear Connor, you really shouldn't put all the blame on yourself. Some things are out of our control." She gently patted Connor's face.

"You're telling me that my marriage was doomed to fail from the start?"

"No, I'm not saying that at all. It's just that many times in our life, there are situations that arise that are guided by a much higher purpose."

"What purpose would it be? Are you saying God had a hand in the downfall of my marriage?" Connor asked.

"That's not what I'm implying at all. God has a purpose. Maybe the downfall of your marriage was God's way of putting your life back on track. Let me try to explain what I mean."

"Go ahead."

"Where shall I begin?" she said.

Gert sat in deep thought for what seemed like many minutes and then looked at Connor and said, "One of the most interesting points you make in your books is the need for a couple to feel connected to each other. Your grandmother believed, as I do, that connectivity exists on a much larger scale."

"What would that be?"

"Be patient with me, please."

"My apologies."

She went on. "I know you also feel this connectivity. It's the reason you've moved here and into your grandmother's house, isn't it?"

Connor finally looked at her and said, "You're right. As long as I can remember, I've always felt like I belonged there the minute I walked through the door."

"Like it or not, this connectivity is what gives life a sense of purpose. My sense of purpose is the charitable foundation I run. Your grandmother and I used to have long conversations about you. She told me how you felt your sense of purpose was to help others. She was so happy when you decided to go into counseling. She felt that you have the ability to read and understand people better than they understood themselves."

"If I had such a wonderful ability, how come I didn't even notice my marriage falling apart? I couldn't see we were drifting apart. I just don't get it."

She looked at him and said, "Noise."

"Noise? What do you mean by that?"

"Your grandmother and I used to watch your talk show every week. It always seemed like you knew what one of the persons was going to say before they said it. She and I both believed it was because you could read or hear their thoughts. The reason you couldn't see what was going on in your marriage is subconsciously, other people's thoughts and feelings have barraged you. It's this constant bombardment that causes the noise and can sometimes mask the issues at hand. It's what drives your inner desire to help others. It's because you know their needs."

Connor stood, walked to the French doors, and looked out at the lake, deep in thought. "I wish I knew my own needs."

"If you search your feelings, you will know I'm right. You came here for a reason today."

"Yes, I did. You invited me," he said.

"No, there is another reason. You came here to seek the truth."

"What did you just say?" he turned and stared at her.

"Don't stand there with your mouth wide open. I said you came here because you need to seek the truth."

Surprised, he looked at her and asked, "How did you know that?"

"She told me about it, which is why I invited you here. You feel lost and need help finding your way."

"Who is she?" he asked

"Why, your grandmother, of course," she replied.

"Look, I don't know if you think this is funny because I sure don't. As you well know, she has been dead for quite a long time."

Connor began to walk toward the door.

"Where are you going?" she asked.

"I'm leaving. I think I've heard enough for one day."

"Please, hear me out. When I have finished talking, my driver will take you home, and I'll never bother you again if that's what you want."

Connor sat down. "Out of respect for my grandmother, I will stay and listen, but don't expect me to believe this load of crap you're peddling me."

"Fair enough," she said.

"Let's move on."

"Do you know how and when I met your grandmother?"

"No, I guess I don't. I just assumed you had been friends for a long time."

"Your grandmother and I met at a get-together for people who wanted to play cards. While we were playing Pinochle, she kept talking to somebody who wasn't there about what card to play next. She was a mean Pinochle player, by the way."

"I know she and all my aunts and uncles would gather on Friday nights and play triple-deck Pinochle until the break of dawn. My grandmother always seemed to know what the next card coming was. It seemed uncanny to me at the time. Playing Pinochle with the whole family is one of my fondest memories."

"Anyway, Connor, I asked your grandmother who she was talking to, and she said Harry, my dead husband. I proceeded to tell her what I thought and still do. I believe the soul generates energy that ties humanity and the world together, and we carry this energy into our afterlife. I also believe some people can feel and sense the energy here on earth and can put it to good use. Some channel this energy in the ability to heal others, while some people use this energy to communicate with souls who have passed on. Do you want me to go on or have you heard enough?"

"I'm still with you, so please continue," he replied.

"Your grandmother told me she always felt connected to you and that you can read and sense the thoughts of others. Once you are willing to open yourself up and learn to control your energy, you will be able to sort out the important noise from the stuff that isn't."

"You're right. I've always felt I could sense what other people were thinking. But what I don't understand is how can I know what's important?"

"You will have to learn to narrow your focus and concentrate. When you learn how to do it, the useless and unimportant noise will fall away. I have friends who can help you learn how to focus your energy on what's important."

Connor rose and stood to look at Gert. "Well, this is certainly not what I expected to happen today. I am going to need some time to digest our conversation. I feel quite overwhelmed. If you will excuse me, I would like to be going. Give me a few days to think this over, and I'll get back to you."

"I understand and appreciate your needs, but please make a decision as quickly as possible. A life may hang in the balance."

"Well, I'll do my best."

"I'll have Hamilton take you home straight away. I so appreciate you taking your time to come and listen to an old lady babble."

"I don't think it was nonsense at all. It was a real pleasure to see you, Gert, and thanks for lunch. It was great."

"You're most entirely welcome, Connor. I'll see you out. Hamilton will be around with the car in just a moment. By the way, she's just what the doctor ordered."

"Who is?" he asked.

"Why, Julie Strand, of course. Your grandmother told me all about her. She says to tell you that there's nothing chicken at all about her legs."

"What exactly did my grandmother tell you?"

"She told me when you were young, you came to visit your cousin, and the two of you picked on Julie and told her she had chicken legs."

"I don't think that now."

"You like her, don't you?"

"I guess so."

"You're dating her, aren't you?"

"We are dating, but it's casual."

"Well, your grandmother tells me Julie is your soul mate, and you need to treat her nice. Do you think you can do that?"

"I don't know if we are soul mates, but I promise I'll do the best I can." Connor shook his head as he walked to the door.

"There is something you should know. Your grandmother tells me you have to listen better."

"Listen to who?"

"The voices in your head."

"What voices?"

"The ones who are asking for help."

"Since you seem to have a direct path to my grandmother, why don't you tell her to send in help."

"She has my dear boy. She has sent you."

"I wish I'd had a hand in that decision."

"You did."

"I did? When did that happen?"

"It happened the moment you decided to move into your grandmother's house. Connor, we are all born with certain God-given talents. I firmly believe this course has been set for you, so you can take advantage of it."

"Maybe I just want to be left alone!"

"That would be a grave decision."

"For whom? Me?"

"For the ones you have been sent to help."

"I'm not following you."

"Look, Connor, you hear voices in your head, don't you?"

"Yes, from time to time."

"Well, the most likely reason is they are souls from the other side who are acting as a pathway for people who are still alive, needing your help. You walk out on this now, and you will most likely seal their fate."

"Thanks a lot, God. I needed more pressure lumped on me," he said, throwing his hands up in the air in disgust.

"Is that what you think? That God is unfair?"

"I came here to get my life back on track. I just don't see how this is going to help."

"It's not about you, Connor."

"It needs to be."

"No, it doesn't. Don't worry, you will get your life back on track."

"I don't think I can do this alone."

"You won't be. It's why God has put Julie into your life. Besides, your grandmother and I will be here to keep you from falling again."

"Great, it should make my mother happy that you're looking out for me. Where the hell were you when I fell the first time?"

"I am truly sorry, my boy. The important thing is that I won't let you fall again."

"Look, I'm sorry, but I have to go. I think I need to digest all of this."

"No problem, I will have Hamilton drive you home."

When he got home, Connor sat down in an overstuffed, wingback chair and started reading an Edgar Cayce book he'd found on his grandmother's bookshelf. Without realizing it, he soon drifted off to sleep.

Chapter 6

The Seattle Police Department

Hawk stood patiently, waiting in the doorway of Caleb's office. Caleb was doodling in the margins of the newspaper as he talked on the phone. He was doing more listening than speaking, and he was twirling the end of his mustache. He looked at Hawk and shot a glance at one of the chairs situated in front of his desk, which Hawk interpreted as an invitation to sit down. After a few minutes, Caleb finished his phone call and looked at Hawk.

"Hawk, where is Detective Fisher? I need to speak to him."

"He's downstairs, logging in evidence."

Within five minutes, Fish joined Hawk, who had taken a seat in the office. Caleb stood and picked up the newspaper he had been doodling on, walked around his desk, and stood in front of the two detectives. He looked directly at Hawk and spoke.

"Hawk, I need a few minutes with Detective Fisher. I would appreciate it if you could wait outside for a moment."

Hawk started to rise to leave, and Fish cleared his throat rather loudly. Caleb motioned for Hawk to go.

"Look, Caleb, Hawk can stay I don't have anything to hide."

"Very well, Detective Fisher, we can do it your way. Is there anything you would like to tell me about what happened Monday night?"

"Not that I can think of. Why?"

"Well, I know that you had some heated words with Mark Brandt. I heard that he was here this morning. Apparently, someone had beaten the living crap out of him after we left the awards ceremony. I couldn't help but notice the bandage on your hand, Detective. I hope for your sake, Fish, that you had nothing to do with it."

"I won't deny that we had words. Mark was at the Rusted Harpoon and wanted to buy me a drink. I told him no thanks. The bandage is on my hand because of a mirror that I smashed on my boat. I was taking out my frustration with my brother."

Caleb raised an eyebrow and studied Detective Fisher's face for a moment.

"I've got to tell you, Ken, you are walking a very fine line. Your therapy sessions haven't been going very well, and now this. It doesn't paint a good picture of the state of your emotions. If you weren't on an active case at the moment, you would be on desk duty until you could figure a way to get your head out of your ass. Your days of doing it the Ken Fisher way are over. Like it or not, you have to work within the boundaries of our system. Do you understand what I am saying, Detective?"

"Yes, sir, I do."

"Good, because this is the last time we have this discussion. Your days of being a loose cannon are over. So, getting back to the subject of Mark Brandt, would it have hurt to have accepted a drink from the guy? Like it or not, we need to have the newspaper on our side. You're going toe to toe with their favorite son doesn't help."

"I'm sorry, Caleb. That asshole ran his article early, which almost got Eric and me killed. I may not be happy with Mark Brandt, but I would never jeopardize my career over somebody I consider a two-bit writer."

"How about someone who almost got you killed?"

"I had nothing to do with Mark Brandt's face. He was here seeking our help."

"Mark Brandt, was he here to press charges on the person who kicked the crap out of him?"

Fish looked down at his feet, shifted his weight from side to side for a couple of seconds, and then looked at Caleb.

"Not exactly. He asked us to take a look at a surveillance video from the lobby of the Times from yesterday."

"What is supposed to be on it?"

"He asked us to look for something that is not on the video. It's missing an image of a woman that he claims was in the lobby of the Times yesterday."

"I assume you had Fergie examine it. What was her analysis?"

"She found nothing wrong with it."

"So, Fish, at this point, there isn't anything that Mark Brandt can tell us about the girl he saw yesterday. Is that correct?"

"Not exactly, Caleb. The girl he saw yesterday or thought he saw died five years ago in a hit-and-run accident. Her name is Samantha Blake. I checked our files. The driver of the vehicle that killed her was never found. Her file is down in the cold case file storage room."

Caleb exhaled, clasped his hands together behind his head, and looked out his office window deep in thought. After an awkward minute of silence, he spoke.

"Basically, Mark is claiming to have had a ghostly encounter. Did Mark happen to say why she came to see him?"

"She wants Mark to look into her father's death."

"Do we know who her father is and when he died?"

"She told Mark that her father's name is Benjamin Blake."

"Do we know anything about Benjamin Blake?"

"The Coast Guard pulled a boat with no one on board off the shoals near the Alki Lighthouse early this morning that is owned by a Benjamin Blake. There is a strong possibility that it might be her father's. There was a suicide note in the cabin and blood splatter on the outside of the cabin and the port rail."

"Sounds like an open and shut suicide case to me."

"The only problem is the engine controls were damaged enough to disable the use of the engines. Not a likely move by someone who is going to commit suicide."

"Probably not."

"Caleb, we also found a lot of cash hidden on board."

"How much did you find?"

"We counted two hundred and fifty thousand."

"Wow, it's a lot of money to hide on a boat. Do you think this guy was running drugs?"

"His boat was certainly big enough and had twin Detroit Diesel engines, so drug-running is certainly a theory."

"Do you have a better one, Detective Steinbrenner?"

"Not at this moment, sir."

"So, gentlemen, what's the plan?"

"We have the address of Benjamin Blake, the owner of the boat. I think Hawk and I should go out and look around."

"That's a good idea, Fish. Bring in the local cops on this one."

"Okay, but we maintain the lead, Caleb."

"I'll set it up and let them know what we have up to this point. Besides, the local cops can help with door to door canvassing of the neighborhood if need be."

"Sounds like a plan. We'll let you know what we find when we get there. The forensics team is going over the boat as we speak."

"Good. Hopefully, between you and the forensics team, we can figure out what happened. Call me if anything goes astray."

1755 Bluff Point Rd.

When Fish and Hawk arrived at their destination, a patrol car was parked in the driveway. The driveway wound its way through a thicket of tall pines trees that stood like sentinels, guarding it against unwanted or unintended intruders. One of the officers got out and approached their car. Fish rolled down his window, held his badge out, and yelled, "Seattle PD"

"Are you guys Detectives Fisher and Steinbrenner?" the officer asked.

"That would be us."

"I'm Officer George Dettrick. My partner will be with us in a minute."

A woman about 6' tall stepped out of the cruiser and came over.

"I'm Officer Karen Dettrick."

"Doesn't your department frown on married partners?"

"They do, but they allow cousins to work together. So, what have we got?"

"We're not quite sure. A boat belonging to the owner of this house was out on the shoals near the Alki Lighthouse. We found a suicide note and blood splatter on board."

"Was there a body?"

"The Coast Guard is out searching for one as we speak."

"What would you like us to do?"

"Why don't you go to the front door and see if anyone answers. Please approach with caution. We don't know if anyone is still in the house or not. My partner and I will go around back and try to gain entry from the rear."

The home was a large 3600 square foot ranch nestled within the stand of trees. There were stairs on the top of the pine-covered bluff behind the house, which snaked their way back and forth down to the boathouse and a dock that jutted out into the bay. Reaching the back of the house, they found the back door kicked in. Drawing their guns, they shouted, "This is the police. Is there anyone home?"

"Fish, why don't you cover me while I enter?"

"Alright, Hawk, be careful. I'll be right behind you."

They could hear the doorbell ringing. They worked their way to the front door and let the officers in.

"We did a quick check of the house. It looks like it's just us, officers."

"Was the back door unlocked?"

"No, the door was shut and locked. Someone kicked it in, so please be alert. I don't want anyone hurt on my watch. The person who kicked this one in has got to be one big boy."

"Detective Fisher, do you think the owner did this to stage the scene?"

"I highly doubt it. The owner is at least in his seventies. I doubt he would have had the strength to kick in a door. This has just officially become a murder investigation."

Hawk pulled on a pair of latex gloves and started searching the couches and tables for evidence. After a few moments, Hawk spoke.

"I found something." Hawk bent down to pick up an object inside a box of tissues.

"What did you find, Hawk?"

"I found a digital recorder." Hawk pressed the play button.

"Don't forget to water the plants in the morning. Make sure the kitchen is clean. Take out the trash and get rid of the beer bottles. Don't want to make Maggie mad. She hates to come home to a mess."

"It sounds like he leaves himself reminders so he won't forget to do his chores. Hawk, you might as well turn it off."

Just then, there was a loud crash on the recording. Fish moved closer "Let's keep it playing. From the sound of the noise, I bet it was from whoever kicked the door in." There was a new voice on the recording

"Don't flinch or you're dead. Do you remember me, Doc?"

Slight Pause

"Of course I do, Mr. Jensen. What are you doing here?"

"I would like to introduce you to one of my associates. His name is Tank. I think it fits him to a tee, don't you?"

"I guess."

"You guess? Look at him. He's a big guy. Wouldn't you agree?

"Yes."

"Now that the introductions are out of the way, my friend and I just thought we would pay you a visit."

"Why now? You said it was a government project."

Benjamin Blake's breathing quickened and got shallow.

"Relax, Doc. I wouldn't want you having a heart attack on me."

There was another slight pause. The breath sounds lessened.

"That's better, Doc."

"I told you that your secrets would always be safe with me."

"Let's call this a little bit of insurance. One can never have enough coverage, don't you think?

"What kind of insurance?"

"The kind of insurance that makes sure all loose ends are tied up."

"I suppose you're right."

"Of course, I am."

"Why now? What do you guys want?"

"Let's just say we're here to tie up a loose end or two."

"Loose ends. I didn't leave any loose ends."

"We're sure you didn't."

His voice was wavering. "I know I didn't. So why are you here?"

"I think tonight is a good night to die, don't you?"

"I don't want to die. I'm not ready."

"None of us are ever ready. Are we?"

"No."

"But, nonetheless, die we must."

"Look, I've done everything you asked of me and then some."

"I know you have."

"But why?"

"Let's just say we need to erase our tracks."

"What tracks would that be?"

"You, you're one of them."

"But the FBI doesn't kill people who help them, do they?"

"Not usually, but sometimes we do make exceptions."

"Exceptions?"

"Yes, unfortunately, Benjamin, you're an exception to the rule."

"I don't understand?"

"I'm sorry, but we can't take any chances."

"I've already told you I would never say anything."

"So, you did, Doc. I hope you have your affairs in order."

"You're not with the FBI, are you?"

"Bingo. See, that's the problem. You're a bright guy. You would have figured it out eventually, and that's a chance we're not willing to risk."

"If you don't work for the FBI, who are you working for?"

"Let's just say we are serving a purely selfish interest here. We all have our reasons, just like the reason you had to take the job for us in the first place. I'm sure you can understand where I'm coming from, can't you?"

The doctor's voice trails off. "Maggie."

"What does she know about our little arrangement?"

"She doesn't know or suspect anything. There's no need to get her involved."

"Since you're involved, she's involved, like it or not."

"I promise you, she doesn't know anything."

"You don't have to worry. We've taken care of everything."

"What the hell have you done to her?"

"Don't worry, Doc, she never felt a thing."

"You son of a bitch, she was all I had left?"

"We just couldn't take a chance. I'm sure you must understand our position."

The doctor's voice trailed off again.

"Maggie, what have I done?"

"Look, Doc, most wives usually know when things aren't right. Don't you think she suspected something when you bought the boat?"

"But why her?"

"She was a liability. I don't like liabilities. Do you?"

"No."

"Besides, it was fun."

"Fun? How can you think that killing someone is fun?"

"We considered it bonus work."

"You think you can kill me and no one will investigate?"

"That's about right, Doc."

"Someone will ask questions."

"It's highly unlikely."

"Why?"

"Because we're not going to do it."

"Who then?"

"You will. The newspapers will report that you left a suicide note. It will state you were distraught over the loss of your wife, so you decided to end it all. Such a sad story, don't you think?"

"You bastards."

"What a great night for a boat ride, Doc."

"Look, as I said before, I won't tell a soul."

"Don't worry, Doc, we believe you."

"If I give you back the money, will you leave me alone?"

"We're not here for the money, Doc. It's just a drop in the bucket to us."

"One million is just a drop in the bucket? Who are you guys anyway?"

"We're your worst nightmare, Doc."

"I'm begging you, please don't do this."

The man he knew as Mr. Jensen put his hand on his shoulder and patted it.

"Didn't your mother teach you not to beg?"

Another long pause.

"Well, Doc, it's time to go and meet your maker."

The recording ended.

After a minute or two, Hawk turned off the recorder.

"That seems to be it, Fish. I guess that the Doc was in way over his head, and it probably cost him his life."

"Hawk, we need to report this to Caleb. Grab the recorder, and let's head back."

"You're right. I'm sure the techies are going to want to analyze the voices on this recording."

Fish turned to the two officers. "Can you guys get your crime scene unit out here? Our team is busy going over this guy's boat."

"We'll call it in, Detective Fisher."

Fish and Hawk separated and began looking through the other rooms. The contents of each room were in a pile on the floor. After a few minutes, Hawk called Fish.

"Hey, Fish, can you come here? I think you're going to want to see this. I'm in the last room on the left."

Not only had the contents of the room been dumped on the floor, but there were blank spots on the wall where objects had hung.

"My guess, is that the contents of this room have a direct connection to whatever Benjamin Blake got himself caught up in that cost his life."

Fish pointed to a square impression in the carpet next to an oak office desk. "I wouldn't be surprised if a file cabinet sat here, Hawk. The question is, did the perp's take it, or is it just circumstance?"

Just as Fish finished speaking, the doorbell rang. A woman in her fifties was standing at the door holding the leashes of two Collies. Fish opened the door and looked at her. She was short and slightly on the heavy side. Her gray hair was pushed back around her ears. She was wearing blue jeans and a pair of slippers with the face of a bunny on them and a loose-fitting brown Carhart jacket. Fish studied her face and could tell by the look on her face that she was distraught.

"Is Doc Blake alright?"

"We're not at liberty to say at the moment."

"I'm Sharon Cross. I live across the street." She turned and pointed to a two-story brick colonial.

"Ever since Doctor Blake's daughter died, my husband and I have taken the responsibility to watch over him and his wife."

"I'm Detective Steinbrenner, and this is Detective Fisher. We're with the Seattle PD." They handed her a business card.

"It was the two men, wasn't it?"

"What two men?"

"I was getting ready to walk my dogs last night. I looked out the window in my front door to see if it was safe to go out. I saw a Black Cadillac Escalade going slowly past Doctor Blake's house. It turned around in our driveway and then parked on the road in front of his house as I was looking out. I saw two guys get out and walk up the driveway."

"What did they look like?"

"I'm sorry, Detective Fisher. The only thing I could see was that one of them was tall."

"What would you call tall?"

"I would guess he was probably at least six and a half feet tall."

"What about the other one?"

"He was quite a bit shorter than the other one. But he was one of the biggest persons I have ever seen."

"Big, as in fat?"

"No, big like the Incredible Hulk."

"Oh."

"Mrs. Cross, did you see them leave?"

"No, after they went up to the driveway, a car pulled up next to the Escalade."

"What kind of car was it?

"I'm not sure."

"What happened then?"

"A person got out of the car, opened the door to the Escalade, and got in."

"Did they leave with the two who went into the house?"

"No, the odd thing, Detective Fisher, is from what I could tell, there was just one person in the Escalade when it left."

"Do you usually notice cars go by your house?"

"Detective Fisher, Bluff Point Road ends at the point. I don't watch television, so the house is quiet enough that I can hear cars as they are approaching."

"Is there a possibility a car came and went after you were asleep last night?"

"Detective, I work out of my house. I do my best work at night, so I am quite sure no cars left or came up the road before I went to bed at 7:30 this morning."

"Do you mind answering some questions?"

"Sure, Detectives. I'm not sure I'll have the answers you're looking for."

Hawk removed a small notebook and a pen from the inside pocket of his suit jacket and started asking Mrs. Cross questions.

"How long have you known Mr. & Mrs. Blake?"

"We've known Doctor Blake and his wife, Maggie, about twelve years."

"You refer to him as Doctor Blake. What did he practice?"

"I'm not quite sure what he did. I just know that Maggie called him Doc. Until their daughter died five years ago, they only came here on weekends. After she died, they moved here to stay. They never talked about their past. I think that something died inside them when their daughter did. A couple of years ago, they started coming out of their shell when Doc bought the boat and started working on it. It was like he was reborn."

"How did his wife take the fact that her husband was so involved in restoring a boat?"

"In a lot of ways, I think she was glad he had a new sense of purpose. About a year before Doc bought the boat, Maggie started going to Tacoma to take care of an elderly parent."

"Mrs. Cross, did they get along with all the neighbors?"

"I know everyone who lives on this road. I've never heard anyone speak an ill word about the Blakes."

"I just have one last question for the time being. Did you ever see the Cadillac Escalade here before?"

"Not that I can recall, Detective."

"That's all the questions I have for now. I appreciate your help."

"You're entirely welcome, Detective Steinbrenner."

"I would like to send one of the local cops over here to take a written statement if it's okay with you?"

"That would be just fine, Detective Fisher. I would be happy to."

"Mrs. Cross, thanks again for your assistance. You have our cards. If you remember anything else, please call."

Mrs. Cross left Benjamin Blake's house. Hawk was standing on the front porch, watching her walk away. After reaching the edge of the driveway, she stopped, turned around, and walked back toward the house.

"Detective Steinbrenner, I don't know if this will help at all, but I have a surveillance camera pointed toward the road. You're welcome to have a copy of it if you would like."

Fish, who had overheard the last comment from Mrs. Cross, spoke up.

"I'm sure that Detective Steinbrenner would be more than happy to review the surveillance video. Hawk, why don't you go with Mrs. Cross? In the meantime, I'll call Caleb and tell him that we are going to stay out here and work with the crime scene team when it gets here."

Chapter 7

The Seattle Police Department

Hawk walked into the lobby of the Seattle Police Department at a brisk pace and glanced at the clock. He looked over at Bill Towns, who was the acting duty officer for the day and smiled.

"It's good to see you, Bill. How's the back?"

"It's coming along, Hawk. I'm getting there. Caleb is waiting for you in conference room 1A."

"Is Detective Fisher here yet?"

"Fish's been here for over an hour. He's in the conference room with the rest of the group. I will call them and let them know you're on the way."

"Thanks, Bill," Hawk smiled at Bill.

"Just doing my job. You have yourself a good day."

Hawk quickened his pace as he headed for conference room 1A. It was the largest of the conference rooms at the station. The wall along the aisle was all glass, making it impossible for Hawk not to be noticed as he approached. Caleb was standing in front of a large whiteboard. He spotted Hawk as he neared the conference room door and immediately glanced toward the clock on the wall.

"Cutting it a little close this morning, are we not, Detective Steinbrenner?"

"It is only 7:45, Caleb. We don't need to be here until 8:00 if I am not mistaken."

"You're not mistaken, but I expect everyone to get here at least half an hour before the start of their shift to get their morning pleasantries out of the way. Is that clear, Detective Steinbrenner?"

"Yes, sir."

"You can fix yourself a spot of tea and help yourself to a crumpet."

"They are doughnuts, Caleb, not crumpets."

"Call them what you want, have one, or don't."

"Thanks, but no thanks."

"Please have a seat then."

Hawk sat down in the closest available chair. "What's up, boss?"

"I know it's early. The sooner we get this started, the sooner we can get to our daily duties. Fish, since you're the senior lead on the team, I'm going to let you lead us off. The object is we need to get everything we know listed on the board. So, Fish, take us away."

Fish stood and walked to the whiteboard, grabbed a dry-erase marker, and began to write.

"Caleb, Hawk and I have learned the following:

1: The yacht Il Dono di Maria ran aground near the Alki Lighthouse with no one on board.

2: There was a suicide note on the boat, supposedly written by the owner, Benjamin Blake.

3: A trail of blood led to the rail.

4: Almost 275,000 dollars was on the yacht.

5: The controls to the engines had been disabled.

6: Benjamin Blake's house was turned inside out. We're not quite sure what the perps wanted. Hawk and I spent last evening going through the Blake house with the crime scene team. The team is going through what we collected and should have a report sometime later this morning.

8: During our search of Blake's house, Hawk discovered a hidden digital recorder. It gave us the following documented evidence.

A: Benjamin Blake was involved in something that led to his death.

B: Two men broke into his house with the intent to end his life.

C: Benjamin Blake was familiar with one of his assailants.

D: This assailant used falsified FBI credentials to solicit Benjamin Blake's help.

9: The assailants entered Benjamin Blake's house by smashing the rear door.

10. One of Benjamin Blake's neighbors, a Mrs. Cross, saw the two assailants arrive at the Blake residence.

11. Mrs. Cross also witnessed the arrival of two other people. One of them drove the assailant's car away.

12. The two assailants forced Benjamin Blake to leave with them in his boat.

13. There were a lot of items recently removed from the Blake house. At this point, we can assume that the items removed belong to Benjamin Blake."

"Thank you, Detective Fisher. The list is quite a baker's dozen."

"Yes, it is, Caleb."

"Let's move onto what the forensics team found on the boat. Adam, since your the team lead for the forensics department, it's your turn in the barrel."

Adam Carter stood, straightened his tie, unbuttoned his lab coat, and walked to the center of the room.

"Caleb, James and I went over the boat with a fine-tooth comb. We took a few different blood samples. All of which belonged to the same person, most likely to the owner of the boat, Benjamin Blake. As we speak, we are working on confirming who it belongs to. We also lifted two different sets of fingerprints. We got a hit on one of the fingerprint sets. It was listed in the national database as classified. I tried to use my security clearance to access the file with no luck."

"Adam, what organization is denying access to this file?"

"I'm not sure."

At that moment, Fish's cell phone began to vibrate. Fish stared at the screen. Caleb looked at Fish with a pained expression.

"Would you like to share the news with everyone at the table, Detective Fisher?"

Fish briefly looked around the table and spoke.

"I just received a text message from Captain Stevens. They found a body floating this morning. It's most likely Benjamin Blake, the owner of the boat."

"When do they expect to be back in port with the body, Fish?"

"Within the hour."

Caleb stood and looked at the people around the table.

"Fish, I want you and Hawk to meet the medical examiner at the boat. Adam, I want you and your team to keep working on the evidence from the boat and go through anything collected from the Blake house."

"What about our classified fingerprint, Captain?"

"If I haven't burned all of my bridges, Mr. Carter, I may be able to get some help with that one. Let's all plan on regrouping back here at 3:00."

They all replied with a simultaneous yes, sir, and left the conference room.

A Floater

Jessica Stilton, the Medical Examiner for the City of Seattle Police Department, was standing at the pier, waiting for the Cutter Albemarle to arrive. Detective Fisher recognized her in an instant. She was wearing a lab coat emblazoned with the Seattle Police Department logo; the letters M.E. were under it. Detectives Fisher and Steinbrenner acknowledged she was there with a wave.

She looked up and exclaimed, "You guys are late!"

"Jess, we're only 15 minutes late. Traffic was a little slower than usual."

"Where's our boat, Detective Fisher?"

"I'll check," he said, Dialing a number on his cell phone.

"Captain Stevenson, this is Detective Fisher. How long before you dock? You're about ten minutes out. Good, we'll be waiting."

It took twenty minutes before the Cutter Albemarle was at the dock, and the gangplank lowered.

Captain Stevenson disembarked and stood next to Detective Fisher.

"Captain Stevenson, have you met Dr. Jessica Stilton, our medical examiner?"

"No, I can't say I've had the pleasure," she said, extending her hand. "It's nice to meet you, Doctor Stilton."

"Likewise, Captain. You have a body for me?"

"Yes, we do. We picked up the body of a male with a single gunshot wound to the head."

Two crewmen came down the gangplank, carrying a body bag. They set the bag down in front of Captain Stevenson and saluted.

"Fish, it looks like the guest of the party is here," Hawk exclaimed as he pointed to the body bag.

"You might not want to look at this. A spinning propeller of a boat hit the body. It's a little bit ugly," Stevenson warned.

Jessica Stilton bent over to open the body bag. She looked at the remains, sucked in a deep breath of air, and then slowly exhaled.

"Based on the damage to the body, getting an identification might prove to be difficult. I need to get it back to my lab so I can do a more thorough examination. Fish, you and Hawk are welcome to join if you want."

"If I can chime in here, I can help with the identification."

Fish, Hawk, and Jessica Stilton all turned to look at Captain Stevenson.

"We require all boat owners to take a boating safety course. I pulled the registry for the class that he took and started calling people who were there at the same time to see if they could identify Benjamin Blake. I came across a guy named John Tidwell who helped restore the engines on the boat. He sent me a text message with a picture of himself with Benjamin."

Captain Stevenson brought up the attachment and handed the phone to Jessica Stilton, who was standing closest to her. Jessica looked at the picture and nodded.

"Based on what I see, Fish, I would say that we have the body of Benjamin Blake." Jessica passed the phone to Fish, who looked at it and then handed it to Hawk.

"I agree with you, Jessica. I think Hawk and I will pick up John Tidwell and bring him in for a positive I.D. nonetheless. We'll meet you in the lab as quickly as we can."

"Sounds like a plan to me, Fish. I'll get started on the workup for the autopsy as soon as I get back."

"Thanks, Jessica."

"Just call me and let me know when you get there so I can have the body ready to be identified."

Detective Fisher turned to look at Captain Stevenson. "Good work, Captain. You can tell your boss we appreciate the fact you guys went back out to look."

Fish flipped open his cell phone and called Caleb.

"Caleb, this is Fish. The Coast Guard has retrieved Benjamin Blake's body. Hawk and I are going to pick up someone who we hope can give us a positive I.D."

There was a pause as he listened to Caleb.

"Sure, Hawk and I can do it."

"What did you sign us up for, Fish?"

"It looks like it's going to be a long day and maybe a long night. As soon as we get done at the M.E.'s office, Caleb wants to have a meeting."

"Why?"

"The only thing he said is that he is escalating the priority on the case."

The Medical Examiner's Office

Jessica Stilton answered her ringing phone. "Hello, this is Jessica."

"Fish, where are you?" She listened for a moment. "You're here. Good, I will meet you in the lab."

Within a few minutes, Fish and Hawk were standing at the window of the lab on either side of John Tidwell. Jessica walked out into the hallway to talk with John Tidwell. She looked at John; his face was ashen.

"I'm Dr. Stilton, the medical examiner. Are you okay, Mr. Tidwell?"

John took in a deep breath and slowly exhaled.

"I'll be okay. I've seen dead bodies before."

"Probably not like this, you haven't. Do you want to go inside the room, or do you want to look through the glass?"

"Out of respect for Benjamin, I'll go in. Can I ask how he died?"

Fish answered John's question.

"John, this is an active criminal investigation, so we're not allowed to say at the moment. You'll probably figure it out on your own once you see his body."

They went into the lab. Blake's body was lying on a metal examining table underneath a white sheet. Fish and Hawk walked up to the table, flanking John Tidwell. Jessica slowly pulled back the sheet to expose Benjamin Blake.

"John, is this Benjamin Blake?" the M.E. asked.

John took a long look at the body on the table and then studied the face. He looked up at Jessica Stilton; his eyes were moist. He was doing his best to fight back the tears.

"Yes, it is. I saw him once with his shirt off when he was working on the boat. I remembered the purplish scar on the left side of his abdomen. It's him for sure."

John quickly covered his mouth with his left hand, turned, ran to the nearest trash can, and promptly emptied the contents of his stomach. Jessica waited for John to finish and handed him a towel to clean up. Fish grabbed John's arm, walked him out of the lab, and helped him sit down in a chair in the hallway.

"You okay, John?"

John shook his head, indicating that he was all right. Fish walked back into the lab. He noticed the worried look on Jessica's face.

"Don't worry, Jess, John will be okay. Do you think it was a suicide as indicated by his note?"

"No, I don't. Chemical analysis of his blood indicates the presence of some seriously strong arthritis medicine. I don't think he would have had the strength to pull the trigger. I was able to retrieve the bullet that killed him. The deceased had a metal plate in his head that prevented the bullet from exiting. I will have it cleaned up and ready to review. We can compare it to other ones in our database on the outside chance that we might find a match."

A digital image of the bullet was entered into a program to check for matches. Within minutes, the analysis ended.

"Gentlemen, there are no matches to it in our system."

"Jessica, can you check it against the national database?"

"That was my next step."

It took about ten minutes for the computer to check the national database. Fish was checking a message on his cell phone when Hawk spoke out.

"Look, the computer is flashing the word match in different colors."

"That means that it found more than one record of a match for this bullet, Hawk," Jessica replied.

"Jessica, can I see your computer screen?" Hawk asked.

She moved away from the computer so Hawk could sit down. He sat down at the workstation and began to read.

"The most recent match is to a bullet taken out of a dead Hispanic fellow. His body was found two days ago by some hikers in the Grand Canyon."

"Does it mention a name for the victim?"

"The body might belong to a petty criminal named Hector Gonzales."

Hawk continued to read the report. "It says that the victim was carrying multiple identification cards. The one closest to the victim indicated that his name is Hector Gonzales. It also states that he had no intact fingerprints."

"That must be why there was no positive ID."

"This guy has been arrested at least a half-dozen times. He's done a couple of stretches in prison."

"Where did he do his last stretch?"

"He was in the Sheridan Federal Correctional in Sheridan, Oregon, for three years."

"When was that?"

"He was released on early parole about eight months ago."

Fish stood motionless, deep in thought, before he asked Hawk to bring up the second match. Within seconds, the file for the next match was on screen. Hawk began to read what he saw.

"A third bullet from the same gun came from a Don Giovassi. He had a single gunshot wound to the head and was slumped over the wheel of a grey 2003 Toyota Camry nine months ago at a scenic overlook in Idaho. There were no witnesses and no signs of a struggle."

"Shit," Fish exclaimed.

Hawk looked at Fish with a puzzled look on his face.

"What's wrong, Fish?"

"When we were reading the report on Samantha Blake's death, I remember reading that a witness saw a grey 2003 Toyota Camry pass him, driving at a high rate of speed within minutes of her death. I know this could just be a coincidence, but it needs checking out."

Detective Fisher's cell phone began to ring. "This is Detective Fisher."

"Caleb, Hawk and I are in the process of wrapping it up here." He paused for a minute to listen before hanging up.

"What was all that about, Fish?" Hawk asked.

"Caleb is chomping at the bit to get the review started. It's time we head back."

"Sure, Fish."

"Thanks, Jessica."

"Hawk, if you ever want to come back and help, I wouldn't mind," she said, winking at Hawk.

"Cool your jets, Jessica. Detective Steinbrenner is officially off the market."

"I am not," Hawk corrected with a growl.

"Quit whining about it, Hawk. You're so off the market it is not even funny."

"Well, Detective, if you become available, here's my card. Don't hesitate to call."

"No problem, Jessica. I just might do that," Hawk flirted.

"Don't waste your nights sitting by the phone, Jessica. He's not going to call you."

"Fish, how the hell do you know I won't call?"

"It's all in the book."

"For God's sake, will you give the Love Doctor a rest?"

"If it will get us out of here and back to the office."

Chapter 8

Caleb Clarke's Office

Caleb Clarke was pacing back and forth in his office, tossing a tension ball into the air and catching it repeatedly. Hawk knocked on the door to Caleb's office. Caleb looked over at the door and motioned for Fish and Hawk to come in. Hawk started to talk, and Caleb held his hand in a stop position. Hawk stopped talking and looked at Caleb as he continued to pace back and forth. After a few minutes, Caleb quit tossing the ball, turned around, and stood in front of Fish and Hawk.

"I tried to track down the classified fingerprint from the boat. I wasn't having any luck with it, so I called a friend who has connections."

Caleb turned around and picked up a sheet of paper off of his desk and handed it to Fish, who read it and gave it to Hawk.

"Caleb, you have friends in Mossad?"

"That doesn't matter, Fish. What's important is that this document stays here between the three of us. I don't want anyone asking questions about how I got this information."

"Not a problem," both detectives responded in unison.

Fish looked at Caleb.

"Caleb, this can't be right. The other set of fingerprints are from a former Marine named Gary Danzig, who is supposedly dead. What the hell is going on?"

"Look, Fish, I intentionally left out part of the document. He went missing on a covert mission. He was part of a highly specialized Fast Insertion Strike Team. These types of operations are highly classified. The government can't even risk acknowledging their existence."

Fish sank down on the brown leather sofa and rubbed his chin, deep in thought. After a couple of moments, he looked at Caleb and spoke.

"I think the shit is about to hit the fan if it already hasn't. So, where do we go next?"

"Well, I think we need to chase every possible lead, and we have to do it quickly. I was reading the file Jessica sent over. I want the two of you to head to the Sheridan, Oregon, Federal Prison. I've made arrangements for you to talk with the guy who shared the cell with Hector Gonzales."

"When do you want us to go?"

"Hawk, the time to go is now. I've made arrangements for a flight down to the prison. The sooner you two get to the Pacific Sun Coast Aviation Terminal, the quicker we might be able to get to the bottom of this mess."

Hawk started to respond to Caleb. Before he had hardly uttered a word, Fish grabbed him and pulled him out of Caleb's office.

"Damn it, Fish, I wasn't finished. Why did you pull me out of there?"

"Look, Hawk, I didn't want you to say something that you will regret saying later."

The Pacific Sun Coast Aviation Terminal was on the south side of the Seattle Tacoma Airport.

Fisher eased a red Jaguar F type convertible into a parking spot next to the terminal lobby door.

"Wow, how sexy," a voice came from behind him.

Fish's face flushed red with embarrassment.

"Take it easy, Ken. I was talking about the car."

"Lynn, you know how to slam a guy back down to earth."

Lynn Keiffer was the pilot for their journey to Sheridan.

"Wow, Ken, a new Jaguar convertible. This must have set you back a bunch."

"It would have if it was mine. It belongs to my dad. He is staying with us for a couple of months, so he let me drive it."

"Well, your dad has great taste."

"Is Eric here yet, Lynn?"

"Yeah, he's been here for about a half-hour. Are you ready to go?"

"I'm ready, let's get going."

They walked into the passenger area. Hawk stood and waited for them to arrive.

"I think Caleb hates me."

"Why do you think that, Hawk?"

"You'll see."

Fisher began to laugh as they stepped out onto the tarmac.

"Go ahead, laugh at my expense."

The only aircraft parked on the tarmac was a six-seat Sikorsky Helicopter.

"I'm sorry, Hawk, I think it's funny."

"Caleb knows I hate flying. What's more, I hate helicopters."

"What I don't get is, how did you ever make it through being in the Navy Seals if you hate helicopters?"

"I did it because I cared about the mission. The success of the mission depended on everyone. We all had to execute our jobs to perfection."

"If you could suck it up then, you can surely suck it up now."

"Look, let's just get this over with."

The liftoff was smooth, as was their trip. They landed on the helicopter pad at FCI Sheridan. within a few hours, and walked towards the main gate.

"See, Hawk, you survived the trip."

"It doesn't mean I liked it. Are you sure this place is a federal correctional institute?"

"I'm quite sure it is. Why?"

"This place looks more like a college campus than it does a prison. If the inside looks as nice as the outside, I can understand why people commit crimes to get back in."

In a few minutes, they were standing in the lobby of the administration building at the sign-in counter.

"Please show your identification, gentlemen."

"I'm Detective Eric Steinbrenner, and this is my partner, Detective Ken Fisher. We are with the Seattle PD. We have an appointment with Warden James," Hawk informed as they presented their badges.

The guard picked up a phone and pressed a button.

"Warden, your appointment is here."

Within minutes, Warden Peter James walked into the lobby.

"Good afternoon, Detectives. I'm Warden James. Would you please follow me to my office."

They entered a stairway and went up to the second floor. The warden's office was in the east corner of the building. Walking into the room, Warden James picked up two business cards and handed them to the detectives.

"Warden James, I'm Detective Fisher, and this is my partner, Detective Steinbrenner. We appreciate the fact you're meeting with us on such short notice. We are here to see Hector Gonzales' cellmate."

"Why are you interested in Hector Gonzales? What is he involved with now?"

"The only thing we can tell you about Hector is that he is dead. Can we meet with his cellmate? We have a couple of questions for him."

"It's not possible at the moment, Detectives. There's been an incident involving his cellmate, Chris Felton."

"Is he alright?"

"I'm not sure, Detective Fisher. He's in surgery at the hospital in Salem as we speak."

"How can we get there from here? We'll want to talk with him as soon as possible, Warden."

"I'll arrange for a car. It's about half an hour or so to Salem from here. It will be anybody's guess on what shape you'll find him in."

Forty-five minutes later, Fish and Hawk were walking into the hospital in Salem, Oregon. They stepped up to the information desk and presented their badges to the receptionist. She carefully studied them and looked at both of their faces.

"How can I help you, Detectives?"

"We need Chris Felton's status. He was brought here from Sheridan Prison."

"Let me check for you." Elizabeth, the receptionist, typed Chris Felton into the patient directory. "Detectives, Chris Felton is listed as being in post-op recovery on the third floor. The elevators are to your left. When you get to the third floor, exit the elevators to the right. The post-op waiting room is about halfway down the hallway on your right. I'll send a message to the nurse's station so they can let his doctor know."

Within a couple of minutes, they were sitting in the waiting room. After an hour, a woman wearing hospital scrubs walked in.

"I'm Doctor Parker. Are you the detectives inquiring about Chris Felton?"

"Yes, we are."

"Chris is lucky to be alive."

"Is he awake and alert enough so we can speak with him, Doctor?"

"Chris is awake at the moment. I can't guarantee how alert he is. You're welcome to try to talk to him. He's just down the hall in room 386."

There were two officers posted at the entrance to the room. Fish and Hawk showed them their badges as they approached. Chris Felton was in a hospital bed with multiple wires hooked to him, along with an I.V. drip in his arm.

"Chris, I'm Detective Fisher, and this is my partner Detective Steinbrenner. We would like you to answer a few questions about Hector Gonzales."

Chris Felton managed a faint smile when he heard Hector's name. His voice was weak, but he answered anyway.

"What's Hector done now? I don't think he knows how to stay out of trouble."

"Chris, we are not sure why, but Hector was shot to death four days ago."

"Shit, is that what this is all about? Hector always told me that if he ever turned up dead, I would be next."

"Look, Chris, your attack may be related to his death, but it's hard to say. We're looking for some information about Hector Gonzales. If you help us out, we'll make sure you're protected."

"What about my mom?"

"What about her?"

"Who is going to protect her?"

"It doesn't look like you have a choice considering your present predicament."

Fish flipped open his cell phone and made a call.

"Caleb, this is Fish. We're at a hospital in Salem, Oregon. Someone attacked Hector Gonzales' cellmate, Chris Felton, this morning. We are going to have to provide some protection for him until this mess gets cleared up. Can you get a transfer order for him?"

Fish listened to Caleb for a moment.

"Where do I want to move him? I'm not sure. That's for you to decide. Eventually, I want to put him in the Witness Protection Program. We can work out the rest of the details when we get back."

Fish listened again to Caleb.

"Yes, Caleb, it's the right thing to do."

Fish closed his cell phone.

"Hawk, Caleb gave us the go-ahead. Warden James will have the release paperwork by noon today."

"Detective Fisher, what about the witness protection program?"

"Chris, first things first. As soon as you're well enough to travel, we will get you out of here. It will take a few days to get you into the Witsec program."

"What about my mom?"

"We can't make any guarantees about your mom. I can promise we will do our best to make it happen."

"Detective Fisher, you've got a mom, don't you?"

"Yes."

"Then, you have to understand how I feel about her."

"Sure I do, Chris. We need to ask you questions about Hector Gonzales. Please answer them to the best of your ability."

Hawk opened his briefcase and produced a picture for Chris to see.

"Chris, is this Hector Gonzales?"

"Yeah, it's him. But you guys already knew it, didn't you?"

"Hector had his fingerprints removed, so we weren't 100 percent sure. Nobody has claimed him missing."

"Detective, Hector always said it was just him and his brother. He had a small apartment behind his brother's garage, but they never really saw each other."

"Can you tell us where?"

"I'm pretty sure it's somewhere in the San Francisco Bay area ."

"Can you be more specific?"

"No, but I saw a picture of his brother's garage once. The name on the garage was the Automobile Fixorium. He said it was near a pizza joint."

"Did he mention the name of the pizza joint by chance?"

"Yeah, it was Giancarlo's Pizza."

"Did Hector talk about his friends or family?"

"No, not very often."

"Did Hector talk about anybody at all?"

"Yeah, he said he liked to hang with this guy named Johnny Two Fingers."

"Did he ever mention Johnny Two fingers name?"

"Not that I can recall."

Fisher was making notes as Chris Felton spoke.

"Did Hector ever say why he and his brother hardly talked to each other?"

"Not that I remember."

"What did Hector talk about the most?"

"Collecting."

"Collecting what?"

"He said he was collecting for his future. He never said what he was collecting."

"We looked at the visitor's logbook. Hector never had any visitors. Do you know if it bothered him?"

Chris Felton's voice was starting to trail off, and his eyes were closing. Doctor Parker, who had been standing in the background, stepped in.

"I'm sorry, guys, that's all Chris is going to be able to tell you for now. It'll probably be tomorrow before he's alert again."

"Hawk, it looks like you and I are going to San Francisco to corroborate what Chris told us."

Chapter 9

The Fixorium

The Automobile Fixorium was on Santa Rosa Street in Sausalito, across the bay from San Francisco. It was next to Giancarlo's Pizza shop. The Fixorium was in an arc above the large roll-up door to the garage. To the left of the roll-up door was a small door with the words Ricardo Gonzales Proprietor on it. Fish and Hawk went inside. A girl in her early twenties was typing on a computer behind the counter.

"Excuse us, miss, is the owner here?"

She raised a hand and said, "Give me a couple of minutes, please. I just need to finish this invoice."

After a couple of minutes, she turned around, smiled and pointed to Detective Steinbrenner.

"Hello, where have you been all my life?"

She looked through the appointment book and said, "We're booked up until the middle of next week." Looking at Detective Steinbrenner again, she stated. "My, aren't you pleasant to look at. I'm free at five if you are."

Detective Steinbrenner pulled out his badge.

"Sorry, miss."

She interrupted.

"Kaylene. My name is Kaylene Irvine."

"Kaylene, I'm Detective Steinbrenner, and this is my partner Detective Fisher. Is Ricardo Gonzales here?"

"I'm sorry, Ricky isn't here at the moment."

"Could you please tell us when he will be back?"

"He just went out for some lunch. He should be back any moment. You can wait if you would like."

Just then, a voice came from behind them.

"If you guys need your car fixed, I'm booked until next week."

The two detectives turned around.

"Are you Ricardo Gonzales?"

"Who wants to know?" Ricardo replied

The two detectives showed him their badges.

"The Seattle Police Department wants to know."

"I'm Ricardo Gonzales. I assure you I'm running a legitimate business here. Just what brings you two all the way from Seattle to speak with me? I've never been to the state of Washington, let alone Seattle."

Fisher began to speak. "Mr. Gonzales, we're not here to question you about your business practices."

"What are you here for then?"

"We would like to ask you some questions about Hector Gonzales. He is your brother, isn't he?"

"Do I have to claim him as my brother?"

"You don't get along with your brother?"

"My brother and I are like vinegar and water. We never mixed very well. Kaylene, would you please take these sandwiches out to the guys."

He set a box full of sandwiches on the counter.

"Would you guys like something to drink?"

"We're fine, thanks for the offer."

"No problem. What kind of trouble is my brother in now?"

"The worse kind of trouble."

"What did Hector do now?"

"Mr. Gonzales, would you like to sit down?"

"This isn't going to be good, is it? Where is my brother?"

"I'm sorry to tell you that your brother is dead."

Ricardo Gonzales sank slowly down to the bench meant for waiting clients. A tear ran down his cheek.

"When did it happen?" he said, obviously distraught at the news.

"His body was found last week in the Grand Canyon."

Gonzalez sucked in a deep breath; his body shuddered.

"You sure it was my brother Hector?"

"We wouldn't be here talking to you if we weren't. Do you know what your brother was doing there?"

"I'm sorry, I don't know. We didn't talk very often. I haven't seen Hector in a long time."

"We have information that your brother lived here."

"Yeah, in a small upstairs apartment in our storage building out back."

"How often did your brother come and go?"

"I'm sorry, I have no clue."

"Your brother lived in an apartment that you owned, but you have no idea of his coming and going. I find it hard to believe," Hawk said.

"Detective, my brother and I saw eye to eye on exactly nothing. If I said white, he would say black. If I told him to go left, he would go right. He did it just to piss me off."

"It just seems odd to us you let your brother live in an apartment you owned if you didn't get along with him."

"Call me Ricky. Detective, the only reason I let Hector use the apartment is because I made a promise to my mother on her deathbed. I promised her that I would always take care of Hector, no matter how I felt about him." Ricky made a sign of the cross. "You see, Hector never had a pot to piss in or a window to throw it out of."

"I understand your relationship with your brother Ricky. He sounds a lot like my brother. Did you give your brother financial support?"

"My business covered his rent and utilities, so I don't know if it would be considered financial support. I never gave him money except at Christmas to get himself something, but I never gave him more than a hundred dollars, Detective Fisher."

"How did Hector support himself?"

"He told me he was a part-time consultant."

"What kind of consulting did your brother do?"

"I'm not sure what kind of consulting he did, Detective. Hector went away for long periods. I assumed he went where the work was. I quit caring about him a long time ago."

"Ricky, did you know your brother has done two different stints in prison?"

"I'm sorry, but I had no idea. I can't say that I'm surprised."

"Why aren't you surprised?" Fisher asked.

"As a kid, Hector was always hanging out with the wrong bunch of guys. They would do stupid shit that would get them in trouble. Look, Detectives, I've been so busy trying to keep this business going that I just didn't have the time or the energy to keep tabs on my brother. I guess I failed my mother and my brother."

"Please understand, Ricky, we are not here to condemn your relationship with your brother. Did you ever meet any of Hector's friends or business associates?"

"No, I'm sorry I didn't."

"We would like to search your brother's apartment, but we need your permission to do it. We can get a search warrant if needed."

"You won't need a search warrant. I'll get Kaylene to take you out there."

"Thanks, that would be great."

"Detective Steinbrenner, could you please do me one favor?"

"We will if we can."

"My daughter Rosalita comes here every day after school. I don't want her to know anything bad about my brother."

"It's a deal, Ricky."

"Kaylene, please come here," Ricky yelled into the garage.

Within a couple of minutes, Kaylene sauntered into the office area. Hawk watched her every move.

"Ricky, you called for me?" Kaylene asked.

"When you've finished getting the guys in the garage all worked up, I would appreciate it if you would take these two gentlemen out back and let them into the upstairs apartment."

Kaylene pointed to Detective Fisher. "Are you sure he has to come along."

"I'm afraid I do," Fish replied.

"Gentlemen, you can follow me," Kaylene said as she walked out of the office door and into the shop.

Hawk and Fish followed Kaylene into the shop.

"You guys are here about Hector?"

"Yes, do you happen to know much about him?"

"Not much. I can count on one hand the times I saw him."

The two detectives walked across the backlot to the detached garage. A wooden set of stairs was on the right side of the building, which led upstairs. Within minutes, they were standing in Hector's apartment. There were boxes strewn everywhere.

"Jesus, Hawk, would you look at this. I've never seen so much stuff packed into one place."

"Remember, Chris Felton told us he was a collector."

"This guy wasn't just a collector. He was closer to being a hoarder."

"Look, this is an original G.I. Joe. There must be thousands of dollars of original toys still in the box piled here."

Fish walked over to an end table. There was an answering machine sitting on top of a pile of six boxes. The message light was blinking.

"We may have something. There are eight messages on this answering machine."

Fish pulled out a small notepad and a pen from his pocket and was ready to write. He pressed the play button. He heard a male voice.

"You have eight new messages. Press play, or you can delete them by pressing the delete message now."

Fish pressed the play button again; he heard a woman's voice.

"Hector, this is Deandra. Where's the money you owe me? I may be easy, but I'm not cheap."

The detectives listened to the end of the message.

"To delete this message, press delete. To play the next message, press play."

The next six messages were all from the same person. The last one, however, indicated the caller was now irate.

"Hector, you son of a bitch. Where is the fucking money you owe me? It will be a cold day in hell before I jump into bed with you again."

Detective Fisher checked the phone's caller I.D. log. "Damn, all those calls were from a restricted phone number. It may be impossible to find out who this Deandra is."

Kaylene spoke up.

"I think I know who she is."

"We're all ears, Kaylene."

"I only know her as Dee. I think she's the girlfriend of one of our mechanics. She has called looking for her boyfriend a few different times. I'm pretty sure it's her voice on the answering machine."

"Kaylene, do you know how to get in touch with her?"

"I don't have a phone number for her. However, she lives with Ray Stipple, one of our mechanics. I have his home address. I can give it to you if you want."

"That would be great."

"If you don't mind waiting, I'll go get it for you."

"Thank you, Kaylene." Hawk watched her walk out the door.

"Wow, Fish, she's one smoking hot girl."

"Relax, Don Juan. You're as good as married. I know a girl at a certain Chinese restaurant in Seattle who would be in total agreement with me," Fish replied.

Hawk's face was red. "I keep telling you you're delusional."

"Well, I've got to tell you that your reactions to the mere mention of her are a dead giveaway. So, you can stuff the 'I don't know what you're talking about' bullshit where the sun doesn't shine."

"Will you please drop it? I don't want to talk about it."

"Fine, Hawk, I'll drop it. Sooner or later, you are going to have to confront your feelings for her. Preferably sooner rather than later."

Kaylene re-entered the apartment.

"Who do you have feelings for? Hopefully, you have them for me," Kaylene uttered as she walked over with the address in hand.

Hawk smiled at Kaylene as she walked toward him.

"As I said, Detective, I get off at five."

"I'm sorry, Kaylene. Just the address, please."

"What are you, all work and no play?"

"You could say that."

"That's just too bad. I don't think the Detective knows what he'll be missing."

"I'm sure he does. Can we have the address, please?"

Kaylene handed Fish the paper with the addresses.

"I'll make it easy for you guys. Ray Stipple's apartment is just a short walk from here."

"How short of a walk is it?"

"You can walk there in fifteen minutes or less."

"Good, I'll use the GPS on my phone for directions," Fish said.

"You don't need GPS to get there. It's simple—just take a left out of our parking lot. Proceed about two and a half blocks. There will be a park on your right. Take the first pathway you come to which goes through the park. When you get to the other side, there will be a four-story brownstone building directly across the street. It's the only building with a fire hydrant and a bike rack out front. The apartment you're looking for is on the top floor. They live in apartment 401."

"Thanks, Kaylene."

"Not a problem. I'm always glad to help the police."

By the way, Kaylene, don't tell her boyfriend we're going there. We don't need him showing up while we're trying to talk with her. It may get ugly if he finds out why we're there."

"Don't worry, gentlemen. I assure you, I won't say anything."

"Good. We wouldn't want to have you arrested for interfering with a criminal investigation."

Chapter 10

Ray Stipple's Apartment

It took precisely eleven minutes for the detectives to walk to the brownstone where Ray Stipple lived. The front door was unlocked and opened into a small vestibule that included a locked set of entry doors. A keypad with a microphone and a speaker was to the right. The entry instructions were posted above it.

"Hey, Fish, I don't think this door is closed all the way," Hawk said just as Fish was about to enter the apartment number into the keypad.

Hawk opened the inner door and gained access to the building's apartments. Within a couple of minutes, they were knocking on the door of apartment 401. They heard the slide of the deadbolt as the door slowly moved. A safety chain kept the door from opening all the way. A young woman with a long, slender face stared out at them.

"We're with the police, are you Deandra Parker?"

"Yes, I am. Why?"

"We need to talk to you. May we come in?"

The door moved slightly and swung open as far as the safety chain would allow.

"How do I know you're cops? Can I see your I.Ds?"

The two detectives showed their badges.

"Look, as far as I know, you two are out of your jurisdiction, so I don't have to open the door."

"That's right, Deandra, you don't have to open the door. But if you don't, we'll be back with the locals and a warrant if that's what you want. It would make it a whole lot easier if you just let us in."

"What's this all about anyway?"

"We'd like to talk to you about Hector Gonzales. You know him, don't you?"

The detectives heard the safety chain being removed. The door swung open, and they walked in.

"Gentlemen, we can talk in here."

The apartment was spotlessly clean. The detectives followed Deandra past the kitchen and into the living room. There was a bay window that gave a commanding view of the park across the street. A flat-screen television was on the wall to the left, directly across from a black leather sofa. Two matching overstuffed leather chairs were next to end tables at opposite ends of the couch. Deandra slowly turned around and lowered herself into the leather chair closest to the window. Fish looked at her and smiled. She had a large, protruding belly and was most likely seven to eight months pregnant.

"You'll have to excuse me if I don't offer you gentlemen something to drink. It's hard to maneuver up and down in my condition."

"That's okay, Deandra. We would just like to ask you a couple of questions."

"Do I need to have a lawyer present?" she asked.

"You can if you want, but it's probably not necessary. I'm Detective Ken Fisher, and this is my partner, Detective Eric Steinbrenner."

"What does the Seattle Police Department expect me to know about Hector Gonzales? I've never met him."

"Deandra, Detective Steinbrenner and I know it's not true. We've been to Hector's apartment. We've heard the voicemails you left Hector. Do you think Ray Stipple will be happy to find out you've been to bed with Hector Gonzales and that he paid you for it?"

Deandra started to cry and rub her belly.

"Look, it's not what you think?"

"Given the messages you left on Hector's answering machine, what else are we supposed to think?"

She sat silent and motionless with her head hung low. After a minute, she looked up and said, "I'll tell you what I know about Hector, but you've got to promise to keep Ray out of this. I don't want to lose him. His baby needs a father."

"Are you sure the baby is his and not Hector's?"

"Detective, a few months ago, I was sitting in the park across the street. I was reading a book by Debbie Macomber when this guy comes up to me and starts talking about how she is his favorite writer. He sat down next to me, and we began discussing the book. He gave insights about the characters I hadn't even considered. I enjoyed talking to him.

"You went to bed with him because you both enjoyed the same writer?"

"I went to the park every day to read because it was spring, and the flowers were all in bloom. It was a great place to read. It's peaceful there. Hector came one day and gave me an autographed copy of a book by Debbie Macomber. I told him I couldn't accept it. He smiled and said I could have it for a small favor."

"What did Hector ask you to do?"

"Hector wanted me to go to bed with him. I had just found out I was expecting a baby. I gave the book back and told him no thanks."

"You called him seven different times demanding the money he owed you. In one of the messages, you told him you wouldn't go to bed with him anymore. What are you lying about?"

"I'm sorry," Deandra began to weep openly.

"You're sorry about what?"

"Hector offered me money if I would go down on him. He said we wouldn't be having sex. He didn't want to take no for an answer."

"Did Hector threaten you and then offer to pay you to shut you up?"

"No. Hector offered me one thousand dollars to take care of him. I needed the money for my honeymoon. It was the easiest and quickest money I had ever made in my life. Ray's big dream is to dive the Great Barrier Reef. I only needed the last payment from Hector to cover the cost of the trip and the dive permits, which is why I left the messages for Hector."

"We're sorry to tell you this, Deandra, Hector is dead. You can kiss the rest of the money he owed you goodbye. If your boyfriend finds out about how you earned the money, you're going to have bigger problems than paying for a honeymoon."

"You've got to promise me you won't tell him."

"Like we said before, we just want to ask you about Hector."

"Go ahead and ask. I'll gladly tell you anything I know."

"Do you know what Hector did for a living?"

"He told me he was a consultant, and he traveled out of town."

"When you were with Hector, did anyone come and see him?"

"I was never there very long, so no."

"Do you know if he had a cell phone?"

"Yes, I saw it on his dresser once."

"Did Hector take any phone calls when you were there?"

"Not that I remember."

"Did Hector ever talk about the specifics of his job?"

"No, and I never asked."

"Did Hector talk about any friends?"

"I'm not sure."

"Did Hector ever mention Johnny Two Fingers or someone he called The Hammer?"

"No, not to me. I'm sorry. I've never heard those names before."

"Is there anything you do know about Hector Gonzales?"

"Yeah, lots. Detective Fisher, you haven't asked the right questions yet."

"What can you tell us about Hector?"

"Hector was also seeing one of the waitresses at Giancarlo's Pizza. It's the place next door to the Fixorium."

"Do you know which girl he was seeing?"

"My best guess is he was seeing a girl named Bonnie Bishop who worked there. I found a pair of panties between his sheets one time. They had the monogram BB on them. I asked him if they belonged to Bonnie."

"What did Hector say?"

"He told me no at first. But I went there once for a takeout pizza and saw him flirting with Bonnie. They were sitting in a corner booth. When I asked him about it, he told me it was none of my business. Maybe Hector was killed by Bonnie's father."

"Why would you think that?"

"Bonnie's father watches her every move. I've heard he has connections."

"What kind of connections?"

"The Mafia, of course."

"Is it hearsay, or do you have any proof?"

"No, I don't. I do know Bonnie's father chased off all her boyfriends."

"Why would he chase off her boyfriends?"

"Because he's overly protective. You see, Bonnie is only seventeen."

"Do you know where Bonnie lives?"

"She lives somewhere on Vine Street. She's most likely working at Giancarlo's tonight. You can go there and talk to her for yourself if you want."

"Is there anything at all you can think of that might give some insight into what Hector did for a living?"

"Maybe you can find his notebook."

"What's in this notebook?"

"I'm not quite sure. It was out on the nightstand one time, and I accidentally knocked it on the floor. It fell open when it hit the floor. I picked it up and looked at it, but none of what was in it made any sense to me."

"What was in it?"

"There were dates and addresses and notes on every line of each page. The notes didn't make any sense to me."

"Why didn't they make any sense to you?"

"The notes were a combination of symbols. Letters and numbers. I asked Hector what they meant."

"Did he tell you what they meant?"

"He said it was his insurance."

"Is that all he said?"

"Yeah, he went to another room and put it away. I never saw it again."

"Deandra, we're done for right now. Don't travel anywhere for the next few days. We may have to ask you more questions."

"Seriously, Detective, do you think I'm going to go anywhere in my condition?"

"Probably not but stick around nonetheless."

Fish turned to Hawk and began to speak.

"Hawk, I think we are going to have to stay another day. We need to search Hector's apartment for his notebook."

"It's going to take a while just to remove all those boxes. It would be great if Caleb could get us some help."

"That's a good idea. I'll give Caleb a call."

Fish flipped open his cell phone and dialed.

"Caleb, this is Fish. Hawk and I are going to be here for another day. We need to search Hector Gonzales's apartment. It seems he kept a journal. According to this girl he was seeing, Hector said it was his insurance. My guess is it contains information critical to our investigation."

Fish listened intently to Caleb.

"I believe we can, Caleb. It would be helpful if you could get us some help. Hector's apartment has so many boxes you can hardly move through it. We are going to have to get the boxes out of there before we can even begin our search."

Fish paused to listen to Caleb again.

"Thanks, Caleb."

"Fish, what did Caleb say?"

"He said he would get us help for tomorrow. He says we have to wrap it up down here. He wants us back in the office the day after tomorrow. Hopefully, we'll find what we're looking for."

"I hope we can go through all that stuff in one day, Fish. I'm not sure we'll be able to."

"Maybe not, Hawk, but try we will."

Chapter 11

Giancarlo's Pizza

Giancarlo's Pizza restaurant was to the right of the Automobile Fixorium. Once in the restaurant, a tall and very thin young man with purple hair greeted the detectives.

"Welcome to Giancarlo's, gentlemen. Would you like a booth or a table?"

"A booth would be just fine," Fish replied.

Their host led them to a booth halfway down the wall on the left-hand side of the restaurant. There was a set of wood-fired brick pizza ovens on the right situated, behind a four-foot-high counter concealing the pizza preparation area. Brightly colored bowls and platters adorned the walls.

"Hey, Fish, this is a nice place."

"Yeah, it is. I hope the food is as good as the ambiance."

"I'll second that motion. Are you going to try the pizza Chris Felton mentioned to us? You know, the one so hot if you eat the whole thing, it's free?"

"First of all, Hawk, my days of eating a whole pizza are done. Secondly, I don't like what hot food does to me. But be my guest and go for it."

The same young man who'd seated them came over to take their order.

"My name is Madrid. Is this your first time here?"

"Yes, it is."

"Are you guys ready to order?"

"What do you recommend?" Fish asked.

"We make everything fresh right here. We grow herbs and heirloom tomatoes outback. The pasta is made on the premises as well. Whatever you choose, I'm sure you'll enjoy it," the waiter answered.

Fish studied the menu. "I'll have the spaghetti with the cheese stuffed meatballs. Hawk, you like hot food. Are you going to go for the so hot if you eat its free pizza?"

"I was thinking about it."

Hawk looked at the waiter. "Which pizza on this menu is the spicy hot one?"

"The Fuoco Diavoli pizza."

"Do people eat the whole thing?"

The waiter pointed to the wall at the end of the dining room. There were pictures of people holding up a tee-shirt saying, "I survived the fire," posted on the wall.

"As you can see, there are quite a few people up there. You know what they say, no guts, no glory."

"Hawk, you don't need to worry. You probably won't have much of a gut left after you eat it," Fish chuckled.

"You know, I'm going for the proverbial brass ring," turning to the waiter, "I'll have the Fuoco Diavoli pizza."

"It sounds good to me, gentlemen. I'll go put in your order," the waiter replied.

Fish began to chuckle.

"What's so funny?

"Do you know what Fuoco Diavoli means? The pizza you ordered is named the Devil's Fire. You've probably never eaten anything like it before."

"For your information, I eat spicy food all the time."

"I'll bet you a hundred bucks you don't make it through this one. There's no way you're going to eat the whole pizza."

"You're on. I'll take the bet. I'm going to enjoy taking your money bite by bite."

Hawk pulled five twenty-dollar bills out of his wallet and threw them down on the table.

Fish removed a hundred-dollar bill and placed it on top of the five twenties already on the table.

"Hawk, you know what they say."

"No, I don't. What do they say?"

"They say that a fool and his money are easily parted. This is going to be the easiest money I've ever made."

"We'll see about that."

A woman's voice came from over Hawk's shoulder.

"Well, look what the cat dragged in."

Fish looked up and spoke.

"Kaylene, are you here for dinner or just picking something up?"

Kaylene slid into the booth next to Hawk.

"It depends on Detective Superhero here," she answered, touching Hawk's arm.

"If he's buying, I'm interested."

"Kaylene, your information was helpful. Buying your dinner isn't a problem."

"I appreciate it, Detective. I am here to pick up a take-home order, so I'll pass."

"You can give us the bill for your order anyway,."

"I paid for it when I called it in. Maybe Detective Steinbrenner can come back and buy me dinner sometime."

"There's always a possibility we will have to come back looking for more information."

"Did you guys get what you needed about Hector from Deandra?"

"We mostly came away with more questions than answers."

"Is there anything I can help with?" Kaylene asked.

"Possibly. We came in here looking for a waitress who works here."

"Who would that be, Detective?"

"We are looking for Bonnie Bishop. We would like to talk to her about Hector. Deandra told us Bonnie knows Hector."

"I'm sorry, Detective. I've talked with Bonnie a few times, but I have no idea if Bonnie knows Hector or not."

Madrid had approached the table and was listening.

"You guys are looking for Bonnie Bishop?"

"Yes, we are."

"So is every guy who comes in here."

"Why do you say that, Madrid?"

"Bonnie Bishop is one of the nicest people you ever want to meet. Once you meet her, you'll know why."

"Will she be coming in tonight?"

"No, she won't. Besides, you guys can't talk to her because she's underage."

"How do you know we can't talk to her?" Fisher asked.

"You guys are cops, aren't you?" Madrid replied.

Fisher pulled out his Seattle PD badge. "My partner and I are with the Seattle Police Department. We think Bonnie has information we need."

"Look, I'm in my second year of law school at the San Francisco School of Law. I know that legally, you can't talk to her without the consent of her parents," Madrid replied.

"Madrid, do you know when Bonnie will be back at work?" Hawk asked.

"Bonnie is out of town until next week. There was a death in her family. Is there any way I can help?"

"You wouldn't happen to know a guy named Johnny Two Fingers?"

"No, I don't. Why do you think Bonnie knows him?"

"Seattle PD has the reason to believe she knows a Hector Gonzales. Johnny Two Fingers is an associate of Hector Gonzales. Hector turned up dead last week, so we were hoping Bonnie knows Johnny Two Fingers. We want to question Johnny about his death."

"Wow, Hector is dead. Bonnie is going to be so upset about it!" Madrid commented.

"Why would Bonnie be upset about Hector's death?"

"Detective, Bonnie is a super nice person. She treats everyone like they have class and dignity. I think it impressed Hector. He would always ask for Bonnie whenever he came in to eat. Bonnie told me Hector always left her great tips."

"We were told Bonnie might have been getting more than just good tips," Fisher commented.

"I'm sorry, Detective. I'm not sure what you mean."

"It doesn't matter what I mean."

"I'm sorry I can't help you. You may want to stop in at the Dock Side Bar & Grill after you leave here. My older sister is the bartender there. She knows anybody and everybody in this city."

"Does your older sister have a name?"

"Jasmine Rose, but she goes by JR."

"Where do we find the Dock Side Bar and Grill?"

"Go to Water Street. It's the only building with a ship's anchor outside. Dress down before you go. The Dock Side Bar & Grill is a place where the locals hang out. You guys go there dressed in suits like you are, absolutely nobody is going to talk to you."

"What's wrong with our suits?"

"Nothing. They just scream: look at me, I'm a cop."

"Thanks, Madrid. Trust us, it's a point well taken," Fisher replied.

"No problem, Detective. Your food should be coming out in about fifteen minutes."

The food was served within twelve minutes.

"Here you go. One, it's so spicy hot if you eat it all, it's free pizza. I'll be back in a minute with the spaghetti and a plate for the pizza."

Fish looked at the pizza in front of his partner.

"Damn, Hawk. I don't think I could even identify all the peppers on your pizza. It even smells hot."

"I know you're just trying to psyche me out. I'll tell you what, I'm taking the hundred dollars to the bank."

Fish began rubbing his eyes with his napkin.

"One thing's for sure, it's hot enough to make my eyes water."

"Your eyes are watering because you're a wuss around spicy food."

"I learned my lesson about eating spicy food a long time ago."

The waiter returned, carrying the bowl of spaghetti and the plate for the pizza.

"Here's your dinner and the plate for the pizza. Is there anything else?"

"I have a question for you," Fish said to the waiter.

"Sure, what would you like to know?"

"What kind of peppers are on his pizza? It's so spicy hot, my eyes are watering."

"Sir, the Fuoco Diavoli pizza has a combination of peppers: Jalapenos, Serranos, Habaneras, Datils, Pequins, and Naga Jolokia. Each pepper I mentioned is hotter than the one before."

"Bon Appetite, Hawk," Fish said.

Fisher began to eat his meal. After a couple of minutes, he looked over at his partner.

"I've got to tell you, this pasta is amazing. How's the pizza?"

Fish looked over at Hawk. He was on his second slice of pizza. The sweat was running down his face.

"Is your pizza getting to you already?"

"I'm fine."

"You're fine? How on earth can you say that? The pizza is so hot, sweat is pouring off your face, for God's sake."

"I'm fine. It's just hot in here."

"Well, like I said before, the hundred dollars is as good as mine."

After starting on his fourth slice of pizza, Hawk looked at Fish and exclaimed, "You're right. I can't eat the whole pizza. I give in—the money is yours."

"You want the rest boxed?"

"No, it can stay where it sits."

Fish picked up the money and handed it back to Hawk.

"What the hell is this for?"

"It was worth the price of admission just to see the Great Eric Steinbrenner, defender of woman's honor, admit defeat. How about we get out of here and check out the Dock Side Bar and Grill?"

"Sounds like a plan to me."

Chapter 12

The Dock Side Bar & Grill

The exterior of the Dock Side Bar & Grill had faded from the weather. The detectives parked in the municipal lot down the street. Fish started to walk when he realized that his partner was not yet moving.

"Eric, is everything okay?"

Hawk was standing like his feet were cast in concrete. Fish walked up and placed his hand on his partner's shoulder.

"Hawk, what's wrong?"

Fish looked at Hawk, who pointed to a powder blue 1966 Mustang convertible.

"My dad had a Mustang just like this when he left us. I still have this stupid notion that one day, he's going to show back up in my life. I'm sorry, Fish. I didn't mean to get all sentimental on you."

"It's okay, I understand. Are you ready to get going?"

"Ready as I'll ever be. Let's go."

Within ten minutes, the two detectives walked into the restaurant. The inside had nautical charts posted all over the walls. The end wall was all glass and overlooked the water. Sailboats were lazily moving up and down the bay. An observation deck contained outside seating. The hostess stand was immediately on the right and was staffed by a woman with graying hair.

"Good evening, gentlemen. Welcome to the Dock Side Bar & Grill. Would you like to sit inside or out? It's a beautiful night, and there's a nice breeze coming in off the bay. Personally, I would pick outside."

"Thanks for the recommendation. We're just here for a drink," Fisher replied.

"The inside entry to the bar is just past the restrooms. Take the hallway to the right," the hostess instructed.

"Thanks," the detectives replied.

The bar was U-shaped, in a large room next to the dining area. The detectives quickly assessed the bar. A young couple was sitting at the end, a woman in her late fifties sat to their right. She was playing a video poker game while sipping a beer. Two couples were playing pool. The detectives walked up to the bar and sat down. The woman behind the bar was dressed in blue jeans and wore a leather vest adorned with pins sporting motorcycle brand logos. She handed a bar menu to the two men.

"Gentlemen, this is our bar menu. Appetizers are on the first two pages. Our beer and wine collection is on pages three and four. The last four pages contain our specialty drinks. If you can't find something to suit your fancy, then you're probably at the wrong place."

"Do you have any craft beers?" Fisher asked.

"The top half of page three contains our craft beer list."

"It's a little slow in here, isn't it?" Fish said as he sat down.

"In another hour and a half, this place will be mobbed," the bartender replied. She pointed toward the deck outside. "It's music on the deck night. The band playing tonight is Reggie's Reggae Rebellion. They are a lot of fun to watch. Have you ever seen them perform?"

"We can't say that we have," Hawk replied.

"Well then, you should stick around to hear them play. It's a blend of Reggae, Fusion, and Calypso music. They put on an amazing show," the bartender explained.

"Thanks. We're looking for a woman named Jasmine Rose. Is she here?" Fisher asked.

"Yes, the last time I checked, I was here," the bartender replied.

"Can we call you JR?"

"I only let my family and friends call me that."

"We met your brother a little while ago, and that's what he said to call you."

"What else did the little brat tell you?"

"He said you might be able to help us."

"That will depend on what kind of help you guys need."

"JR, we're looking for information."

"So, the little shit sent you to me?"

"Yes, he did. He told us you know just about everything and everyone in this town."

"I am going to kick the crap out of him the next time I see him."

"Madrid was just trying to help us out. So, go easy on him."

"I know just about everything and everyone in this town because I've earned their trust. What is said here and what goes on here, stays here. I don't gossip about other people."

"We can compel you to talk with us if we have to."

She looked at the two detectives and was irritated.

"As I said before, what goes on here stays here!"

She picked up the bar menu and handed it to Detective Fisher.

"I suggest you take this menu and go find a seat out on the deck and order yourselves a drink. I would take a long look at the craft beer section. The first six beers on the list are made right here. If you don't like the offering, you can always leave the same way you came in."

"Come on, Hawk. We might as well go grab a seat on the deck and enjoy what's left of the daylight," Fish said, tucking the menu under his arm. Turning back toward JR, "We will be back tomorrow. Trust me, you will end up talking with us."

JR gave a mock salute to Detectives Fisher and Steinbrenner as they walked out onto the deck.

The detectives looked out over the water. A large catamaran was gliding across the water. Farther off to the right, a group of harbor seals were sliding in and out of the water off a large pile of rocks that jutted out from the shore.

"You know, Hawk, I could get used to a peaceful kind of easy life. I picture myself at the helm of a sailboat as it eases out of the bay into the ocean for a long journey."

"The way you dote about your boat, *The Salt Life*, I find it hard to believe that you would trade it for a sailboat. That requires work."

"I never said anything about trading my boat. It's just that sometimes a sailboat seems more laidback to me."

"Sounds good to me. I'll come along as you're first mate and call you skipper."

"You know, I was trying to be serious. I really wouldn't mind walking away from all this sometimes."

"Yeah, I know what you mean. I haven't been in this game as long as you have, and I'm already starting to feel burned out. I want to thank you."

"You want to thank me?"

"Yeah, I do."

"What on earth for?"

"For talking me into joining the Seattle PD. It's kind of like owning a boat."

"How the hell is being on the force like owning a boat?"

"They say the best two days of a boat owner's life are the day he buys the boat and the day he sells it. The way I look at it, probably the best two days of my life will be the day I joined the force and the day I leave it."

"I'll second the thought. Let's drink to that."

"You know, it pisses me off that we're going to have to come back here tomorrow. I hate the bullshit we get from people."

"Tell you what, let's order a drink, relax, and just kick back for the rest of the evening."

Fisher opened the menu to peruse the craft beers. There was a note inside the protective sleeve in front of the craft beer list, which contained the following information: 7:00 a.m., Golden Gate Recreation Area, Conzelman Road parking area. Be prepared to run.

Fish looked over at Hawk. "It looks like we're going for an early morning run."

"You know damn well I'm not a morning person. In fact, running in the morning is about the furthest thing from my mind when I wake up. Is this your brilliant idea of mindless torture? If it is, I'll throw in the towel now."

"I just figure you're going to want to work off the pizza you ate."

"Will you give the pizza a rest? I threw in the damn towel, after all. I'll give you the hundred dollars if you shut the hell up about it."

"You have my word. I won't bug you any more about the pizza."

Members of Reggie's Reggae Rebellion were setting up their equipment on the stage on the left-hand corner of the deck against the outside wall of the restaurant. A man with dreadlocks wore a tie-dyed g-shirt with the name of the band in black lettering. He looked up and caught Hawk's eye and smiled.

"So, Fish, do you want to stick around for the music?"

"Not really. You can if you want to. I don't mind taking a taxi back to the hotel."

"Are you afraid to cut loos,?"

"Not at all. My friend who got us into the hotel wants to stop by tonight. Besides, I need to file our daily report before I go to bed."

"While you're at it, make sure you call the boss."

"Why do I need to call Caleb?"

"I wasn't talking about our boss. I was talking about your boss. She will start calling me to make sure you're okay if she doesn't hear from you. Since you've got us running tomorrow morning, I am going to need a good night's rest. The last thing I need is your wife waking me up to make sure her husband is all right."

Fish started chuckling.

"Fine. I will call her as soon as we get checked in at the hotel. I am going to tell her about the pizza you tried to eat. I'm sure that she'll get a kick out hearing about the facial contortions you were making."

"That's not even funny."

"Oh yes, it is. The crowning touch will be the picture that I took of one of those contortions."

"Just remember I don't get mad. I will get even with you when you're least expecting it."

Chapter 13

Golden Gate Recreation Area

Detectives Fisher and Steinbrenner walked out of the Casa Madrona hotel toward their rented car.

"Fish, how on earth did you get us in here?"

"I called a friend who works for SFPD. His sister is a convention coordinator and gets hotel discounts."

"Enough of one to meet our expense report requirements?"

"No, not quite that big."

"Caleb is going to blow a gasket when he sees the expense report for this trip."

"The way I see it, it's a lot easier to ask for forgiveness."

"This is one time I'm glad you're the team lead. You're a lot better at asking for forgiveness than I am. I've got to tell you the room was amazing. The view alone was worth the price of admission."

"I take it you slept well?"

"I slept just awesome. I can't remember ever having a better night's sleep. You must have called your wife."

"Yes, I did. I wanted to have her give you a call and wake you up. She gets a kick talking to you."

"I appreciate the fact that you didn't. Are you ready for our morning run?"

"Almost. Would you mind driving?"

"What, you never let me drive. Are you not feeling okay this morning?"

"I feel fine. I just didn't get enough sleep. The couple in the room next door were having a headboard banging marathon, if you know what I mean. I had trouble getting to sleep."

"I hate it when that happens."

"They didn't run out of steam until about 2 o'clock this morning."

"You know, you could have got them to stop, don't you?"

"How the hell was I supposed to get them to stop?"

"You have a gun, don't you?"

"How about we get in the car so we can go?"

"Do you think she'll show up?"

"Hopefully. The way I look at it as this will probably be our only chance to stretch out our muscles today."

The ride from the hotel to the Golden Gate recreation area only took about ten minutes. They pulled into the Conzelman Road parking lot at precisely 6:45 a.m.

"We're the only ones here."

"Give it time. She'll show."

"I hope you're right."

A motorcyclist pulled into the parking area at five minutes to seven. She removed her helmet and walked over to the two detectives who were standing by the car.

"See, Hawk, I told you she would show up."

"Wow, a 1936 Harley Davidson Model R Flathead," Hawk said, impressed.

"It just goes to prove that even cops are smart. Don't worry, I would have known you guys were cops even if Madrid hadn't told me. Are you into Harley's, Detective...?" JR replied.

"Steinbrenner, I'm Detective Eric Steinbrenner, and this is my partner, Detective Ken Fisher. You can call us Hawk and Fish if you want."

"Isn't that cute. You guys have code names? I bet the guys in your fan club even have a secret handshake."

"What fan club? Fish asked

"You know the Barney Miller fan club. Hawk and Fish, it's just so rich." She laughed. "So, tell me, Detective Eric Steinbrenner, excuse me, I mean, Hawk, do you guys wear decoder rings?"

"Fish, JR is getting funnier by the minute. I can hardly keep myself from laughing."

"I take it, Hawk, you're into motorcycles?"

"I own a couple. Your motorcycle is in mint condition."

"I would hope so. I've spent a lot of hours restoring it."

JR removed her leathers. She was wearing blue running shorts and a matching tee-shirt emblazoned with the words Villanova Cross Country printed in white.

"You ran cross country at Villanova University?"

"Detective Fisher, I was a four-year starter on the cross-country team there."

"Do you run out here very often?"

"I run out here every day, rain or shine. The views are tremendous, and the hills give me a great workout."

"How far do you go?"

"The trails all connect, so I run five to ten miles, but sometimes I go farther."

"That's a lot of dedication," Fisher said.

"I was an alternate for the last Olympics. I don't intend to sit out the next one."

Fisher examined the panorama as he removed his sweatsuit.

"The view here is fantastic, don't you think, Hawk?"

"I would have to agree. Where else are you going to run where you have the Golden Gate Bridge and the City of San Francisco over one shoulder and whales surfacing in the Pacific Ocean over the other?"

"JR, how far had you planned on running today?" Fish asked.

"This is my ten-mile loop day. It's about five miles each way. There are out stations on the way that I use. If you guys prefer just to run, it's okay."

"We don't want to change your workout. If you lead, we will follow. Is there an area where we can get stretched out before we run?"

"Sure, the first workout station is at the head of the trail and is set up for stretching."

They jogged over to the workout area and started stretching.

"Detective Fisher, Madrid says you guys are looking for information about Johnny Two Fingers."

"Yes, we are. Do you know him?"

"Not very well. He's come into the bar a couple of times."

"Can you tell us what his real name is?"

"I'm pretty sure his name is John Pierce."

"What's with the nickname Johnny Two Fingers?"

"He earned the nickname Johnny Two Fingers for two reasons. First, he only drinks Two Fingers Tequila. Secondly, he always wants his glass to be filled just two fingers high."

"Do you happen to know what he does for a living?"

"The scuttlebutt around town is that he is into high tech electronics."

"Do you know who he works for?"

"I think he's a consultant."

"Do you know for who?"

"I'm sorry, I don't, but I believe it's a company in the electronics industry."

"He must be pretty good if he is consulting with the electronics industry."

"Fish, he was in the bar one night and told this guy he was with that he holds roughly twenty patents."

"I wonder how he got involved with Hector Gonzales."

"I've never heard the name Hector Gonzales before. Maybe Hector was one of Johnnie's customers. Rumor has it for the right kind of money, Johnny Two Fingers will build you any high-tech electronic gadget you want."

"When was the last time you saw Johnny Two Fingers?"

"I haven't seen him in two or three weeks."

"Do you know where Johnny Lives?"

"I heard him mention he is a silent partner in a group that purchased the old Edelman Factory site over on Kippen Street."

"Can you give us a description of Johnny Two Fingers?"

"Johnny is about one hundred forty-five pounds soaking wet. He is about 5 feet 10 inches tall and has short brown hair. He wears short-sleeve shirts that are buttoned all the way up and khaki pants. He always has a pocket protector full of pens and mechanical pencils in his breast pocket. If you looked up the definition of geek in the dictionary, you would probably find his picture."

"Thanks, JR, you've been helpful."

"You're welcome, Detective Fisher. Are you guys ready to run some hills?"

"I think Hawk and I are as ready as we're going to be."

"Well then, what do you say we get going? Do you want to set the pace, Detective Fisher?"

"No, I'll leave it up to you."

"Are you sure, Detective? I wouldn't want to be responsible for hospitalizing two detectives."

"We're positive. Let's do this."

After two hours, they returned to the Conzelman Road parking area. Hawk was bent over at the waist with a hand on each knee, attempting to catch his breath.

"Hawk, are you alright? You're breathing like a freight train."

Hawk gave a thumbs-up gesture to his partner.

"Detective Fisher, I'm impressed. You held your own out there. You're not too bad for an old guy. You must work out a lot."

"I try to keep in shape. I play tennis whenever I get the chance."

JR looked over at Hawk. "Is your partner going to make it?"

Hawk was still slightly gasping for breath.

"I'll be fine," Hawk replied.

"Hawk, I wasn't sure you had recovered enough to talk."

"Where on earth did you learn the stomach crunches you were doing at station eight? I tried to do a couple of them. They were killers," Hawk asked, still gasping.

"From my cross-country coach at Villanova."

"I'm impressed. I sure as hell couldn't do very many."

"Trust me, Hawk, the first time I tried, I wasn't successful either. Maybe you and Fish could add them to your workout routine."

"I don't know if I could be that cruel to my body."

"Did I tell you JR won the NCAA Cross Country title twice?" Fish asked.

"No, you didn't. Had I known, I might have objected to her taking the lead."

"Put it this way, what doesn't kill you can only make you better."

"You can be sadistic."

"Put a sock in the complaining. We need to get a move on it."

"Can we go back to the hotel and shower before we head over to Gonzales's apartment?"

"That's exactly what I thought we should do next."

"Since it's going to take a while to get all those boxes out of there. Why don't we let the guys the local section chief is sending over to do part of the work? We can go in and search for the notebook once all the boxes are out," Hawk recommended.

"Just what are we going to do while they are removing all the boxes?"

"I figured we would go over to the Edelman Factory complex to see if we can find Johnny Two Fingers."

"I'll call Caleb and let him know what's going on."

Chapter 14

The Edelman Factory Complex

Detectives Fisher and Steinbrenner parked in front of a sign at the Edelman Factory Complex, indicating it was the entrance to the rental office.

"Fish, did you notice the cornerstone of the building as we drove by?"

"No, I can't say I did."

"The cornerstone was dated 1878. Judging by the impressive looks of the building, I bet this place is on the National Historic Register."

The detectives walked through the door labeled office. A sign with an arrow pointed up the stairs to the right.

"Shall we head up?"

"Since it's our only choice, it sounds like the thing to do."

Framed photographs of the interior of the factory hung on the right wall of the staircase. When they reached the top, a sign indicated that the rental office was down the hallway. A door marked "office" was at the end. They opened the door and walked in. There was an L-shaped counter, two chairs were to the right of the door, and two more were on the wall to the left. A round coffee table was in front of the two sets of chairs. A binder labeled Edelman's Restoration was in the middle of the table. There was a sign on the

136

counter that read: We are out showing our property. Please have a seat and wait. A Keurig coffee maker was on a small table at the end of the counter, accompanied by a carousel containing various K cups coffee flavors.

Hawk spun the carousel around and commented. "The coffee is free. Do you want a cup?"

"No thanks, I'm good."

Hawk pulled a K cup out of the carousel.

"Ah, here's something I've always wanted to try. Pumpkin Spice Latte. You sure you don't want something?"

"I'm good. Thanks anyway."

Fisher picked up the binder from the table, sat down, and began to flip through the pages.

"Hawk, you should look at the pictures in here. The apartments for rent in this place are seriously upscale. Someone has sunk a ton of money into this place."

Hawk sat down with a cup of coffee in hand and took a sip.

"Wow, this coffee is good. You should try it."

"Coffee tastes like someone ran water through a sweaty pair of gym socks to me. You add Pumpkin Spice to sweaty gym socks, and I get a mental picture that could ruin the whole mystique of Thanksgiving dinner for the rest of my life."

"This is Latte. Latte is not coffee."

"Coffee and Lattes are in the same category. I'd have to be dead to drink either."

The sound of high heeled shoes was coming from beyond the counter. A young woman, about six feet in height, walked into view.

"Good morning, gentleman. Do you have an appointment?"

"No, we don't."

"I'm sorry, gentlemen, we are booked up for the rest of today. We have some open time tomorrow afternoon." She turned around and walked away from the counter.

The detectives walked up to the counter and presented their badges.

"I'm sorry, but you're going to have to make your next appointment wait. Or you can tell them to come back."

"I'm sorry, gentlemen. I said you need to make an appointment." Her words trailed off as she turned around.

"Look, miss, I'm Detective Fisher, and this is my partner Detective Steinbrenner. We need to ask you a few questions. So, please show us to your office so we can talk."

The rental agent walked over and unlocked a hinged panel in the counter so the detectives could gain access to the office area.

"My office is the third one on the right. Please wait for me there. I should only be a minute or two. I need to wait out here for my next appointment."

The detectives went into the office and sat down. Within five minutes, the girl entered the office and sat in a rolling office chair.

"I'm Cassandra Stone, the head leasing agent here. What does the Seattle PD need to know about our property?"

Fisher removed a notepad from his briefcase and flipped it open.

"Ms. Stone, we need to ask about one of your investors. A gentleman by the name of John Pierce." Fisher said.

"What name was that?" Cassandra asked.

"Pierce, John Pierce. Perhaps you might know him by Johnny Two Fingers?" Hawk answered.

"I'm sorry, gentlemen. I'm sure I've never heard either of those names."

"Perhaps you could share your list of investors with us."

"I'm sorry, gentlemen, I work for Pacific Coast Real Estate Property Management Company. I couldn't begin to tell you the names of the people who own this property."

"We believe the man we are looking for lives and works on this property. We would like to see a list of the tenants."

"I will have to get it cleared by my boss."

Cassandra picked up her phone and hit a speed dial button.

"Mandy, this is Cassandra. Is Carlton there? Please put me through to him."

"Carleton, this is Cassandra. I have two gentlemen from the Seattle Police Department who are asking questions about one of the investors."

Cassandra listened to the man on the other end of the phone for a couple of minutes. She placed the phone down and spoke to the two detectives.

"Look, gentlemen, I would like to help you, but my hands are tied. Per my boss, I am to give you the name and address of our lawyer."

She pulled out a notepad and began writing. "All requests for information will have to go through them." When finished, she slid the note across the desk.

"You can tell your boss we can get a search warrant for his office and this property if we need to. It would go a lot easier for everyone involved if you guys don't interfere with a police investigation."

Cassandra started to relay the message to her boss when she stopped talking after the first word and began to listen. After a moment, she placed the phone in its cradle and looked at the two detectives.

"My boss wants me to tell you to do what you feel compelled to do."

"You can tell your boss we're going to come back with a warrant tomorrow. We'll take this place apart brick by brick if we have to. It would be wise for him to cooperate."

"I will pass it on to him, Detective Fisher."

"Let's go, Hawk."

Fish and Hawk walked out of the office and down the stairs to the exit. When they got into their rental car, Fish handed Hawk a portfolio of the rental property.

"There's a map of this entire complex inside this portfolio. The map inside is two-sided. Side one shows the commercial property and side two has what is residential."

"What good is this going to do us?"

"My guess is if John Pierce is here, then most likely, we can be sure of two things. First, he is probably in a building last on the schedule to be updated. Secondly, if this guy is an electronic whiz, we just need to look for high-tech gadgets."

"Based on those assumptions, we need to proceed down the road to the left to the end of the main building here and turn right. According to this, the last buildings to be renovated are out back in the right-hand corner of the property. They are the ones on the edge of the water and are the most secluded," Hawk instructed, pointing at the map.

"Looking at this map, I couldn't agree more with your assumptions. I bet we're going to find some high-tech surveillance in place when we get to the alley leading up to the buildings."

They pulled out of the parking lot and turned to the right, toward the end of the building. Halfway down the building, there was another entry door. A keyless entry pad was to the right of the door. The words Building 'A' were on a large piece of stone above the door. They turned at the end of the building between buildings A and B. There was a door on the front corner of building B. The words The Cork and Fork Restaurant were on the door, along with the hours of operation.

"Hey, Fish, did you notice the sign on the door as we passed?"

"What about it?"

"The Cork and Fork sign said it opens at 11:30 a.m. Maybe we can catch some lunch. After the workout we had this morning, I'm starving."

"I know where there's some leftover pizza, Hawk."

"I thought you were going to give it a rest?"

"I just couldn't resist the dig. Maybe we can try it out for dinner if time permits."

"Sounds like a plan to me."

They continued to the end of building A, which was two blocks long. Buildings C and D were on their left and right, respectively.

"There sure are a lot of buildings here. I wonder what they used to manufacture here."

"Based on the equipment pictures we passed on the way up to the rental office, I think they probably made furniture."

"Hawk, did you notice the motion-tracking cameras?"

"No, I'm sorry I didn't."

"While you took the time to read when the Cork and Fork is open, I was looking at the cameras mounted on the building."

Fisher stopped the car, and they got out.

"Hawk, start walking toward the alley. As you walk, notice the camera on top of Building D."

"I see what you mean. The camera is tracking our motion. That's not normal for a surveillance camera."

"Exactly. Whoever or whatever is down this alley, wants plenty of advanced notice. Someone has gone to a lot of expense and trouble. I'm willing to bet it was our electronic genius boy wonder, John Pierce, AKA Johnny Two Fingers."

"Do you see what I see?"

"I'm not sure what you're talking about."

"Well, maybe it's because I'm younger than you," Hawk teased.

"I sure as hell wasn't the one sucking wind after a two-hour morning run. You may be younger, but I'm a lot fitter than you are."

"Regardless, my eyes are a lot keener than yours. If you had my youthful eyes, you might be able to tell the lenses on all the cameras have been shot out."

"Well, Mister Eagle-eye, if we get out on the tennis court, those keen eyes of yours aren't going to help you one bit. You'll be wondering what the hell just happened after my serves go whizzing right by you. You'll be left standing there flat-footed, saying come on, Fish, hurry up and serve will you."

"Did I ever tell you that you're one of my favorite comedians?"

"It's all part of your training."

"That's exactly what I'm talking about. Your old man brain is having a lot of trouble keeping the facts straight."

"Just remember, I have a gun."

"Alright, my mother taught me to respect my elders, so I give in."

"Good, let's get back to business. We should probably call the local police for backup. I doubt whoever took out those cameras is still here, but I, for one, don't want to be surprised."

Within twenty minutes, a local squad car from the Sausalito Police Department arrived. Fisher and Steinbrenner displayed their badges as two officers got out.

"I'm Detective Fisher with the Seattle Police Department, and this is my partner, Detective Steinbrenner. Thank you for responding, Officers."

"I'm Sergeant Billings, and this is Officer Allen. So, Detective Fisher, what are we looking at?"

"We're not sure, Sergeant. We came here looking for a possible suspect in a crime named John Pierce.

We have reason to believe he builds high tech electronics on-site here."

Fisher opened the sitemap of the Edelman complex and showed it to the officers.

"We believe the lab is in this back corner."

"Do you think this guy is locked and loaded, Detective Fisher? Do we need to approach with caution?"

"Someone with some seriously good sniper skills, has taken the time to take out all the lenses on these cameras. My guess is whoever shot out these cameras is long gone. But I would rather err on the side of caution."

"Do you guys have bulletproof vests? It's probably a good idea if we all wear one."

"Thank you, Sergeant, bulletproof vests are a great idea," Hawk said.

Within minutes, they were outside of Building K. The entrance door was missing.

"I believe we are in the right building. I can hear the ultrasonics from the motion detectors firing inside the building. Someone is protecting the contents of the building."

"Look at the door, Fish. We've seen this type of work before."

Sergeant Billings walked over to the entry door.

"This door has been kicked in. You guys have seen this before?"

"We're working a case in Seattle where entry to a house was gained the same way."

"It's got to take one big son of a bitch to kick in a steel door. I suggest we proceed with extreme caution."

They entered the building and started searching rooms carefully.

They heard Officer Allen cry out. "In here, we've got a body."

The other three rushed to where the body was. The body was slumped over and tied to a chair.

Fish walked over and lifted the man's head.

"Gentlemen, meet John Pierce."

The victim's shirt had been ripped open. The buttons from his shirt were on the floor.

"Are you sure this is the guy you are looking for, Detective Fisher?"

"Yes, Sergeant, we're sure. There is a picture of him in the other room, receiving an award with his name on it. It looks like whoever shot him in the head attempted to beat information out of him," Hawk said.

Deep, purplish bruises had formed on the victim's torso and face.

"Sergeant, can your guys process the crime scene?"

"I'm sure we can. Are we looking for anything in particular?" the sergeant asked.

"Based on the fact the entry door is off its hinges, I highly doubt there is anything to discover here. It would be great if we could find out who he was building high-tech electronics for," Fish responded.

Officer Allen entered the room where the body was. "I would say it's going to be highly unlikely. I found an empty open file cabinet in the other room. There was also a keyboard and a wireless internet router there, but no computer. Whoever did this didn't want any information given up."

Hawk picked up a piece of electronic equipment from a workbench on the left wall. "Hey, Fish, do you recognize this?"

"Yeah, I do. It looks like this guy built the portable fingerprint scanner we use. So, if this guy has made stuff that is used by police departments, we should be able to find out information on his company one way or another."

Chapter 15

Hector Gonzales's Apartment

Detectives Fisher and Steinbrenner walked into the office at Automobile Emporium. Kaylene looked up as they entered.

"Well, if it isn't my favorite Detective and his sidekick. Are you ready to take me up on my offer, Detective Steinbrenner?"

"I'm sorry, Kaylene. I sincerely appreciate your offer. I'm just not into one-night stands."

"Who said anything about a one-night stand, Detective? I would be surprised if you could last that long."

"I think it's time we change the subject. Are the detectives from the local office here?"

"Two female detectives arrived with a moving van and a warrant to search the apartment. I went ahead and let them in."

Ricardo Gonzales came into the office from the repair bays and slammed the door.

"Detective Fisher, can I ask you a simple question?" He asked.

"Sure, Ricky, go ahead and ask."

"Why did you take boxes from my brother's apartment? I read the search warrant; it didn't say anything that said you could take boxes."

"We had to remove the boxes so we could search for a notebook your brother kept."

"The only thing you're after is a notebook my brother had?"

"That's correct."

"Then why did the detectives clearing the apartment say it was all going to be taken to their office and placed in the evidence locker there?"

"You told us your brother didn't have a pot to piss in or a window to throw it out of, right?"

"Yeah, but so what? It doesn't give you guys the right to take anything from the apartment unless it's on the search warrant."

"The fact is there are thousands of dollars of vintage and new toys in the boxes up there. If the money used to purchase them was from crime, then we have every right to confiscate them."

"I see your point, Detective Fisher. I just don't think of my brother as a criminal. I'm sure you are right about it, but it's still hard for me to stomach."

"I'm sure it is. As far as I'm concerned, it would be difficult to prove that the money was earned from Hector committing a crime. I'll tell you what, once we get this stuff inventoried, we'll hold it until you decide what you want to do with it."

"I can live with that, Detective."

"Good, I don't want any bad feelings."

"Today is Taco Thursday. I bought extra so you and your crew could have some." Ricky said, handing Fish a box full of tacos.

"Thanks, Ricky."

"You're welcome. If you like pork, you might want to grab one of the pulled pork tacos—they're good."

"It sounds great to me."

The detectives walked through the garage, carrying food. Two female detectives were placing boxes into the back of a cargo van. Fish and Hawk presented their badges to the detectives.

"We're Detectives Fisher and Steinbrenner of the Seattle Police Department. We're the lead detectives on this case. Would you ladies like to take a lunch break?"

"We haven't had a better offer all morning, Detective Fisher. I'm Detective Mitchelson, and this is my partner, Detective Secourt."

"What are you two doing with the boxes you're removing?"

"We were instructed by our boss to remove all these boxes and put them into storage. We're going to take them to our office and put them in the evidence locker."

"Did your boss tell you this stuff was evidence?"

"No, we just assumed that is where it's all going."

"All this stuff belongs to the brother of the deceased. Are you guys cataloging the items you are removing?"

"Yes, we have a complete inventory upstairs."

"Is there a lot left to bring down?"

"We've only cleared the kitchen, living room, and one of the two bedrooms. There was so much stuff packed into every nook and cranny, it made it slow going, getting it cataloged and removed."

"Have you found any notebooks yet?"

"Not yet, Detective, but we've been concentrating on clearing out the boxes more than we have been searching."

"Detective Fisher, what does it feel like to work with a real-life hero?" Detective Secourt asked.

"I would like to think every police officer who is out there putting their life on the line is a hero."

"I would agree with Detective Fisher, but it's not every detective who gets the key to the city and a day in his honor."

"I hate all the notoriety it has brought me. I saved a woman from a rape. It doesn't have to make me a hero, Hawk said.

"Is it true what I hear about you, Detective Steinbrenner?"

"I don't know, Detective. It depends on what you've heard."

"The scuttlebutt around our office is that you're going to be the featured hunk on next season's television show, 'The Bachelor.'"

"What a crock of bull shit," Fish muttered under his breath.

"What did you say, Detective Fisher?"

"What I said, Detective Secourt, is I hate to burst your bubble. Detective Steinbrenner won't be appearing on any television shows or calendars."

"Too bad, he's a hottie."

"Well, Detective, there's a certain girl in Seattle who is so head over heels in love. She would have an issue sharing Detective Steinbrenner with anyone."

"I can speak for myself, so why don't you let me?"

"I figure if I keep stepping in and nudging you in the right direction, you won't accidentally think with the wrong muscle."

How the hell are you so sure about the direction I need to go?"

"It's all in the book."

"I don't remember reading about this in the field detective's handbook."

"I was talking about the book on Love and Relationships I gave you."

"For God's sake, will you please give the Love Doctor a rest."

"Mark my words, Hawk, I will get you to read it yet."

"I'd have to be on my deathbed before I would read such a load of crap."

"Just remember, it's like you said, I do have a gun."

"When the two of you get done thumping your chests at each other, can we get back to the task at hand?" Detective Mitchelson chimed in.

"Detective Mitchelson is right. Let's get the rest of the boxes out of the apartment and into the van."

"Detective Fisher, I think it would be best if we have one person log the boxes while the rest of us remove them."

"I agree with you, Detective."

Within an hour and a half, they finished removing the last of the boxes.

"Fish, there must be thousands of dollars worth of collectibles here. I carried out two original G.I. Joe fighter pilots along with countless other new in the box G.I. Joe's. The last time I checked, the fighter pilots alone are worth about seven thousand dollars each."

"It doesn't matter what it's worth, Hawk. None of it belongs to us. If Ricky doesn't have his brother's will, it might all belong to the State of California."

Within an hour, they were finishing up the search for the notebook when Hawk called out. "Fish, I found a trunk in the closet. It's heavy." Hawk struggled to pull the trunk out of the closet.

"Is it locked?"

"Yes, it is. It should be easy to pick."

"That might not be necessary, Detective. I found some keys on a key ring in the nightstand next to the bed," Detective Mitchelson replied.

She brought in the keys and handed them to Hawk.

"Thanks. Hopefully, one of these is the magic key." The third key Hawk tried was the correct one. The lid popped up, and Hawk opened it all the way.

"Holy shit, guess what I found?"

"Hawk, I was hoping you were going to say a notebook, but some reason I don't believe it is what you were going to say. Was it?"

"No, I was going to say a Honus Wagner."

"I'm sorry, a Honus what?

"This guy has a Honus Wagner baseball card."

"Is that supposed to mean something to me?"

"If this baseball card is original, it is worth over a million. There are only a few of them known to exist."

Hawk lifted a tray out of the trunk that contained baseball cards. Fish was now standing and looking over Hawk's shoulder.

"Now we know why the trunk was so heavy. There must be at least a dozen guns in this trunk."

"We'll have to get the lab to examine these guns and see if they were used to commit a crime."

"I highly doubt it," Fish said, picking up a World War II German Luger. I think these guns are collectibles."

"If there's no notebook in there, Detective Steinbrenner, then it has to be somewhere else," Detective Mitchelson said.

"I wouldn't be so sure, Detective Mitchelson. Hawk, let's carry this box out to the kitchen table," Fish said.

They placed the now empty box on the table.

"Hawk, do you see anything unusual about this box?"

"Besides the fact it's now empty, no."

"You have much to learn, my friend."

"What the hell do you think I need to learn, Fish?"

"You need to learn the power of observation, my young friend."

"What exactly didn't I observe?" Hawk asked.

Fish reached both arms into the box and started feeling the bottom of the box.

"Here's what I was looking for."

"What did you find, Hawk."

"I noticed the interior of the box wasn't as deep as the box is tall, which can only mean one thing—that this box has a false bottom."

Fish pulled a tray out of the bottom of the box. He reached back in and removed a Ziploc bag, which contained a key. The key had a white tag with lettering in black. It read 128 Pearl St. Fish handed the bag to Hawk, who removed the key.

"So, we didn't find a notebook. Maybe this key belongs to wherever the notebook in question is."

"You're probably right, Hawk. But this key could have no significance to the case at all. To top it off, I would bet that there are at least a few hundred addresses across the United States that are 128 Pearl Street, maybe more. We can feed the information back to our techies in Seattle and let them see what they can come up with."

"We ought to run it by Ricky. Maybe this address will mean something to him."

"Great idea, Hawk. Maybe we'll get lucky."

Detective Michelson's cell phone rang.

"Detective Mitchelson, speaking;" Looking at her watch. "At five… we can be there." She closed her cell phone and said, "Detective Secourt and I have a meeting in our office at 5:00 p.m. I am supposed to tell you there is a meeting in our command center at 9:00 a.m. tomorrow that you two need to attend. Do you guys need a hotel recommendation?"

"Detective Mitchelson, Fish here has us checked into Casa Madrona."

"Casa Madrona? How the hell did you guys manage it? The place is way out of our travel allowance."

"Detective Mitchelson, Detective Fisher believes it is easier to beg for forgiveness than it is to ask for permission," Hawk said with a chuckle.

"Don't forget to tell her my connections got us sixty percent off of our rooms."

"Detective Fisher, here is a copy of the list of inventoried items for you guys. Detective Mitchelson and I will make sure it all gets put away under lock and key. If you two don't require our assistance anymore today, we are going to make a mile," Detective Secourt announced.

"Detective, I believe we're all set for now. I appreciate that you're going to make sure it gets put away safely. I would hate to explain to Ricky Gonzales how a baseball card worth over a million dollars was lost. Thanks for the help. Detective Steinbrenner and I will see you in the morning."

The detectives left to return to their station with the items they had removed from the apartment.

"Hawk, we need to get a copy of this inventory list to Ricky."

The detectives walked into the garage. Ricky was working on the engine of a 1963 Corvette.

"Nice car, Ricky. Is it yours?"

"I wish, Detective. It belongs to a real estate developer. There's more money in restoring classic cars than there is in fixing the newer ones. But if I didn't fix the newer ones, I wouldn't be in business. I need to build my reputation to get more work. I was hoping to eventually just do restorations. Did you find what you were looking for?"

"No, we didn't," Fish said, handing Ricky the inventory list. "Can you make a copy of this inventory for yourself? It's a list of the items we removed."

"Do you think what you removed is worth much?"

"I would say so, Ricky. One piece is worth over a million."

"Detective Fisher, what the hell did my brother have worth over a million?

"He had a rare Honus Wagner baseball card."

Ricky walked over and sat on a stool in front of a workbench.

"Jesus, Mary, and Joseph. Do you think he stole it from someone, Detective Fisher?"

"That's certainly one possibility. We will run the inventory list against known robberies. If it isn't stolen goods, then it belongs to whoever Hector designated it to in his will."

"What if there is no will or no one who was designated to have it, Detective Fisher?"

"Then it would most likely belong to the State of California. I certainly hope your brother left a will."

"Me too!"

"Ricky, does the address 128 Pearl Street mean anything to you?"

"Pearl Street, I can't say that it does, why?"

"We found a key hidden in the same chest where we found the baseball card. Since your brother took the time to hide it, obviously, it has some significance."

"Can I see the key Detectives?"

"Sure."

Ricky examined the key and handed it back to the detectives.

"We were hoping that you might know what it goes to."

"I'm sorry, I don't, but if anything comes to mind, I have your numbers. I'll be sure and call."

"Thanks, Ricky. Oh, you might want to make sure that you stick around here for the next few weeks until our investigation is over."

"It's not a problem. I don't have any trips planned. You will let me know when this mess is over, won't you? My brother and I weren't close at all, but I feel like I owe him a proper burial."

"I doubt that you owe your brother anything at all."

Chapter 16

The phone rang non-stop in Hawk's hotel room. He finally picked it up and uttered an almost unintelligible hello.

"Good morning, sunshine. It's time to get your ass out of bed."

Hawk looked around the room, which was pitch dark, as he tried to clear the cobwebs from his brain,

"What the hell time is it, Fish?"

"It's precisely 4:35 am, and it is time to get moving."

"You're in a snit this morning. What the hell is eating you? Did the couple in the next room keep you up again?"

"Let's just say that some things are out of our control."

"I thought that we didn't have to be in San Francisco until 9:30? I was not planning on rising for another three hours."

"I hate to cut your beauty rest short, pal, but had you not turned off your cell phone, you would have gotten the text from Caleb saying that he wants us back in the office before noon. We've been booked on the first flight back to Seattle."

Hawk picked up his cell phone and looked at it.

"Shit, I forgot to charge my phone. I can meet you downstairs in thirty minutes."

"You better make it twenty minutes, or the bus will leave without you."

"I don't know who is more sadistic, you or Caleb."

Hawk was downstairs to meet Fish in less than twenty minutes. Fish shot a perturbed look at Hawk.

"What did I do to deserve that look?"

Fish continued to ignore Hawk and gave him an icy stare. At 11:03 am, they walked into the main lobby of the Seattle Police Department. The duty officer, who was on the phone, paused his conversation and spoke to the detectives.

"Caleb is in the situation room, gentlemen. He's expecting you."

When they opened the door to the situation room, Caleb was pacing back and forth, a bouquet of flowers was in the middle of the oval conference table.

"I hope that you didn't drag us back to Seattle because someone sent flowers, Caleb."

"The flowers are for Detective Steinbrenner, but that's not why I dragged you back to Seattle. I dragged you back gentlemen, because last night, the Police Commissioner escalated your case to the highest priority."

"Why? Has something else happened?"

"Someone shot and killed Sharon Cross last evening. I sent Detectives Reese and Caron out to the crime scene. Mrs. Cross was just in the wrong place at the wrong time."

Fish let out a curse under his breath and sank into the closest chair. His eyes were darting left and right rapidly as if his brain was in overdrive, searching for what to say next. Tears were beginning to well up in the corners of his eyes.

"Just from the few minutes that I spoke with her, I could tell how much she cared and watched out for the Blakes. Caleb, is someone with her husband?"

"His kids are headed home to be with him. I sent Jane Pritcher out to stay with him until they get there. This case has now become priority number one, Sharon Cross's brother-in-law is Councilman Blaine Cross. With people dropping like flies, the mayor wants to keep it out of the news for the time being. He doesn't want anyone to think that there is a serial killer on the loose and create widespread panic throughout the city."

"How are we going to keep this out of the papers, Caleb?"

"That's where you two come in. I've agreed to let Mark Brandt work on the investigation team."

Fish started to speak, but Caleb placed his hand up in the air and made a motion for Fish to stop.

"Fish, I know that working with Mark is the last thing you want to do. I need to pull out all the stops and get this case solved. Mark is on the team—end of discussion."

Fish got up from the chair, turned, and looked out the window for a few moments. He shook his head as if he were clearing out the cobwebs.

"Caleb, I'll work with Mark as long as we get full control of the release of information. If I even get a hint of him leaking the tiniest bit of information, it will take all the king's men to keep me from going ballistic on him."

"I'm one step ahead of you. I've already had a meeting with Mark and his editors at the paper. I have put them on notice that if they print any information, no matter how insignificant, I will charge them with tampering with an investigation. Trust me, they got that message loud and clear."

"I certainly hope so. I would hate to have to take Mark Brandt apart one piece at a time, and you know that I will."

"You're going to have to do a much better job at keeping your emotions in check, Fish. With the mayor's office weighing in on this, I won't be able to help."

"You have my word. I'll be on my best behavior."

"I'm glad. I'll need you to stay focused on the task at hand. I read your report and went over the list of electronics you found in John Pierce's lab. We talked to Scan Pro, the company that built the portable fingerprint scanner. The design came from a company named Imagine Electronics. Unfortunately, we can't get any information on Imagine Electronics. I have our forensic accountants looking into it. It seems that Imagine Electronics was a shell company. We are having difficulty finding info on John Pierce. It seems that he managed to stay off the grid."

"Since his computer was missing and his filing cabinet was empty, how on earth are we going to get information on this guy?"

"I thought we would start with John Pierce's parents. They live in Bellevue. I have detectives on the way there now to talk to them. We're going to have to be careful about how we dig for information, so I've enlisted some help. You had better sit down."

Fish sat down next to Hawk. His face had a puzzled look to it.

"I need to talk to you about your daughter."

"Why? What has Hailey gotten into now?"

"Trust me, she's not in any trouble."

"So why are you bringing her up now?"

"Hailey has been working for me."

Fish shot up out of his chair—the veins in his neck were bulging.

"What gives you the right to involve my daughter?"

"You did when you asked me to keep her out of jail when she got caught hacking the City of Seattle school records. Did you think that I got her out of trouble and into Carnegie Mellon University on a full-ride scholarship all on my own? Things are beyond your control, and unfortunately, what your daughter does or doesn't do is one of them."

"You're a son of a bitch," Fish said through gritted teeth.

"I'm paid to make the tough decisions. It was a decision that needed making."

"What the hell have you got her doing?

"I asked her to look into John Pierce and his activities along with Gary Danzig, the owner of the other fingerprint from Benjamin Blake's boat. I need to know how someone who has come back from the dead, just like Lazarus, is involved. I asked to utilize her skill set to find some records."

"You're telling me that my daughter is hacking a database hoping to find information vital to the case?"

"Yes, I am."

"Why couldn't you have one of your buddies back in Scotland Yard or MI-6 do the dirty work?"

"You know as well as I do, I can't ask the Brits to do any hacking. It won't look good if they get caught."

"Gee Caleb, do you think? It won't look good if my daughter gets caught either."

"I know you're worried about Hailey getting caught. She's a bright girl. I think she'll be able to protect herself."

Fish shook his head in disgust and glared at Caleb.

"She got caught hacking the city school district website. How the hell do you think she won't get caught this time?"

"I had a long discussion with Hailey. She is going to search the dark net for clues."

"It's called the dark net for a reason. Bad people hang out there."

Fish leaned over and placed his hands on Caleb's desk; he was as close to Caleb as he could get.

"So, help me, if my daughter gets hurt, there will be hell to pay."

Hawk grabbed Fish and pulled him away from Caleb.

"Easy does it, Fish. You better back off before you do something you might regret."

Fish shook his shoulder hard as he pulled away from his partner and snapped at him.

"Keep your fucking hands off of me, Eric."

"I'm just trying to help you. You know I'll do everything I possibly can to help to keep Hailey safe."

Fish looked at Hawk and grimaced but said nothing.

"Let's get one thing clear. You need to stay focused on the case. If I get any hint or idea that you're going off-script again, your days as a detective will be over. There is no more safety net. You're going to have to do it by the book for once. Do I make myself clear, Detective Fisher?"

"I don't think that I'll find anything in that book of yours that will cover putting my daughter in harm's way, will I?"

Fish waited for Caleb's reply, which was not forthcoming.

"Detective Fisher, have I made myself clear?"

Fish sucked in a deep breath and replied.

"Perfectly, sir."

Hawk looked at Fish and then at Caleb and spoke.

"Caleb, what's up with the flowers?"

"Detective Steinbrenner, the flowers are for you, so I thought that you might tell us why you received them?"

"Honestly, I have no idea."

"Are you sure that you don't want to confess?"

Hawk shuffled his feet for a moment. His eyes darted back and forth as if he was trying to decide what to say next.

"Nothing is going on."

"Hawk, you know how I feel about mixing business with pleasure at the office, don't you?"

"Yes, sir, I do. I promise it won't happen again," Hawk answered.

"Well, considering the nature of why you received these, I am willing to overlook that rule since congratulations are obviously in order here."

"You have me at a loss. I have no idea what you're talking about."

"Well, Hawk, maybe this will help."

Caleb opened his coat closet and removed a giant helium balloon from the vase of flowers that read: Congratulations, Dad.

Fish, who had been scowling, smiled a wide-eared grin and leaned over and spoke to his partner.

"As I said, Hawk, you're so off the market it isn't even funny. Tell me again, you don't know what I'm talking about. You really should read the book, you know."

"Hawk, there's a card attached to the vase of flowers. Should I read it for you?"

"That's not necessary."

"Good, since that's out of the way, let's get back to business. Here are the images of the bullets we have retrieved. They came from the bodies of Benjamin Blake, Don Giovassi, and Hector Gonzales. The fourth one, removed yesterday, came from John Pierce. As you can see, they are all from the same gun. This confirms that the deaths are linked."

"What information did you get from them?"

Caleb handed him a FedEx overnight envelope.

"The car that was found in a scenic overlook in Idaho was owned by Don Giovassi. The Boise police sent some items found in his car. Go ahead and take a look."

Hawk moved closer to Fish as he removed the content of the envelope. There was a photo stapled to a page.

"We've seen this picture before, haven't we?"

"Mark Brandt's ghost keeps popping into this equation."

Fish pulled the picture off the paper. The paper was labeled Samantha Blake. It was a listing of her daily routine.

Fish leaned against the conference table and started rubbing his chin.

"Caleb, it looks like Samantha Blake's killer expected that it would push her father over the edge to do whatever they needed him to do. Benjamin Blake did what they wanted, and now someone is getting rid of anybody who might have a clue as to what it was that Benjamin did."

"I would say you summed it up in a nutshell, Fish. I'm having our forensic accountants look for clues. They're pulling his tax filings for the last ten years. Hopefully, they will give us a better idea of what he did for a living."

"Besides the death of Mrs. Cross, has anything else that happened while we were gone?"

"Fish, the crime scene unit found a key at Benjamin Blake's house labeled storage unit."

"Maybe the key was what whoever killed Mrs. Cross was looking for."

"That's a possibility. We went through Benjamin Blake's financial records to see if we could find the location of the storage unit. We didn't turn up anything. He must have paid cash for it."

"Was a thorough search of the boathouse done?"

"I'm not sure, but we'll get it done if need be. Is the boathouse on Blake's property?"

"It's at the bottom of the cliff, behind the house. Since Benjamin hid money on his boat, perhaps he also hid things in the boathouse."

"You make a good point. I'll get Adam Carter and his CSI team back out there if need be. The black Cadillac Escalade did a drive-by while we were executing our search there."

"If the black Cadillac did a drive-by, why didn't we keep 24/7 surveillance on the Blake house?"

"We didn't know about it until we reviewed the footage from the security camera at the Cross house, which was after her husband found her. Trust me, Fish, I wish we had round the clock surveillance on the house."

"Were they able to get an image of the driver from the security tape?"

"Unfortunately, we weren't able to get a clear image. We did check the earlier footage. It was the same vehicle that Sharon Cross told you she had seen. My guess is they were coming back to search the premises."

"Did we at least get the license plate number?"

"The plates were covered with dark plastic. Later that day, the Tacoma Police Department reported a black Cadillac Escalade had been abandoned and was on fire. They were able to get the VIN. The Salt Lake City Police Department reported it stolen. There's no way to know if it was the same vehicle Mrs. Cross saw in front of Blake's house or not."

"Caleb, maybe another search of Blake's house should be done."

"I already have a team out there. By the way, we relocated Chris Felton to a safe house at your request."

"I wanted to have another crack at him. I was hoping maybe he could shed some light on what we discovered here."

"Fish, I could have him held for a few more days until you and Hawk, talk with him."

"That would be good."

"In the meantime, can we get someone in San Francisco to look into Sun Coast Properties? Hopefully, we can get the list of investors for the Edelman Property. They also need to take a close look at Hector Gonzales's brother, Ricardo. We don't expect to find anything illegal. We would be remiss if we didn't take a look at his finances."

Chapter 17

Seattle Bound

The air was crisp, making the surface of the snow glisten. An Alberta Clipper had brought bitter cold air and thirty mile an hour winds out of Canada. A car pulled into the driveway of the large Victorian house. A passenger got out bundled from head to foot and trudged up the front steps to ring the doorbell, snow crunching under her feet as she approached.

The call of the doorbell awakened Connor. His neck and back ached from falling asleep in a chair. He stood up and stretched, trying to ease the pain. He called out to the person ringing the doorbell.

"I'll be right there. Give me a minute, will you?"

He peered through the peephole and quickly opened the door. He was standing there looking at who he assumed to be none other than Gertrude Lane. She was wearing heavy white winter clothing. Had it not been for the dark, wraparound sunglasses that covered her eyes, she would have blended entirely with the layer of snow on the ground. As Connor opened the door, a cold blast of air forced its way into the house. Snow brought in by the wind was quickly covered the wooden floor.

"It's freezing out there, Gert. Please come in."

Gertrude Lane stomped her feet to shake off any additional snow and stepped inside. Connor Darke quickly closed the door behind her. She unwrapped the scarf, removed her sunglasses, and pushed the hood of the parka back to expose her head. Connor started to laugh at the sight of Gert but stopped because of a muscle spasm in his back.

"Is everything all right, Connor?"

"Yes, why?"

"I received a very distressing phone call about you today."

"Did my mother call you? I'm sorry if she did."

"Most mothers have a deep-seated connection with their children. That's why it's called motherhood. Your mother didn't call me. I doubt she even realizes that you know me. It was Doctor Strand who called me."

A very puzzled look came across Connor's face.

"Julie called you? Why?"

"She said you called her twice during the night and hung up both times as soon as she answered. She tried calling you back."

Connor ran his hands through his hair and then rubbed the stubble on his chin.

"You're sure that Julie said I called her last night?"

Gert looked at Connor and pointed one of her crooked fingers at him.

"I may be old, but I can assure you that I'm not senile, nor would I have come out in this bloody cold weather if it wasn't important. I am sure that you called the poor girl last night."

"I don't remember calling her."

"When you didn't answer her repeated calls, she called me and asked if I could come over to make sure you were all right."

Connor checked his cell phone log.

"Wow, she called fifteen times. I can't believe I never heard them."

"Well, obviously, you must have needed your rest. I told Julie that it was no problem for me to come over. We had a nice talk. She is a keeper."

"Don't push me into a relationship that I'm not ready for."

Gert reached over with the same crooked finger and tapped Connor three times on the chest in the area of his heart.

"Like it or not, Connor, your heart has already taken you there."

"We'll see about that."

"Did you stay up too late?"

"I didn't think I had," Connor replied with a bewildered look on his face.

"Are you sure you're okay?"

"I guess so, why?"

"You look like hell. You didn't sleep well, did you?"

Connor pointed to a nearby wingback chair.

"I fell asleep in that chair, so I'm a little stiff this morning."

"It's not morning."

"What time is it?"

"It's almost 1:30 in the afternoon."

"It can't be."

"Well, it is."

"Wow," shaking his head, "I never sleep that late. Crap, I missed my daily run."

"I am glad to see you're here and all right. Besides, it's way too cold to be running outside today. Connor dear, we need to talk."

"About what?"

"Seattle."

"What about Seattle?"

"It's what your grandmother said to me, of course. It's also the message that you left on Julie's answering machine."

"What did my grandmother tell you about Seattle?"

"She said that when you saw an article in the newspaper it struck a nerve with you."

"She told you that?"

Gert shook her head yes.

"I'm sorry, this is just too weird for me."

"Why do you say that?"

"I know you believe in this connection and my psychic abilities. I'm just not sure about all this yet."

"Don't worry, in time, it will all make sense. Do you mind if Hamilton comes in? I would rather not make him wait for me in the car."

"Please, have him come in."

"Good. I'm glad you don't mind because he's got our lunch. I took the liberty of picking up some Chinese food for us."

"Lunch," exclaimed Connor.

"I haven't even had breakfast yet."

"We've already wasted too much time. If you want some breakfast, we brought egg rolls."

"That's not quite the same thing as eggs."

"I know it's not. Do you want to have some food or not?"

"I guess I can handle that. Do you mind if we eat in the kitchen? I haven't got around to unpacking the boxes in the dining room yet."

"Not at all. Please, lead the way."

Hamilton entered and carried the bag of Chinese food into the kitchen and set it on the table. He removed three boxes and three egg rolls from it.

"We picked up Seafood Lo Mein and Sweet and Sour Chicken, I know you like them equally as well."

"It seems like you know everything there is to know about me, Hamilton."

"We all tend to be creatures of habit that can and do often change. The things I don't know about you and what lies ahead."

"Besides being Gert's aide, what exactly is your part in all of this?"

"My duty is to see that no harm comes to you while you find your way down the path we call life. I am someone who has your back."

"That's just wonderful," Connor muttered under his breath.

"What was that? I didn't hear what you said."

"I said, of course you do."

Gert, who had wandered into Connor's kitchen, yelled out. "Connor, dear, where are your plates?"

"The plates are in the cupboard to the left of the sink. The silverware is in the top drawer below the cabinets with the plates."

Gert grabbed plates, forks, and spoons and set them down on the kitchen table, then spoke to Hamilton and Connor.

"Do you two think you can relax long enough to come in here and eat?"

A simultaneous yes came from the two men who went into the kitchen and sat down at the table opposite from one another.

"Gert, getting back to the reason you're here. Did my grandmother tell you anything besides mentioning the article in the Seattle Times?"

"She told me to tell you that the time to act is now."

"What got you all charged up to come over here."

"You did, of course."

"I did?"

"Yes, you did,. I know that you read the newspaper article about Seattle."

"What does it matter? A lot of people across this great country probably read the same article. What makes me so important?"

"Because, out of all the people who read the article, you're the only person who knows that there is a connection between the article and the voices in your head."

Connor rubbed his face with both hands and looked at Gert, frustrated.

"Connor, you can wipe that look off your face. It's not going to work with me. So, are you going to tell me about Benjamin Blake?"

"Who?"

"Benjamin Blake, dear. Are you going to tell me about him?"

"I'm sorry, I'm at a loss."

"For some reason, I don't believe that at all. You know as well as I do, you're here because of Benjamin Blake's daughter, Samantha. She's been in contact with you, Connor, hasn't she?"

"I don't know what on earth you're talking about."

"There's one thing you don't do very well."

"What would that be?"

"You don't lie very well. Samantha is attempting to contact you, isn't she?"

"In a manner of speaking, yes, she has. I just don't know where to go from here."

"You have to go to Seattle, of course."

"Why should I go?"

"You won't be happy with yourself if you don't."

"What about my needs?"

"It's not about you anymore."

"I'm not ready for this. I can't lose myself again."

Gert put her arm around Connor. "You have to take control of your life."

"I don't know if I'm ready for that."

"You better be ready, Connor. You've been wallowing in self-pity for far too long."

"You think by going to Seattle, I'll be in control of everything going on?"

"I know one thing for sure. It's a step in the right direction, and the only way you can travel the path of life is by taking one step after the other."

"I don't think I'm ready for the journey you think I need to take."

"You need to pull it together. Please do it quickly. I've got you scheduled to fly to Seattle today."

"You bought plane tickets for me to leave today?"

"No, I didn't."

"How am I supposed to get there?"

"My private jet is fueled and ready to go."

"But I have commitments."

"They can be changed."

"I'm supposed to take Doctor Strand's son to the Syracuse basketball game. I don't want to let him down."

"Don't worry, I've already taken care of that."

"You have?"

"Yes, I did."

"Why?"

"Because you know you have to go."

"I was looking forward to bonding time with her son Zachary."

"Don't worry, your uncle J.C. is more than happy to help."

"Great, now you've got my uncle involved."

"He graciously accepted since he is your biggest fan."

"But JC hates basketball."

"I know, but he loves you."

"What am I supposed to do when I get there? I'm not even sure where I need to go when I get there."

"I made the necessary arrangements. You and Hamilton will be staying at the Alexis Hotel in downtown Seattle."

"Why is Hamilton going?"

"There has never been someone who had your back. I want to make sure someone does. I can't go because of health reasons, so I'm sending Hamilton with you in my place."

"Wow, I don't quite know what to say."

"There's no need to say anything."

"How long am I going for?"

"That depends on how much help you can give. I've got you scheduled to see Mark Brandt of the Seattle Times tomorrow."

"Can I have some time to digest all this?"

"Sure, you can. You can take all the time you need, just do it while you pack your bags to go. Hamilton and I will be waiting right here for you."

Within fifteen minutes, Connor was downstairs with his bag packed.

"Good, you're ready. The sooner we get on the road, the sooner you will be in Seattle to help."

Chapter 18

Seattle or Bust

Hamilton Gardner pulled the Tesla into the parking lot of the Sair Aviation terminal at the Syracuse Airport. Connor looked out the passenger window of the car.

"It looks like a storm is moving in. Are we going to be okay?"

"Not to worry, Connor, the plane is safe within the hangar. As long as you don't dawdle, Hamilton will have you off of the ground and above the storm before you know it."

"How is Hamilton getting us off of the ground?"

"He's the pilot, which is the other reason he is going."

"Is there anything Hamilton doesn't get behind the wheel of?"

"Not much. If it moves, he can drive it."

Connor looked over at the entrance to the hangar lobby and noticed a familiar car.

"What's Julie's car doing here?"

"She wants to go to Seattle with you."

"You're pushing me, Gert. I asked you not to, remember?"

"Look, after last night's phone calls, she is worried about you and wants to go with you."

"Of course, you told her yes because you want to be the match that lights the flame of our romance, don't you?"

Gert smiled at Connor and started whistling the song "Matchmaker" from Fiddler on the Roof.

"Julie told me that she was going to buy a ticket and follow you to Seattle if she had to because she would worry herself to death while you're gone. I figured that since you and Hamilton were going anyway, I could save her the airfare. I called her while you were upstairs packing. It just so happens she has re-arranged her schedule so that she could go."

"I don't think her going is such a good idea."

"I do."

"Well, I don't."

"I'm not giving you a choice. She is going. End of discussion. Besides, it wasn't my idea. It was hers."

"Why does she need to go?"

"Your grandmother says that her going with you is important to your physical and mental wellbeing."

"I'm sure you had a hand in her decision to go."

"Not in the least. She is about as smitten as it gets. You laid that groundwork a long time ago, and now you are reaping the fruits of your labor. Besides, it will be a chance for you two to get to know each other."

"You've added matchmaker to your dossier?"

"I thought about being a reporter once. Try this headline on for size. The "Love Doctor" finds love."

"You're pushing, and I asked you not to push."

"Relax, Connor. I'm just teasing you."

"Since you've read my books, you of all people should know love takes patience and time."

"I couldn't agree more. It's just this one has been simmering for twenty years, my dear boy."

"It might not be safe for Julie to go."

"Don't worry, that's the other reason I'm sending Hamilton with you."

"You're sending Hamilton so that he can protect me?"

"That's a good way of putting it."

"You've thought of everything then?"

"Probably not, but the more bases I can cover for you, the easier it will be."

"I can't win, can I?"

"You did when you met Julie."

"What will she do with Zachary?"

"She is going to leave Zachary with her mother."

"Is there anything else I need to know about?"

"Not at the moment."

Connor got out of Tesla and walked to the back of the car to retrieve his bags. Julie walked over, pulling her suitcase behind her.

"How is my favorite patient today?"

"I would be a lot better if you weren't going."

"That point is moot, Connor, I am going, and it's final. Besides, it will give us time to talk about the cause of your headaches since they are not of a physical nature."

"Are you a qualified psychiatrist, Julie?"

"You know very well I'm not. It's just you know more about their cause than you are willing to talk about."

"Can you guys finish the scintillating conversation you're having once you're onboard? I would like to have wheels up before the storm gets any closer," Hamilton interjected.

The group walked through the hangar onto the tarmac, where the Dassault Falcon sat with its engines running. Seth Martin, the co-pilot, was standing in the doorway.

"Boss, the flight plan is filed. As soon as we finish the pre-flight check, we can go."

"Thanks, Seth," Hamilton replied.

The trio set their bags down and walked up to the stairs of the aircraft. The interior had six brown leather swivel chairs.

"You guys can sit wherever you want. If you get tired, all the chairs recline flat for sleep. The plane's emergency instructions are in the holder on the wall next to each chair. Please familiarize yourself with it. Buckle your seatbelts. When you see the seatbelt light go out, you are free to move around the cabin. The restroom is through the door at the back of the cabin. Food and drinks are available in the cabinet to the left of the door. You two are the only ones on the plane. Whatever happens between the two of you stays on the plane."

Within minutes, they were off the ground and above the incoming storm.

"Connor, you're not happy with the fact I'm here. I'm a big girl. Besides, I think by now, you know I want to be with you."

"Julie, I'm thrilled to see you. I'm just worried about your safety."

"That's why Mrs. Lane sent her aide along."

"Do you think Hamilton is going to protect us?"

"I would certainly hope so. According to Mrs. Lane, Hamilton was special ops for MI-6 and is extremely well trained."

"That just makes me feel warm and fuzzy all over."

"You don't have to be so melodramatic."

"I'm sorry, you're right, I don't."

"Since we have a few hours before we land in Seattle, why don't you tell me what's going on in your head?"

"I'm not sure there is anything to tell."

"All your test results are back. There is nothing physical causing your headaches. That leads me to believe there is a non-physical cause for them."

"I don't quite know what to tell you."

"Why don't you start by telling me about what happens when you get the headaches? I hope I've moved beyond just being a doctor to someone you can have intimate conversations with."

"I'm not sure I'm ready to open up."

"If you keep all this angst inside, it's going to destroy you. Back there on the ground is a twelve-year-old boy who worships the ground you walk on." Julie started to cry lightly.

"Why are you crying?"

"For God's sake, I lost you twenty years ago. I'm not going to let the only man I've ever loved walk out of my life a second time. You know, for a relationship counselor, you sure as hell suck at reading the signs in front of your face."

"I see the signs loud and clear. I'm just scared to jump into the deep end again."

"Let's take this leap together."

"I started having these headaches when I moved into my grandmother's house five and a half months ago."

"But you're not just getting headaches, are you?"

"No, I'm not. As the headaches subside, I sometimes see images of people and hear voices in my head. As the headaches disappear, so do the voices and the images."

"What does Gertrude Lane have to do with this?"

"You remember how you told me you watched my show religiously?"

"Watching your show was my guilty pleasure."

"You know how I always knew what the people were going to say before they said it?"

"Yeah, I kind of thought it was just part of the show's way of sucking the audience in."

"You thought I received information before I asked questions?"

"It's just that I've heard most of the talk shows on television are fake."

"The only thing I know, is that my shows were genuine. I was fed information, but not the way you think. I could always sense what their thoughts were."

"When did you meet Gertrude Lane?"

"I met Gert a few years ago when we worked together distributing Thanksgiving dinners to the poor. I didn't know Gert was none other than Gertrude Lane, the philanthropist, until yesterday. Gert and my grandmother both believed they had psychic abilities. I have the same abilities, which is why we are heading to Seattle."

"What do you expect to do in Seattle?"

"I hope to help the Seattle Police Department solve a cold case of a missing girl."

"Why do you think the police can't solve it?"

"Because the case they're working on has a dark side. I am going to Seattle to help fill in the gaps. I am going to give them the answers they have no hope of getting."

"You're going to give them answers to questions they can't get? They are not going to understand or comprehend how you know them."

"That's it in a nutshell."

Julie got up from her chair and walked over to Connor.

"I'm not going to stand here blowing smoke up your shorts and tell you that I understand what you're going through. I love you with all my heart, and I am going to stand by you no matter what."

She bent over and kissed Connor lightly on the lips.

"Connor, Hamilton said it was going to be at least a six-hour flight, and what happens in here stays in here. How about you fulfill one of my fantasies?"

"What fantasy would that be, Julie?"

She leaned over and whispered in Connor's ear.

"You mean like here on the plane, as in right now?"

"That's exactly what I mean. After all, Hamilton did say what happens on the plane stays on the plane."

Chapter 19

Seattle

The trip to Seattle took about six hours. Hamilton landed the Dassault Falcon at the Pacific Sun Aviation Terminal at the Seattle Airport. After opening the cockpit door, Hamilton spoke to Connor and Julie.

"I hope the two of you made the most of the flight."

"We'll decline to comment. After all, you were the one who said what happens on the plane stays on the plane."

"Did you at least like the landing?"

"I didn't even realize we were on the ground until the plane stopped."

"Hamilton prides himself on quick takeoffs and smooth landings," Seth Martin replied.

Hamilton walked to the rear of the airplane and removed the luggage from the cargo hold. They grabbed their bags and walked into the passenger area of the Pacific Sun terminal. Stopping at the pilot's office, Hamilton picked up the keys to a dark grey Audi SUV.

"Hamilton, what is the plan from here?"

"The first order of business at the moment, is food. Since we are in Seattle, I think some seafood for dinner would be very appropriate."

"That would be great," Connor and Julie replied.

"I know an excellent restaurant on Pier 56 called Elliot's Oyster House. Have you been there before?" Connor offered.

"I haven't, so I'm open to a new culinary experience."

Hamilton Gardner and Seth Martin got into the front seats of the Audi while Connor and Julie occupied the second row of seats. Before long, they were walking into Elliot's Oyster House. Hamilton stepped up to the host stand and asked for a table for four. The girl wrote his name down on the waitlist and then looked over at Connor.

"Oh my God, I can't believe it," she exclaimed as she stepped out from behind the host stand and hurried over to Connor. "I've read every one of your books, Mr. Darke. You probably don't remember, but I met you at one of your book signings four years ago."

"I'm sorry, miss..."

"Stiles, Melanie Stiles."

"I'm sorry, I don't remember the name. My apologies."

"That's okay, Mr. Darke, when I met you, my last name was Brown. I won't ever forget meeting you. You told me if I found my love for music again, that love would find me. I met my husband while I was looking for a piano for my apartment. His name is Keith. He has helped me take my music to a whole new level. I don't think I'll ever be able to thank you enough."

"That's alright, Melanie. Just knowing you followed your heart is thank you enough for me."

Grabbing four menus, Melanie showed them to a table.

"Wow, Connor, that was impressive," Julie commented.

"That's why I hate going out in public."

"That bothered you? I don't understand."

"Don't get me wrong. I enjoy it when I learn I've helped someone. It's just for every person like Melanie, there are half a dozen critics. I have a hard time dealing with the flack from people who haven't read my books or refuse to listen to their hearts."

"You know, it's not any easier in my shoes."

"I'm not sure where you're going with this."

"People have always doubted what I've told them they need to do to feel better. If you can walk away knowing you've given it your all, then you have done what you've set out to do."

"Thanks, Julie, I appreciate it," Connor replied with a smile.

"Connor, may I add my thoughts to this conversation?" Hamilton asked.

"By all means."

"I agree with Mrs. Lane — your talent to help seems to be God-given. Maybe all these people who criticize you are agents of darkness. Their sole purpose is to slow down the work you've been doing. Perhaps the things leading to your bout with depression and drinking were intended to get you off track. You have to learn to rise above it all."

"That was some fascinating insight."

"If you don't mind Hamilton, since the hotel is just a few blocks away, I would like to walk there," Connor announced after dinner.

"That would be fine. I will have your luggage placed in your room. You can pick up your keys when you get there."

"Thanks, Hamilton."

"I would like to walk with you if you don't mind," Julie said.

"You look exhausted. Are you sure you don't want to ride to the hotel?"

"I don't feel tired. There isn't anything I would rather do at this moment than walk with you."

Within a few minutes, they had reached the lobby of the Alexis Hotel. A young man with spiked hair looked at the couple as they walked up to the counter.

"Mr. Darke, I haven't seen you for quite some time. Welcome back."

"Andy, are you working nights now?"

"No, I'm just filling in. Here's the room key."

"Don't we both have a room key, Andy?"

"Your reservation is for our grand suite. It has two separate bedrooms. If that doesn't suit the two of you, we can change you to separate rooms."

"I'm sure the present arrangement is fine."

Within a few minutes, they were at the door of their suite. Connor opened the door, and they walked in.

"Oh, my goodness, Connor, I think this is bigger than my first apartment and a lot nicer. You've stayed here before?"

"On a few different occasions. I used to stay here when my television show would go to different locations. The people working here are some of the nicest people I have ever met."

"I don't think I've ever stayed in a hotel room with a fireplace."

Connor kissed Julie lightly on the forehead. "There is a first time for everything."

"Are you worried about tomorrow?"

"No, I don't think I would be here if I couldn't help. I'm concerned that I haven't come soon enough."

"I can understand that. You need to remember two things. The first is, life can only be taken one step at a time. Secondly, being here is like playing the lottery—you can't win if you don't play, so being in the game is like starting on the right foot to save a life."

"Thanks, Julie. I needed to hear that."

"You know what else you need to hear?"

"What would that be?"

"Mrs. Lane and Hamilton aren't the only ones who have your back. I do, too. You know, they say behind every good man is a good woman supporting him. These last few months I've gotten to know you as I've never known someone before. There is a warmth in your heart and soul that arrives before you do."

"What about Zachary's father?"

"I met Zachary's father in a bar when I was out drinking with friends. I married him out of necessity because I was still in medical school. Zachary was the only thing we had in common. He treated Zachary and I like we were one of his possessions. When he got tired of us, he traded us in for a newer model."

"I'm sorry to hear that."

"Don't be sorry. I'm not."

"Doesn't your ex-husband come and see Zachary?"

"He has absolutely nothing to do with him. It hurt Zachary so much that he withdrew into a protective world. To see how you have been able to draw him out of his shell has touched the depth of my soul."

"I think Zachary has been as good for me as I have been for him. So, as much as I pulled him out of his shell, I think he's done the same for me. When I moved into my grandmother's house, I did it to escape the world. I wanted to wall myself off from the past."

"You have provided something for me I thought I would never, ever have in my life."

"What's that?"

"Love. You've taught me how to do something I've never known before. You taught me how important love is. I love you, Connor. I understand if you're not ready to respond to me. I don't want to push you. I just want you to know when you're ready, I'll be here."

Julie turned away from Connor and walked into the room where her suitcases sat. Connor watched her walk away and sighed. He desperately wanted to grab her and sweep her up into his arms and never let her go, but he knew he wasn't ready to give all of himself to her.

Chapter 20

The Seattle Times

Connor's sleep had been restless. Doubt had gnawed at him like carrion on a rotting corpse. He heard pounding on the bathroom door.

"Connor, are you alright?" Julie asked

"I am. Why do you ask?" Connor answered, turning off the shower

"Because you wrote a message on the table in the main room."

"I did?"

"I know I didn't do it, and it looks like your handwriting."

"What did it say?"

"I would rather you saw it for yourself."

"Give me a couple of minutes to dry off and get dressed."

In a few short minutes, Connor opened the door to his room. He was wearing just a pair of blue jeans. He walked over to where Julie was standing in front of the table.

"Wow, Connor, I don't think I have ever seen such fine muscle tone. You must spend a lot of time working out."

"Working out gave me a way to detach my brain for a while. When I was in my alcohol recovery program, I decided to concentrate on getting my body in the best shape it had ever been in."

"From my point of view, I like the shape you're in." she admired, placing her hand on Connor.

"What about this message you asked about?"

Julie stepped aside, written in black magic marker on the table was the following:

'Like the sands of the hourglass, time is short.'

Connor looked at the writing on the table for what seemed like an eternity to Julie.

"Is everything okay,?"

"No, it's not. I don't remember writing this. I'm not even sure I did."

"If you didn't write it, who did?"

"Who wrote it isn't important. What matters most is that lives will be lost if we don't act quickly."

"I will get ready to go."

"Go where, Julie?"

"Why with you, of course."

"I don't think it's a good idea."

"Like it or not, I am coming with you."

"There is one thing I know for sure about you."

"What would that be?"

"I know you are one of the most persistent people I have ever met."

"I'll take it as I hope you meant it as a compliment."

"That's exactly how I meant it. Why don't you go ahead and get ready? I told Hamilton we would meet him downstairs at 8:00."

Connor looked at Julie as she walked out of her room.

"Wow, Julie, I like the look. I feel like I'm a thorn next to a beautiful rose."

"Why do you say that?"

"I've never seen your hair up before. It looks nice. I feel like the ugly duckling next to you."

"Just remember, the ugly duckling turned into a beautiful swan, so there is hope for you. Besides, I think we're more like Mutt & Jeff."

"Am I Mutt or Jeff?"

"That's for me to know and you to find out. After all, isn't half of the fun in the chase?" she replied with a laugh.

A few minutes later, they were walking into the lobby. Hamilton Gardner rose from where he sat.

"I trust you two liked your accommodations?"

"Yes, the room was great," they agreed.

"Are you ready to go? We don't want to keep Mark Brandt waiting."

Within fifteen minutes, they were in the lobby of the Seattle Times. Connor Darke walked up to the receptionist's desk.

"Good morning, I am Connor Darke. I am here to see Mark Brandt."

"If you'll sign the guest register, I will let Mark know you're here," the receptionist replied.

After a short wait, Mark entered the lobby.

"Good morning, Mr. Darke. It's a pleasure to meet you," he greeted, extending a hand to Connor.

"Mark, it's nice to meet you. I would like to introduce you to my companions, Dr. Julie Strand and Hamilton Gardner."

Mark shook their hands.

"Welcome to the Seattle Times. I thought we could go into our first-floor conference room. So, if you will all follow me, we can get started."

Windows lined two sides of the conference room. The table had chairs spaced evenly around it. They took a seat. Mark set a pen and notepad down.

"Mr. Darke, do you mind if I take notes while we talk?"

"You can take all the notes you want. Please, call me Connor. I look for my dad when people refer to me as Mr. Darke."

"That's fine, Connor. So, you're okay if I write about you in my column?"

"I would prefer you don't, Mr. Brandt."

"I'm sorry. I thought the reason for your visit to Seattle was to announce you're back in the game."

"I don't quite follow you. Back in what game?"

"Why the Love Doctor, of course. You had the top-rated talk show on television before you decided to take a year's sabbatical. I guess I thought you were here to announce your return to daytime television."

"I don't have any intention of doing any such thing."

"If you're not here to announce your return to public life, what are you here for?"

"I'm here to discuss an article you wrote about a fire at Hidden Shores and to talk about Samantha Blake."

Mark stood motionless, just staring at Connor Darke. After a couple of minutes, he sucked in a deep breath, ran his hand through his hair, and spoke to Connor.

"Wouldn't it have been easier to pick up a phone and call me? I know you're living in Syracuse, New York. That's a hell of a long way from Seattle."

"I am here because I have information about the article you wrote about the fire at Hidden Shores five years ago. Besides, if I had called you and told you that I know about Samantha Blake, we would probably not be having this discussion."

"You know, I don't think this is funny."

"Trust me, there is nothing funny about this. We need to talk about Samantha Blake."

Mark sneered at Connor as he spoke.

"Who the hell put you up to this? Was it Ken Fisher or Eric Steinbrenner of the Seattle Police Department?"

Mark's face contorted, and the muscles in his neck had tightened.

"Mark, you need to relax."

"It just seems to me that someone has fed you information. There isn't any other way you could have known about Samantha Blake."

"No one has put me up to this."

"I'm sorry, I don't believe you. There are only a small handful of people who even know about it."

"I know about it."

"How on earth do you know about it? I don't get it,."

"That's because Samantha told me about it."

"You've seen her?"

"Not the way you did."

"I don't understand."

"Samantha Blake was here not long ago, standing in your lobby, asking you to investigate the death of her father."

"How do you know about her visit? The list of people who know is short."

"That list now includes my companions and me. Samantha Blake was here, standing in front of you a couple of days ago. The first thought you had when you saw her was that you had never seen a more beautiful woman in your entire life. You were hoping to get her into your bed. Is that about, right?"

"Yes, that pretty much sums up my encounter with her. I just don't understand why she came to me."

"I believe she came to you because of the award you won as an investigative reporter. She told you she wanted you to investigate her father's murder."

"But I won that award after she was dead. How could she possibly have known?"

"How and why she knew doesn't matter, Mark. What matters is that you and I have a job to do."

"What job is that?"

"We have to help save lives."

"Save lives—whose lives do we have to save?"

"Mark, you can trust me when I say this. There is something very sinister tied to the death of Benjamin Blake, which is why I'm here asking for your help."

"But how can I help?"

"By accepting the invitation, you received from the Seattle Police Department yesterday."

"This all seems too impossible to believe."

"I'm sure it is, but we don't have time to debate this. You're going to have to put faith in what I'm telling you."

Mark shook his head back and forth, exclaiming vehemently as he did.

"No, Mr. Darke. I can't take this based on faith."

"There is something else Samantha Blake told me. It's something she didn't tell you," Connor said, placing a hand on Mark's shoulder.

"What would that be?"

"She told me the make, model, and license plate number of the car that killed her."

"Nobody has ever come forward with information. The only way you could know it is if she told you, isn't it?"

"That's right."

Mark shook his head in disbelief.

"This is getting way too weird for my liking, Mr. Darke."

"Like it or not, it is what it is. So, are you going to help or not?"

"I don't think I have a choice. I guess we have to go and talk with the Seattle Police Department."

"Yes, we do. The sooner we can talk with them, the better."

"I'll call them and tell them we're on our way."

"Before we head over to the Seattle Police Department, there is one more thing I need to discuss with you."

"What would that be?"

"I just wanted to say congratulations."

"Congratulations on what Mr. Darke?"

"I want to congratulate you because you're going to be the father of twin girls."

"Now, you're just showing off, aren't you?"

"I don't do it to show off. I said it because I want you to know we're not alone. The people who have gone before us can have a dramatic effect on us, both in life and in death."

Chapter 21

The Seattle Police Department

Fish poked his head into Caleb's office.

"Caleb, do you have a minute?"

"Sure, Fish, what's up?

"I wanted to tell you that I thought about what you said about working with Mark Brandt and keeping him in the loop. He might be able to help with this case, so I'm okay with it."

"I'm glad to hear it. Is Hawk available?"

"I believe so, why?"

"I need the two of you to meet me in conference room 2A in fifteen minutes."

"Not a problem. What's going on?"

"Mark called. He is on his way over and should be here in fifteen minutes or less. Grab Hawk and get down to conference room 2A."

"I'm on my way."

"Hawk, we have a meeting to go to," Fish announced, stepping into Hawk's office.

"I don't have any meetings on my schedule. What's come up?"

"A pain in my ass."

"Does this pain in your ass have a name?"

"Yep, its name is Mark Brandt."

"Let me sit between the two of you when he gets here. I wouldn't want you to beat the crap out of him."

"I'll behave. I promise."

"What do we owe the honor of his visit to?"

"He wants to be a contributor and not a bystander. He had a response from the article he wrote about the disappearance of my niece. I guess he's all hopped up about it and is on his way over."

Hawk and Fish walked into the conference room. Caleb was already there.

"Where is Mark?" Fish asked.

"He's on his way up. He has come with an entourage."

Within a few minutes, Mark walked into the conference room with Connor Darke, Hamilton Gardner, and Julie Strand following close behind. Caleb jumped up at the sight of Hamilton Gardner and looked hard at him. He rubbed his bald head, pointed at Hamilton, and smiled.

"I don't believe my eyes. If it isn't Hamilton Gardner. I heard you retired at the ripe old age of forty-two."

"That's not entirely true, Caleb. I'm semi-retired."

"You look great, Hamilton, even without the hair."

Hamilton rubbed his bald head. "It's so kind of you to notice. I see that we have suffered the same fate."

"Unfortunately, we have."

"How is Gale these days?"

"Gale is great. She is basking in the glory of being a grandmother for the very first time. I heard about Adrianna. What happened?"

"I lost her ten years ago. She was killed by a drunk driver while running one morning. I was working deep undercover when it happened. I didn't find out about it for five and a half months."

"I had no idea. I'm so sorry. Adrianna was such an exceptional woman."

"She had to be. She put up with my sorry butt. When I came home and found out she was gone, I couldn't do undercover work anymore. I sunk into a depression so deep, I thought I would never get out of it."

"The fact that you're here is a testimony that you found your way out."

"I didn't do it by myself. Do you remember Colonel Victor Lane?"

"Why, of course, I do. His death was a sad day."

"It certainly was. Colonel Lane got me the help I needed. I owe him my life. Before he passed, I committed to staying on with his wife. I met Connor Darke through Victor's wife, Mrs. Gertrude Lane. Mrs. Lane was good friends with Connor's grandmother."

"Would that be Gertrude Lane, the philanthropist?"

"One in the same."

"You're tagging along as a favor?"

"Not at all. Gertrude Lane has a deep interest in Connor's abilities. I'm here to make sure no harm comes to Connor or Ms. Strand.

"Mark, why don't you tell me what has got you all charged up," Caleb addressed Mark.

"I ran the article about the fire at Hidden Shores and the disappearance of Detective Fisher's niece. I got a call from Mrs. Gertrude Lane stating that she was sending someone who might have some information. So, here we are, gentlemen. I would like to introduce you to Connor Darke."

Fish stood and walked over to Connor. "I thought it was you, Mr. Darke. I recognized you the minute you walked through the door. It is wonderful to meet you," Fish said, extending his hand to Connor.

"I'm Detective Ken Fisher, and this is my partner Detective Eric Steinbrenner. Eric, this is the one and only 'Love Doctor.'"

"I hate it when people call me the Love Doctor. I consider myself a relationship specialist. You can call me by my first name, which is Connor, Detective Fisher."

"Regardless of what name I call you, I am pleased to meet you."

"Trust me, Detective Fisher, I am always excited to meet people who put themselves in harm's way for the good of their fellow man."

Connor turned toward Detective Steinbrenner.

"I am especially pleased to meet you, Detective Steinbrenner. It's not every day I get to meet a hero. I would like to introduce you to my traveling companion, Doctor Julie Strand. Julie, Detective Steinbrenner saved a woman from a brutal attack."

Julie reached out her hand. "So many people are afraid to get involved, Detective Steinbrenner. The world stands a much better place because of what you did."

"Thank you. That's very kind of you to say." Hawk blushed.

"What kind of information do you have, Mr. Darke?" Caleb asked.

"To start, I have information concerning Benjamin Blake's daughter, Samantha."

"We haven't released any information about Benjamin Blake or his daughter. Samantha is dead.

What information can you possibly have about her?" Hawk asked.

"I know the make, model, and license plate number of the vehicle that killed her."

"How on earth can you know that unless you were the one driving?"

"I wasn't even in Seattle when it happened. I know about it because she told me, Detective Steinbrenner."

"You've seen her ghost like Mr. Brandt claims to have?"

"No, I haven't."

"So, how can you possibly know anything, Mr. Darke?"

"You can believe what I am about to tell you or not, Detective Steinbrenner. Samantha Blake told me she was hit by a silver four-door Toyota Camry. The car had Washington license plates with the number P8722 9C."

"Why should I believe you?"

"Run the plate if you don't believe me."

Eric looked at Connor. "Relax, that plate number does belong to a 2007 Toyota Camry. We found items in the car that lead us to suspect the owner of the car used it to hit and kill Samantha Blake."

"Where is the car now, Detectives?"

"The car is in the police impound yard in Boise, Idaho. It was found in a scenic overlook in Idaho. The owner was in the car dead—killed with a shot to the head. We have boots on the ground in Boise. Our guys are doing a complete forensic analysis with the aid of the Boise PD. Is there anything else you would like to share with us about Samantha Blake?"

"She told me someone murdered her father because of what he was involved in. What exactly he got himself into, she was not sure. She did say there are clues at the house yet."

"Did she say what was out there?"

"No, she didn't."

"Connor, what makes you think there is anything of importance out there?"

"Didn't Benjamin Blake's neighbor report that a Cadillac Escalade cruised by the house more than once?"

"Yes, she did, and how did you know that?"

"Because Sharon Cross has told me that she wants you to find her killer."

"Did Mrs. Cross, by any chance, tell you if she saw her killer?"

"Unfortunately, Detective Fisher, she said she heard a noise and turned to see what it was and saw the same Black Cadillac Escalade from the night Benjamin Blake went missing. She started to run for home and got hit from behind. That's all she could tell me."

"We found the burned-out hulk of the Escalade yesterday. There isn't much evidence that we will be able to pull from it. We've scoured the Blake house twice and turned up nothing."

"Have you posted around the clock surveillance on Blake's house?"

"We didn't find it necessary originally, but we have now."

"Trust me, they went back to look more than once. I suggest you send someone out to look again, and this time, I want to go along."

"How do we know you're not part of the group looking for information?"

Connor threw up his hands in exasperation. "I came here to help the investigation. If you don't let me help, more lives will be lost."

"Whose lives? As far as we know, we are trying to figure out the death of Benjamin Blake and Mrs. Cross."

"Caleb, all I know is the strong sense I have that their deaths are just the tip of the iceberg."

"I was never sold on the crap you used to shovel on your television show. I am going to need something more substantial to go before I agree to put a civilian on an active investigation. I am duty-bound to protect you, Mr. Darke, even if I believe that I'm protecting you from yourself."

"Since you want something more to go with ,Caleb, what about the key the Detectives found hidden in Hector Gonzales's apartment?"

A look of surprise and disbelief crossed the faces of Detectives Fisher and Steinbrenner. Fish spoke up.

"Caleb, I don't know how Connor knows about the key we found, but maybe he's right. I think that we should let him help us."

Caleb threw his hand up in the air, signaling defeat.

"Fine, Connor, you can go out with Detectives Fisher and Steinbrenner. I suppose one more look won't hurt."

"Thank you, Caleb. You won't regret it."

Connor turned and looked at Detective Steinbrenner.

"Detective Steinbrenner, I can tell by your expression you don't believe a word I've said."

"Trust me, I would like to."

"Maybe this will convince you I have a special insight."

Connor walked over to Hawk.

"Let me be the first to congratulate you on your marriage."

"Don't you mean his upcoming marriage, Mr. Darke," Fish replied.

"No, I don't, Detective Fisher. Your partner has been married for four months. His wife, Ming-Wei, is expecting."

"Wow, Connor. I guess you're just full of surprises."

"Here is another surprise for you, Detective Fisher. Detective Steinbrenner read my book on love and relationships. He couldn't admit it to you because he felt embarrassed. He needed my help."

"Hawk, it looks like Connor has you all figured out. It's good you've read Connor's book," Fish patting Hawk on the shoulder.

"I probably would have read it sooner if you had shut up about it, Fish."

"I'm just glad you did, Hawk."

"Me too."

"I would have liked to have witnessed your wedding vows, Eric. Why didn't you wait?"

"We were going to wait. Trust me, it was a spontaneous decision, Fish."

"Congratulations anyway. I wish you all the best. I have to admit it though, you're going to have your hands full."

"Thanks, Fish."

Fish turned to Connor.

"Well, Connor, it looks like you're now officially part of this investigation."

Chapter 22

Evidence Gathering

The detectives stopped in front of Benjamin Blake's house. Connor was sitting in the rear seat. Mr. Cross came running down his driveway, waving at the detectives' car. He was short of breath and panting hard.

Fish put his hand on Mr. Cross's shoulder.

"Are you okay?"

Mr. Cross shook his head and spoke in a short staccato-like manner.

"I just called your office. I can't believe you're here already."

"We're not here in response to a phone call from you. What's going on?"

"Detective Fisher, there was a cop car in front of the house up until an hour ago. It left in a hurry with its siren and lights going. Not long after that, I heard noises coming from the Blake's house. It sounds like someone's destroying the place."

"I want you to go back to your house until we say it's safe."

"Hawk, I think we had better call the local police department for back up."

"I'll take care of it, Fish."

Hawk flipped open his cell phone and called the local police dispatcher. Fish leaned into the car to speak with Connor.

"Connor, I want you to go with Mr. Cross until we come for you."

Before Connor could get out of the car, a shot rang out from the direction of Blake's house and whizzed past Hawk's right ear. It struck the side of a planter on the front left corner of the Cross's driveway, sending a shower of concrete pieces into the air. Fish pulled Connor out of the car and pushed him down below the left side of the vehicle.

"Connor, stay low and don't move until we have this situation under control."

"No problem, Detective."

Sirens were coming toward the house. When they came into sight, Hawk waved for them to stop at a safe distance. He ran toward the lead police car, crouching low with his badge displayed. Four police officers got out of the two vehicles. Crouching low, they moved to where Hawk was.

"I'm Detective Steinbrenner of the Seattle PD. My partner over there is Detective Fisher. The guy crouching down is a civilian assistant to the Seattle PD. We came out here to go through the original crime scene once again. There was supposed to be a patrol car sitting on this house. Do you happen to know why the patrol car left?"

"They were responding to an automobile accident with injuries. When they got to their destination, they found the traffic light was showing green from both directions. It was a real mess with multiple cars and multiple injuries. We got here as quickly as we could. Detective Steinbrenner, what are we up against.”

“We’re not sure, Officer. Multiple shots have been fired.”

Just then, two more shots rang out. The patrolman next to Hawk exclaimed.

“We now know there are at least two shooters. What’s the plan?” the cop next to Hawk exclaimed.

“The house is surrounded by trees, which should give us enough cover to move in on the house. Why don’t two of you come with me, and we’ll work our way to the back of the house. The other two can move in toward the front with Detective Fisher.”

Hawk gave his partner the signal to start moving toward the house. Shots rang out as the two groups went toward the house. They stopped, took cover, and shot back. The gunfire exchange continued for thirty to forty minutes, then abruptly ended.

“We need to move carefully. Whoever is in there may have stopped to reload their weapons,” Fish warned.

They were within fifty feet of the house when the sound of a running motor came from behind it.

“Fish, they must have a boat. Whoever was in there is getting away.”

Within a space of ten minutes or less, the two groups were standing at the top of the bluff overlooking the bay. A twenty-four-foot cabin cruiser was moving out into the bay at a high rate of speed. Fish opened his cell phone and called Captain Danni Stevenson of the U.S. Coast Guard.

“Captain Stevenson, this is Detective Fisher from the Seattle PD. I need the Coast Guard to help me with the pursuit of a boat that just left the dock at Benjamin Blake's house at a high rate of speed. The boat is a blue and white Yamaha about twenty-four feet in length. The occupants are armed and dangerous. Let me know as soon as you get anything. Thanks, Danni."

"Fish, should I go and get Connor? He's still crouching on the other side of the car?"

"I think we'd better make sure there is no one in the house before we get him. I'll take two of the officers through the back while you take the other two and go through the front."

Within minutes, both groups were in the house. Hawk, who had moved into the den, called out to Fish.

"Fish, we've got a body in here."

Fish moved to where Hawk was standing over the body.

"Is he alive, Hawk?"

"No, he's gone," Hawk said after feeling for a pulse. He pulled a wallet out of the man's pocket. "Diego Javier," he read before handing the wallet to one of the patrolmen. "Could you run this for priors, please?"

Fish was next to the body. "There is a gunshot wound to the back of the head."

Fish rolled the man's body over. "There are three more gunshots, two to his chest and one in his arm. My guess is he was severely injured. Whoever was with him decided to finish him off so he couldn't talk."

Fish stood and looked around. "Mr. Cross was right. Someone was in here destroying the house." Every drawer in the house was out, and its contents emptied onto the floor. One of the officers spoke up.

"Do you know what they were after, Detective Fisher?"

"We don't know if they found what they were after. We do have a police consultant out in the car. Hopefully, he'll be able to help. Hawk, would you please go get Connor and bring him in."

"I'll be back in a flash."

Hawk came back with Connor Darke. Connor spent time looking around the interior of the house. He opened cabinets and closets, putting a black X on each area he looked in as he went. Hawk watched as Connor made his way around the house.

"Connor, what are the black X's for?"

"Once I feel that there is no more evidence that will contribute to the case, I place an X as a visual."

"It looks to me that you've cleared pretty much the entire house."

"You're right, Detective Steinbrenner, I have."

"In that case, what do you think?"

Connor stood deep in thought for what seemed like an eternity to Hawk. Hawk was beginning to get impatient when Connor started walking around all the rooms, scrutinizing every inch of the house very carefully. He stopped and turned to Fish and Hawk.

"The thing they were looking for is not here."

"They must have found what they were looking for," Hawk exclaimed.

"Detective Steinbrenner, you're going to have to develop your skills on being patient," Conner remarked.

Hawk looked at Fish. "Did you tell him everything?"

Fish let out a muted laugh. "I swear to God, Hawk, I didn't tell him to say that."

"No, Detective, he didn't."

"Detective Steinbrenner, you've been out here more than I have. Does anything seem odd to you?"

"No, it doesn't. It just looks like a typical crime scene to me."

"Detective, in looking around this house, I have noticed the enormous number of pictures hung everywhere of what I am guessing are family members and friends."

"I noticed that, too, Mr. Darke. You're not telling me anything I didn't already know," Hawk answered.

"Detective Steinbrenner, what don't you notice about all of these pictures?"

"I'm sorry, Mr. Darke. I am not sure what answer you're looking for."

"I will explain it to you then. There are a lot of pictures on these walls. The one thing not in any of these pictures is a pet. When I walked into the bathroom, I noticed a lot of allergy medicines. Based on what's there, one of the Blake's was allergic to animal dander."

"Mr. Darke, that knowledge and a quarter won't even buy a cup of coffee."

"You're right, it won't, Detective Steinbrenner. If you add that there is a grave for a pet named Skipjack outside, which the Blakes most likely didn't own, it suggests there is something other than a pet buried there. In one of the pictures in the den, there was a picture of a young Benjamin Blake with his father. They were standing by a small boat named the Skipjack. I could be wrong, but I'm guessing the grave is where Blake hid information. So, shall we go outside and dig it up?"

"But what if you're wrong?"

"Then I'm wrong, and we rebury Skipjack, but since there are no pictures of a pet hung anywhere in this house, I doubt that I am."

"Hawk, shall we go see if there are any shovels in the garage?"

"Sure, Fish."

Within a couple of minutes, they were digging up the ground in front of the grave marker.

"Stop the digging, gentlemen," Connor shouted when the hole was about three feet deep.

Detective Steinbrenner looked at Connor. "Seriously, you want us to stop digging? I guess I was right after all. You don't have a damn clue what they were looking for."

"That's because, the answer isn't in the ground. It's inside the grave marker. If someone can give me a hand, I will show you what I'm talking about."

Fish walked over to the grave marker. Together, they were able to pull it out of the ground. On the bottom side was a metal plate that had four screws in it.

"This is most likely Benjamin Blake's hiding place."

"Fish, I saw some screwdrivers in the garage. I'll go get one."

Hawk was back in a flash and knelt to unscrew the metal plate from the grave marker. An envelope in a zip lock bag was inside the stone.

"Hawk, do you want to apologize to Mr. Darke?"

"Fish, I want to see what's in there before I start apologizing."

Fish removed the folder from the ziplock bag and started looking through its contents.

"Holy shit. Hawk, you need to see this stuff."

Fish started passing documents to his partner.

"Fish, this guy thought he was doing the bidding of the FBI. I can't believe he thought they would want him to change an entire set of dental records."

"I don't understand it either, Hawk. First off, we know Mr. Jensen is fictitious. For one, that leaves us still looking for who is behind all this. Secondly, we need to find the reason for the cover-up. Thirdly, where the hell is the money?"

"Hopefully, Connor can continue to be of help."

"I'll second that motion, Hawk."

One of the patrolmen walked up to Fish.

"I ran Diego Javier for priors. He has a long list of crimes. There is a warrant out for him for armed robbery. My guess is he was a gun for hire."

Fish looked at the officer's name badge. "Thanks, Officer Jennings. I would appreciate it if you guys could sit on the house until our crime scene team can get here."

"Not a problem, Detective Fisher."

Fish flipped open his cell phone and dialed Caleb's number.

"Caleb, this is Fish. Connor was right. There was someone in the house when we got here. We exchanged gunfire for a while. The scene is secure now. We have one dead in the house, and one or more persons escaped in a boat. I've called the Coast Guard, and they are out patrolling for it as we speak. Connor was able to lead us to a file that Blake had hidden. We know what he was into. We found blood in two different places, which means a second person was injured. Would you send the crime scene out here? We will head back to the office and bring the information we found."

Fish's cell phone rang.

"This is Detective Fisher."

"Detective Fisher, this is Captain Stevenson. We've found the boat you were looking for."

"Captain Stevenson, was there anyone on board?"

"There was a male body onboard with no identification."

"Danni, do you think he was the only one?"

"Probably not, Fish. We got a report that a diver was spotted going overboard. There was a spot for two different sets of scuba gear on board, and we found only one."

"Danni, did you search the immediate area around the boat?"

"We did but turned up nothing. We are going to tow the boat into Seattle. We'll let you know when we get it there."

"Thanks for the update, Captain Stevenson."

"You're welcome, Fish."

Detective Fisher hung up and looked at Hawk.

"Let's get this information and Connor back to the office."

Chapter 23

The Seattle Police Department

Detectives Fisher and Steinbrenner walked into conference room 2A carrying the folder from the Blake residence. Fish laid the folder down in front of Caleb.

"Caleb, Connor was right about the fact there was more information at the Blake residence. We wouldn't have found it without him."

"We've had teams out there more than once, and so has Benjamin Blake's killers. How the hell were you able to find it, Mr. Darke?" Caleb asked.

"I just noticed what no one else had."

"Mr. Darke, why don't you enlighten me on what we didn't notice."

"I noticed there were hundreds of photos hung on the walls of the house. Not one of those photographs had a picture of a pet in it, yet there was a grave marker for a dog named Skipjack outside of the house. I simply made an educated guess."

"What did you make an educated guess about?"

"I deduced what everyone was so desperately seeking was hidden in the grave of a non-existent pet."

"What if you had been wrong?"

"That point is moot, isn't it?"

"I guess it is," Caleb replied as he rose and shook Connor's hand. "Thank you for your effort."

"Not a problem. That's what I came here for."

"Fish, what's in the information Connor helped you find?"

"This file confirms the information we heard on the digital recorder we found at Benjamin Blake's residence."

"Give me the condensed version of the file."

"Benjamin Blake was hired to change dental records by someone who claimed to be working for the FBI.

"Do we know whose dental records he changed?"

"No, that information wasn't part of what we found. Supposedly, he received ten million dollars to do it."

"Do the documents look authentic?"

"Surprisingly, very authenticate. We don't know who Mr. Jensen is, nor do we know who he's working for."

"Maybe Connor can continue to assist us."

"For some reason, I don't think we are going to solve this case without his help."

"I certainly hope we can get to the bottom of this, Fish, and soon. I have a feeling this is going to get ugly before we're done. Oh, and there is something else I need to tell you."

"What that would be?"

"Our young friend you're concerned about has pulled through."

"Thanks for the update."

"Caleb, you are referring to Chris Felton, are you not?" Connor asked.

"How the hell do you know that, Connor? I've kept the need-to-know loop small to protect Chris."

"I'm sorry, I just know."

"That is not a good enough explanation, Mr. Darke. I need to know how the hell you know about him, and I need to know right now!" Caleb's face was red and extremely tense.

"You need to calm down. I'm sure there is an explanation for this," Fish stepped in.

"It better be a good one," Caleb replied.

"All I can tell you is the same voices that asked me to help told me they were intervening with the powers to be on behalf of Chris Felton. To put it mildly, Caleb, he has friends in high places."

"For now, I am going on the fact you couldn't possibly know about Chris Felton. If I found out you were involved in the attack, you will regret the day you were ever born. Is that understood, Mr. Darke?"

"It's perfectly understood, Captain."

"Captain, may I add something to this conversation?" Fish asked.

Caleb had a look of surprise on his face at the request from Fish.

"Isn't this a first, Detective Fisher. You've never asked permission to put your two cents into a conversation. Why start now?"

"You said I need to become a team player."

"I believe I did, Detective Fisher."

"Captain, consider this, that I'm trying to put my best foot forward."

"That's great, Fish. In the spirit of cooperation, Ricardo Gonzales turned over a notebook to the San Francisco PD. He rents out the house that he grew up in, and he remembered that his dad had an old army footlocker stored in the loft of the garage. The San

Francisco PD has faxed us copies of the pages from the book."

Caleb handed a copy to Detectives Fisher and Steinbrenner, who started reading the pages.

"Caleb, these are all coded addresses. I bet this is the notebook that Deandra Parker saw and something to do with the jobs that Hector did."

"That would be my guess, Detective Steinbrenner," Caleb answered.

Fish let out a loud, mournful groan and sank in on one of the sofas. The copies of the pages that he had been reading fell from his hand and scattered all over the floor. He buried his face in his hands and began to weep uncontrollably. Hawk walked over to Fish and waited for him to stop crying. He stopped and attempted to speak. His voice was raspy as he spoke to Hawk.

"Take a look at page three, about halfway down, it's there."

"What's their Fish?" Hawk asked

Suddenly, Hawk yelled at the top of his lungs. It sounded like the death throes of a wounded animal.

"Would either of you mind telling me what's going on?"

"Caleb, the address of Fish's sister's house at Hidden Shores is on the third page. I think we can move the Surley case from being death caused by faulty equipment to murder. Somehow, their deaths are tied into whatever Benjamin Blake got himself into."

Just then, Hamilton Gardner and Julie Strand entered the conference room. Julie ran over to Connor.

"Are you alright, Connor? I heard there was a shooting," Julie stated.

"Don't worry, Dr. Strand. I made sure Connor was out of harm's way," Fish spoke out. His eyes were red and from crying.

"Thank you, Detective Fisher. I couldn't stand to lose him. Are you all right, Detective? It appears that you've been crying?"

Connor spoke up.

"Julie, Detective Fisher just found out that the fire that his sister and brother-in-law died in five years ago was intentional. Their deaths may be tied into the present investigation."

Julie looked at Detective Fisher and spoke.

"I'm truly sorry for your loss, Detective. Where do you go from here with your investigation?"

"Dr. Strand, we are going to press on with our investigation until we get to the bottom of things. Hopefully, Connor will be willing to stay until the end."

Connor nodded his agreement.

"That sounds good to me, Detective. What do we do next?"

"We are going to try and divide and conquer the task at hand Dr. Strand," Caleb answered.

"What can I do to help Captain Clarke?"

"You can go home, Dr. Strand. The best place for you is out of harm's way."

"I want to stay with Connor. There must be something I can do?"

"Caleb is right, Julie. You should go home. It will be safer for you. I'll stay here and see that nothing happens to Connor. Mrs. Lane has traveled here by train. I'm sure that she and her attendants can see you safely home."

"You have my word, Dr. Strand, we will do our best to make sure that no harm will come to Connor."

Julie looked at Hamilton—her eyes were getting moist. Hamilton moved over to Julie and hugged her like he would have embraced his daughter.

"I'll keep him safe," he whispered in her ear.

"I'll take that as your promise to bring him back in one piece," Julie replied.

Hamilton bowed low to Julie, then stood and spoke.

"Caleb, can you have someone escort Dr. Strand to the King Street Station? I will let Mrs. Lane know that she's on her way."

"That won't be a problem."

Caleb made a phone call, and within two minutes, two officers were standing in Caleb's doorway.

"Gentlemen, please see that Dr. Strand gets safely to the King Street Station."

Julie turned and buried her face in Connor's chest for a moment. Choked up, she uttered an I love you to Connor and turned and left with the officers.

"Have we gotten anywhere on John Pierce yet, Caleb?" Fish asked after Julie had left.

"No, but you'll be happy to know that along with the notebook Hector Gonzales's brother also found his will. Hector left it all to his brother."

"Caleb, is the San Francisco PD going to release all the things we took out of Hector's apartment to his brother? If they don't, having his brother's last will won't be worth the piece of paper it's written on."

"They already have, Fish. Hector's brother picked it up yesterday."

"Wow, it's great to see somebody who does so much for his community catch a break," Fish replied."

"I think it's the local community that caught the break on this one."

"How so, Caleb?"

"Ricardo is going to auction all his brother's stuff. He has already sold the Honus Wagner baseball card. He took the proceeds and purchased a building that he is having renovated for a medical clinic for the poor in his community."

"That is amazing."

"It sure is Hawk. Sometimes, the most ordinary people do the most extraordinary things."

"Caleb, I would appreciate it if you could give me a contact number for Ricardo Gonzales. I would like to arrange support for the medical clinic from the Lane Foundation. I'm sure as soon as Mrs. Lane hears about this, she will insist on helping," Hamilton spoke up.

"I will make sure you get the information, Hamilton."

"That would be great."

"I assure you Ricardo Gonzales didn't know what his brother was involved with," Connor volunteered.

"That is pretty much what San Francisco PD believes. The only thing we know for sure is the bullet that killed John Pierce is from the same gun that killed Benjamin Blake," Caleb stated.

"Trust me, John Pierce was involved with the people behind Benjamin Blake's death."

"Connor, I guess the Seattle PD will have to keep digging until we get to the bottom of it all."

"Caleb, I plan on staying in Seattle until this investigation is over."

"Good, Connor, we welcome the help."

Chapter 24

The Seattle PD the next morning

Detective Steinbrenner pulled the stocking cap he was wearing down over his ears to protect them from the icy fog that was hanging in the air like a dead weight. It was a short walk to the main Seattle Police Department building. He headed for Fish's office and found it empty. He continued down the hallway and noticed the lights were already on in one of the conference rooms. Walking into the conference room, he found his partner slumped in a chair, asleep and snoring loudly. He shook his partner's shoulder to awaken him.

"Good morning, Fish. I take it you didn't go home?"

"What?" Fish replied.

"Home Fish. You didn't go home last night, did you? I'm surprised your wife didn't call me to find out where you were."

Slowly clearing the cobwebs out of his head, Fish focused in on his partner and spoke.

"I talked with her last night after you left. She's in Dublin, Ireland, at a conference. I told her I was on my way home. I meant to go. I guess the time got away from me."

Fish stood and tried to straighten up his clothes to make himself look presentable. File folders and papers were strewn all over the conference room table.

"It looks like you got out your sister's cold case file again after I left. You know, I would have stayed behind and helped had you asked."

"You would have stayed?"

"Of course, I would have. You only had to ask, Fish."

"I'm glad you didn't. You look tired, Hawk. Since you're here already, you couldn't have gotten much sleep?"

"I didn't. I kept thinking about how we found your sister's address in Hector Gonzales's notebook. It wasn't something I expected at all."

"Me either, Hawk. I knew I wouldn't be able to sleep, so I decided to stay and work. Fish, why didn't you tell me women get cranky when they're expecting?"

"Had you told me you were going to embark on the journey called parenthood, I would have made you read the book 'What to Expect When You're Expecting.' I expect that we will get some hits on the information we sent out. I was glad that Mark Brandt stayed to help. I can't believe how fast he can type."

"Fish, do you think we will see any of them much before noon?"

"I highly doubt it. Connor was so tired that he could barely keep his eyes open."

Just then, a voice came from the doorway of the conference room.

"Who won't be here before noon? Why on earth would you think that?"

Fish looked over to see Hamilton Gardner and Connor Darke standing in the doorway of the conference room.

"I'm sorry. I just figured that you two were exhausted," Fish said.

"We are exhausted, Detective. Since lives may hang in the balance, this is more important. We can sleep when it's over."

"I've been working on this case for over five years. What makes you think we're going to get to the bottom of this anytime soon?"

"Detective, I think the reason I'm here is to help finish this and do it quickly."

Connor pointed to the papers and file folders strewn across the conference table.

"Detective, is that the contents of your sister's cold case file?"

"Yes, it is. Why?"

"Do you have any pictures in there? If so, I would like to see them."

"Sure, no problem."

Fish opened a folder and extracted three pictures and handed them to Connor. Connor looked at each one, stopping at the picture of Detective Fisher's niece. Hamilton looked at Connor, who was staring at the last picture.

"Do you recognize her?"

"Possibly."

Fish jumped up from his seated position at the table and moved around the table to see which picture Connor was staring at.

"That's my niece. She's been missing ever since the fire. Have you seen her?"

"Maybe, Detective. But not in the sense that you are asking about."

"What does that mean?"

"I'm not sure, but this girl could be one of the images that I have seen in my mind. It could very well be the image that I've seen the most. But I can't be sure. Is there any way you can progress the age of the girl in this picture?"

"I asked our sketch artist to do exactly that the other day. I'll see if she has it finished."

Fish left the conference room and headed down the hallway. In less than ten minutes, he was back. Jan Sikowski, the department sketch artist, was carrying a large pad.

"Connor, this is Jan Sikowski, our sketch artist. She has already completed what she believes to be an updated picture of my niece. I brought her along in case you want her to make any changes."

Jan Sikowski moved next to Connor, who towered over her. She flipped open the large sketch pad that she had been holding and passed it to Connor.

"Let me know if you need me to make any changes, Mr. Darke."

As Connor looked at the updated sketch, the colors drained from his face. Connor swallowed hard and looked at Detective Fisher and then at Jan Sikowski, giving her back the sketch pad.

"You won't need to make any changes to this sketch. This is a perfect likeness of the girl I've seen in my mind. I wouldn't change a thing."

Fish moved over to Jan Sikowski and looked at the updated sketch. His eyes started to moisten.

"Connor is seeing the vision of my niece. Is that the only thing that you can tell us? Do you know where she is or what happened to her?"

Fish grabbed Connor roughly by the shoulder and shook him.

"Come on, Connor, give me something that can help me find her."

Hamilton pulled Detective Fisher off Connor.

"If you would relax for a minute, Detective, I'm sure Connor will share what he knows."

Fish backed off and threw his hands up in the air.

"You've got one hell of a grip, Detective," Connor commented.

"Forgive me, Connor. I don't know what I was thinking."

"I do, Detective Fisher. You are a person who, from time to time, lets their emotions get the better of them. If the visions I am seeing are that of your niece, then she is being held against her will."

Fish spoke to Connor in a very pleading but sorrowful tone.

"Where is she being held? I need to know."

"Unfortunately, I can't tell you what she or I don't know, Detective. The only thing I can tell you is she doesn't believe she will get out alive."

"Does she say why?"

"She has only told me that she believes there are other girls. One of the girls who was with her hasn't returned in a long time. She feels the girl is dead because she tried to escape."

"Connor, did my niece mention the name of the other girl?"

"Detective, your niece told me her roommate's first name was Sharina."

"Did she tell you about the girl other than her name?"

"She told me that she was colored."

"Why do you think she's never mentioned her last name?"

"I'm not quite sure I can answer that, Detective. My best guess as a trained psychologist would be that she's under an enormous amount of stress. Which means she's probably not thinking very clearly."

"If you hear her voice in your head, can she hear yours?"

"I'm sorry, Detective, it doesn't work like that."

"Would you please enlighten me on how it does work?"

"Here is what I believe to be true. The souls of some people who have passed on get trapped between this life and the next. Some aren't technically trapped but are there to not only act as guides to the people who have moved on but to help the people who are still alive."

"I still don't get why you can't talk to my niece."

"Because someone who has moved on has heard your niece's cries for help and has placed me on the receiving end of her pleas. Basically, it's a one-way conduit."

"What you're telling me is that my niece's prayers are being heard by a guardian angel who has sent you to intervene on her behalf."

"I'm not sure that the help she is getting is from a guardian angel or not, but I think you've summarized the situation perfectly."

"There is something I just don't get."

"What don't you get?"

"My niece has been missing for the better part of five years. Why has it taken so long for her message to get to you?"

"I can't explain that. I don't know why I'm seeing your niece now, Detective. I believe that what matters is that I have heard her, and I'm here on her behalf. I, for one, don't want to focus on the why's any longer. I just want to help you find her. Shall we get to it, Detective?"

"Connor is right, Fish. There is hope where you had none before, so let's get on it."

Fish turned to Hawk and smiled. It was a half-hearted smile, but a smile, nonetheless.

"Alright, Hawk. Why don't you pull up the national database for missing children and see if Sharina appears on it."

Hawk stood, started the computer, and returned with the keyboard and a wireless mouse to the conference room table.

"When it's finished booting, I'll bring up the national database, Fish."

"You won't have to do that."

The group looked up to see Mark Brandt standing with a folder in his hand. There were dark circles under his eyes.

"Why not, Mark?"

"Because Detective Steinbrenner, after I left here last night, I went back to my office and ran all the addresses from Hector's notebook."

"That must have taken you a while to do. There were at least a couple of hundred addresses in his notebook."

"There were two hundred and thirty-seven different addresses, to be exact. It didn't take as long as you think it did, Detective Steinbrenner. When I was here last night helping you to compile all the addresses into Excel, I kept a copy of the file for myself. When I got back to my office, I wrote a computer query so it would do the work for me, and here are the results."

Mark held up the folder and waved it.

"I found missing person reports for thirty-seven of the addresses."

A lump began to form in the back of Mark's throat, and his voice began to crack as he continued talking.

"They are all young girls. Most of them are between the ages of thirteen and seventeen."

Mark slumped down into the nearest chair.

"You, okay, Mark?" Connor asked

Mark took two deep gulps and cleared his throat.

"I'll be alright, Connor. I know I have a reputation for being cold, callous, and uncaring toward women, but down inside, I do care. It's just hard for me to think that these poor girls have been deprived of their childhood, and that's something I just can't tolerate. Children are innocent and should never be treated that way."

Fish stood up, walked over to Mark, offered him his hand, and then pointed to the others in the room.

"For once, you and I are totally in agreement, Mark. With the help of everyone in this room, we are going to solve this case."

"What would you like me to do next, Detective Fisher?"

"Mark, how about we agree to be friends, Okay?"

"Sure, I can do that."

"How about you refer to my partner as Eric, and you can call me Ken. Does that work for you?"

"Ken and Eric, it is."

"Mark, is there a Sharina in your file?"

"Let me check. I've arranged them alphabetically."

Within a few seconds, Mark pulled a sheet of paper from his folder.

"Yep. I have a missing report for a Sharina Johnson of Fellows Road in Half Moon, New York. She went missing two years ago. Would you like to see her picture?"

"You have her picture; that's great, Mark."

"I took the time to print all the pictures of the girls I found address matches for."

Fish placed the phone in the center of the conference room in a hands-free mode and dialed Caleb.

"Caleb, this is Fish. I need to commandeer the large meeting room for our team for a while."

"Detective Fisher, I have to tell you that I'm impressed."

"What are you impressed with?"

"You used a word I've never heard from your lips."

"What word was that?"

"You said the word team, Detective. Maybe you're getting the hang of it."

"It's taken me a while to learn that there is no 'I' in team."

"How long do you need the room?"

"Until we have the case solved. Mark has identified thirty-seven girls from the addresses we found in Hector Gonzales's notebook. We need room to spread out."

"Go ahead, Fish. I'll let the duty officers know that the room is off-limits until you're ready to give it back."

"Thanks, Caleb, I appreciate it."

"Not a problem. Fish. It's what I'm here for."

Within thirty minutes, all the pictures of the girls were hanging around the perimeter of the large conference room. Hawk looked around and ran his hands through his hair.

"You know, it sure seems a lot more personal when you put faces with the names. I wonder how many other addresses in Hector's notebook belong to missing girls."

"Hawk, we know for sure that there are thirty-seven. If you start worrying about the others, it is going to eat you up inside."

"What do you want to do next?"

"Detectives, can I make a suggestion?" Connor offered.

"Sure."

"I would like to go to the Hidden Shores development."

"We can do that, but I don't think you will find anything out there."

"Maybe I will and maybe I won't, but I feel that there is a reason I should go."

"Then go, we shall. Do you want to come as well, Mark?"

"If it's alright Detectives, I thought I would go back to my office and spend time getting any additional information I can about the girls."

Fish looked at the clock and spoke to Mark.

"That sounds good to me. Shall we meet back here in the morning?"

"My editor was hoping to corral Connor and Hamilton for dinner. You and Eric are welcome to join us."

"I appreciate the offer, Mark, but I have a late afternoon meeting with my wife's doctor, so I'll pass on dinner," Hawk declined.

"How about you, Ken? Do want to come along for dinner?"

"I work with inner-city youths one night a week, and I don't want to disappoint them."

"No problem, Detective. Connor, is dinner okay with you and Hamilton?"

"We may have to ask for toothpicks to keep our eyelids open, but we're good with it," Hamilton accepted.

Chapter 26

The House at Hidden Shores

Detective Fisher looked in the rearview mirror at Connor Darke. It almost seemed like Connor was brooding.

"Are you alright, Connor?" Fish asked.

Connor made no reply. Hawk turned and looked at Connor in the backseat.

"Fish, based on the look on Connor's face, I don't think he is going to respond to you."

The remainder of the ride to Hidden Shores went without a word. A sentry house guarded the main entrance to the Hidden Shores Community. When they arrived, a guard opened the window of the sentry house. Fish rolled down his window and held his badge out.

"Please state your business at Hidden Shores," the guard said.

"I'm Detective Fisher with the Seattle Police Department. We're here to visit the Surley Property."

The guard passed a clipboard to Fish. "Please write your names and the address you're going to on the sign-in sheet."

Fish signed the sheet for the three of them and handed the clipboard back to the guard. He drove to where the Surley house had once stood and parked. The trio got out of the car and stood there looking at the property. Where a house once stood was an empty lot facing Puget Sound.

Hawk looked around at the expansive homes that all had access to the Sound in one way or the other.

"I bet the lots here are expensive," Hawk commented.

"They probably cost at least two or three years' salary at our pay grades, Hawk," Fish replied.

Connor, who was still silent, bent down and touched the ground. He remained in a crouched position for fifteen minutes before he stood motionless, staring at the detectives.

"Connor, are you alright?" Fish asked.

Connor raised his right hand and turned the palm toward the detectives as if to say stop silently. He stood rigid for almost five more minutes.

"I'm sorry, Detective, did you say something?"

"I asked if you were alright."

"I am fine."

"Are you getting any feelings from standing here?" Fish asked.

"Your sister's house was new, was it not?"

"The house was so new that they had just gotten the occupancy permit the day before. They had just started moving in."

"What was the cause of the fire?"

"The arson investigator determined there was a natural gas leak. The owners never noticed it. Unfortunately, it got cold enough during the night the furnace kicked in. The explosion was instantaneous. They never had a chance."

"How did the hole get in the gas line?"

"I didn't say that a hole caused it. How did you know that?"

"Shall we continue? I can explain how I know later."

"The investigator believes that a nail from a picture punctured the gas line."

"I would guess the cause of the fire was accidental."

"That's right."

"How long did it take for the fire department to respond? Connor asked

"They were here in a matter of minutes," Fish replied.

"Yet they couldn't save the house next door, either?"

"How did you know there was a house next door?" Hawk asked.

"It was an educated guess, Detective Steinbrenner. If you look around, every lot that has water access has a house on it, but these two. I suspect that there was a house here, Detective Steinbrenner, and you have just confirmed my suspicions. It still leaves me wondering why the fire department didn't save the house next door."

"Because they didn't have the access code to get into the community. By the time the gate opened, it was already too late," Fish answered.

"Doesn't it seem odd that the contractors had gate access, and the local fire department did not?".

"We checked it out, Connor. It's just an oversight. We don't believe it was intentional. The gates were new," Hawk explained.

"I suppose Detective Steinbrenner, you are now going to tell me the Moon was in the seventh house and Jupiter was aligned with Mars that day," Connor stated emphatically.

"I'm sorry. I don't like the fact that the fire department couldn't gain access either," Hawk admitted.

"My apologies, Detective Steinbrenner. It's just that all this seems too coincidental. I am getting the sense this was an orchestrated event and not a coincidence, Detective Fisher. Was there a will?"

"Yes, of course, there was. My sister and brother-in-law left everything to my niece."

"Why weren't you included in the will?"
"I wish I had the answer to that. We had become distant in the years preceding the fire. I don't know why. My niece will be well off if we find her alive. Otherwise, a portion of it all goes to the state."

"Why do you say just a portion of it will go to the state if we don't find your niece?"

"My brother-in-law started a biotech company. If my niece is found alive, she gets his share of the company stock."

"Detective, is the company worth a lot?"

"It will be when it goes public this year."

"I'm sure you looked at everyone in the company to determine if anyone stands to gain a lot when that happens."

"We looked at everyone with a fine-toothed comb. No one stands to gain anything significant. My brother-in-law owned the majority of the company."

"I see," Connor said.

"What is the time limit on the will before the property gets turned over to the state?"

"I have no idea."

Connor stood for a long time, looking at the water, lost in thought.

"I can't believe the way he gets lost in thought so quickly. I hope that doesn't happen to him while he's driving," Hawk commented.

After a few more minutes, Connor turned and spoke to Hawk.

"The answer to your question is no, Detective Steinbrenner."

"The answer to what question?"

"Let me refresh your thoughts for you. A few minutes ago, you made a comment to Detective Fisher that you hoped I didn't get lost in thought while I was driving. The answer is no. It only happens when I let it happen. I was trying to make a connection to what happened here five years ago."

"Were you successful?"

"I would say most definitely so."

"What can you tell us?" Fish chimed in.

"I am getting a strong sense of anguish and loss. A woman died in this fire, did she not?"

"Yes, my sister and her husband did," Fish replied.

"Are you sure about that?"

"I am. They are buried together at Brook Lawn Cemetery," Fish replied.

"Therein lies the problem. Your sister died in a fire here some five years ago. But I am getting a strong feeling that your sister's husband didn't die in the same fire."

"What gives you that impression?" Fish asked.

"She does, Detective Fisher. She deeply mourns for her daughter. She keeps telling me that her daughter's life is in danger because she was taken away from her. But she never mentions her husband.

"Connor, could she be so distraught over the loss of her daughter that his presence is shrouded to her?"

"That could be why. It's just hard to say one way or the other."

"Is she telling you who took her daughter?"

"She keeps telling me a tall, sinister-looking man took her daughter from her, and he has a scar down his left cheek and eyes that are empty."

"Empty eyes. What the hell does that mean?" Hawk demanded.

"I believe she is referring to a feeling the guy has a very dark soul," Connor replied.

"I don't think we can put an all-points bulletin out for a tall, soulless individual," Hawk advised.

"Are you getting anything else?"

"The man she is referring to was here with a man of Mexican descent who was killed by the man with the scar."

"Maybe Connor is referring to Hector Gonzales," Hawk exclaimed.

"The Mexican man is telling me he trusted the man with the scar with his life, but he shot him in the head from behind," Connor continued.

"Fish, I believe Connor is definitely referring to Hector Gonzales. Is there anything else, Connor?" Hawk asked.

"There will always be something else, Detective Steinbrenner. Hector is thrilled that his brother is putting his collection to good use."

"That just about nails it for me, Hawk. I think we have found our tie to the Benjamin Blake Case.

Connor, you said you think my brother-in-law didn't die that day. What makes you say that?"

"Please understand it's just a feeling that I'm getting about him not being with your sister."

"There is absolutely no way I can base an investigation on a feeling."

"I wouldn't want you to Detective Fisher. Let me try to explain something to you. When I hear these voices in my head, they will often mention other people. There has been no mention of your brother-in-law, Detective Fisher."

"Does that mean that my brother-in-law is not dead?"

"No, it doesn't mean he is not dead. It just seems unusual to me that there have been no references to him. It could be as I told you earlier, that his soul is between this life and the next. I can't give you any concrete evidence that he's either alive or dead."

Fish looked at the ground and shifted his weight from one leg to the other for the longest time and then stopped and kicked some loose dirt, sending a cloud of dusr into the air.

"Connor, five years ago, I buried my sister and what I thought were the remains of my brother-in-law. If there is even the smallest possibility that he is still alive, then I have to go down that road as far as it will go."

"Fish, maybe we should chase down Hector Gonzales's involvement in your sister and brother-in-law's case."

"Yes, we should Hawk. From this point forward, we need to start working these two cases as if they are one.

"I agree. But aren't we going to need more help?" Hawk asked.

Connor and the detectives got back into the car. When they got to the main gate, Fish stopped to sign them out. Connor got out.

"What is it, Connor?" Fish asked.

Connor walked over to the keypad on the guardhouse.

"What is this keypad for?" Connor asked the guard.

"It's used to gain access to the community when there is no guard," the guard answered.

"Are the residents given a personal entry code?"

"Not exactly. The residents have a special key fob that opens the gate."

"I would like to ask you a couple of questions if I can," Fish began. He paused for a moment. Looking at the guard's nameplate, which read F Chance. The guard realized what Fish was looking at.

"The F stands for Frank."

"How long have you worked for Sound Security?"

"I started the company with my brother nine years ago. The girl who works at this site is on her honeymoon."

"Was she the one working out here on the day of the fire five years ago?"

"No, she wasn't. I can tell you who was."

Chance flipped open a laptop and typed something in.

"I have all the employee records and when and where they worked in a database. It looks like Dewey Longo was working out here the night of the fire, but you probably knew that, didn't you?"

"Yes, we did. Is Dewey Longo still employed with your company?"

"No, he isn't. We fired him a couple of months after the fire. The night of the fire, he was supposed to wait for his relief, but he didn't, so there was no one here to let in the rescue squads. By the time they got here, it was too late. We would have let him go right after the fire, except that he was the sole person responsible for two younger siblings."

"Do you happen to know why the local police and fire departments didn't have passcodes?"

"Normally, that's something we handle, but we didn't have them yet. The gates weren't even supposed to be operational yet. Hell, Detective, none of the homes were even scheduled for occupancy yet. I feel terrible that people died."

"You're going to feel even worse when I tell you that the couple who died was my sister and brother-in-law."

"Your Sister and brother-in-law, shit! I'm sorry for your loss, Detective Fisher. Truly I am."

"Frank, do you happen to know what happened to Dewey Longo after you fired him?"

"Yeah, he's dead, Detective."

"How long ago did he die?"

"Not long after the fire. Longo's sister said he couldn't handle the thought that someone died because he left his post, so he hung himself."

"Do you have his sister's name and address?"

"I'm pretty sure I have it back at my office. If you give me a business card, I'll make sure you get it."

Hawk handed him two business cards and waited for Fish to finish talking with Frank Chance.

"They gained access to the community with a custom-built electronic device," Connor said quietly.

"Who gained access, Connor?" Hawk asked.

"The man who took your niece, Cassie, and the man who caused the fire. The Mexican man you said was Hector Gonzales keeps telling me his friend Two Fingers is with him, and he is an electronics wizard."

"Hawk, he's got to be talking about John Pierce," Fish commented.

"Do you have a copy of the surveillance tape from the night of the fire?" Connor asked.

"It's back at the office. Why?"

"I need to see it."

"We've looked at the tapes. There is nothing there."

"Trust me, Detective Fisher, the fire that burned the house down was intentional. I need to see the security footage."

"If you get in the car, I will take you back to the office so you can review the tape. It's getting late, Connor, and you promised to go to dinner with Mark and his editor. The recordings aren't going anywhere. We can review them in the morning.

"Fine," Connor said and got back in the car. He stared out the window until they were pulling into the parking lot of the Seattle Police Department.

Chapter 26

The Alexis Hotel

Detective Fisher pulled the car up to the front entrance of the Alexis Hotel and turned to speak to Connor.

"I don't know what to make of all this. I can't say that I believe everything you're telling me. I'm doing my best."

"You can trust me when I say this, Detective Fisher. I feel driven by the ones who have called on me to help. I have no hidden agenda. I hope you come to understand that."

"I am working on it. The fact that I haven't thrown you out on your ear is the beginning of a change in my point of view. For whatever it's worth, Connor, I am glad you're on board. Go enjoy your dinner and get some rest. I'll see you tomorrow."

Connor reached over and offered Fish a handshake.

"I'll see you bright and early in the morning, Detective."

"Get there when you're ready. I've had consultant badges made up for you and Hamilton. The duty officer will have them when you come in tomorrow. You'll both be able to come and go as needed."

With that, Connor got out, went into the hotel, and made his way to the elevators. The door to the second elevator slid open, revealing Hamilton Gardner inside.

"There you are, Connor. I was hoping to meet you in the lobby," Hamilton stated.

Connor studied Hamilton very carefully as he exited the elevator.

"I don't believe that I have seen you dressed this casually before, Hamilton. You wear it well."

"Why, thank you. You have about thirty minutes to freshen up before Mark gets here with his editor. Go get ready. We can talk on the way to the restaurant."

"I have just one question."

"Julie is safely on her way home with Mrs. Lane. She will call you when she gets home," Hamilton answered before the question was asked.

"That's great, thanks for the update."

"By the way, I have it on good information that Julie left something behind for you."

In less than five minutes, Connor was opening the door to his room. He looked inside and noticed a small box sitting on a table. There was a card attached.

> *Dear Connor, I know that you're not ready to commit to a relationship just yet, but I just want you to know that I'll be here waiting for you no matter how long it takes. So please wear the contents of the box and know that my heart beats with yours.*

Connor opened the box. There was a dual time zone watch inside. Its two small dials had been set to Pacific and East Coast times, respectively. Connor removed it from its packaging. There were two interconnecting hearts engraved on the back. He donned the watch and headed downstairs. In less than twenty minutes, he was down in the lobby. Hamilton handed a piece of paper to the hotel valet.

"Is Mark here with his editor yet?"

"He's on his way. The restaurant has changed. Instead of taking a short stroll, we're going to the Pellagio. His editor is going to meet us there. You look nice, Connor. I especially like the watch."

Just then, Mark walked over and reached out to shake Connor and Hamilton's hands.

"Wow, you guys look great. I feel like the ugly duckling. Are you guys ready to go? My boss has managed to get us a table at the Pellagio," Mark announced.

"I take it that Pellagio reservations aren't easy to come by," Hamilton said.

"You have to make reservations six to nine months in advance. Apparently, someone owed my boss a favor, and a big one at that," Mark shared.

"It's a good thing the food lives up to the billing," Connor said.

"Do you mind if we take our car, Mark?" Hamilton asked.

"No, that's fine," Mark answered.

They walked outside and waited for the Valet to bring the car around.

"Mark, how long does it take to get to the Pellagio? Connor asked.

"About thirty-five to forty minutes."

"What is the big deal about the Pellagio?" Hamilton asked.

"The Pellagio Mansion is one of the most visually stunning buildings I have ever seen," Mark explained.

"Mark, you're right. This place is magnificent," Hamilton exclaimed as they drew nearer.

Thousands of small lights adorned the trees lining the driveway leading up to the mansion that was now a restaurant. The outside of the classic Roman-style building was lit up by an ever-changing hue of soft yellow, blue, and pale pink light. A large multi-jetted fountain was in front of the restaurant. Plumes of water rose and fell from the fountain as they walked in the Pellagio's entrance.

"This place is incredible. I feel just like I am walking into a Villa on the Italian coast," Hamilton observed.

An impeccably dressed woman walked up to the group as they entered the restaurant.

"Gentlemen, I would like to introduce you to my boss, Sienna Jones," Mark stated.

I know this handsome man is the one and only Connor Darke. I would have known you anywhere. I am a huge fan of yours," Sienna said, walking over to Connor and shook hands.

"The pleasure is all mine," Connor replied.

Sienna then looked at Hamilton Gardner. "I understand you're a personal aide to Gertrude Lane. I am pleased to meet you."

Hamilton looked at Sienna. Her eyes were nothing like he had ever seen. It was almost like they were able to pierce his very soul. Hamilton was so enamored with her looks that he took her hand in his, brought it to his lips, and kissed it gently. "I assure you, Ms. Jones, I am thoroughly entranced by your beauty. I may work for Mrs. Lane, but my heart is now yours."

"You had better be careful, Mr. Gardner. I may not give it back," Sienna said with a blush.

"I could think of a much worse way to die, Ms. Jones," Hamilton replied.

"Please call me Sienna, Mr. Gardner."

"I don't think I can do that, Ms. Jones."

"Why not, All my friends call me Sienna, and since you're now in my circle of friends, I wish you would call me Sienna."

"Truthfully, Ms. Jones, I don't believe that there is a name on this earth that would do your beauty any justice."

Sienna blushed even more at the comment.

"Why, Mr. Gardner, if you keep this up, you may not be the only one losing a heart tonight."

Hamilton smiled at Sienna and bowed low. Just then, a young man in a tuxedo walked up to the group. "Good evening, I'm Robert, your host for the evening. If you follow me, I will take you to your table. You will be dining in the solarium tonight."

He led them to the solarium where the tables were around an indoor pond covered with lilies and assorted plants. A violinist and a cellist were in one corner of the room and were softly performing classical music. The night sky was clear, stars shone down through the glass dome of the solarium.

Hamilton, who had offered Sienna his arm, escorted her to the table. He looked around the solarium and then up through the glass roof. He pulled a chair out for Sienna.

"This is perfect," he exclaimed.

"I couldn't agree more," Sienna Jones said with a smile.

The meal was eight courses and lasted almost three hours. At the end of the meal, Hamilton asked if he could take care of the bill.

"There is no need, Hamilton. The bill is paid in full already. If you pay for six and only four show up, it still costs the same."

"Sienna, I've visited Seattle before but have never been able to get a short-notice reservation. How did you manage?" Connor asked.

"I get preferential treatment because I make sure the paper gives them great reviews."

"I can't imagine this place ever getting a negative review."

"I see it as a win-win situation. The Pellagio gets months of booked reservations, and I get first dibs on cancelations."

"Connor, if you schedule a trip out here, let me know, and I'll get you a reservation. But I'll only get it on one condition."

"Just what would that be, Sienna?"

"That you bring Mr. Gardner with you when you do."

"I'll try, Sienna, but don't ask me to make a promise I won't be able to keep."

"That's fair enough for me. If you gentlemen will excuse me, I need to use the powder room."

Hamilton stood and pulled Sienna's chair out for her and offered his arm so she could stand up.

"If you keep spoiling me, Hamilton, I may never let you out of my sight."

Hamilton grinned at Sienna and watched her turn and walk away. He looked at Connor and turned his head toward Mark, who immediately looked back at Hamilton and chuckled.

Mark, what do you find so funny?"

"If you must know, Hamilton, she's known as the ice queen around the office. I think you melted the tough exterior she puts up faster than Dorothy melted the Wicked Witch. I guess she just met the person she wants to spend the rest of her life with."

"What makes you think that?"

"Hamilton, if you've read any or all of Connor's books on love and relationships, you would know the signs."

"I'm not so sure that she's in love, Mark."

"I, for one, think Mark's right. Sienna has just been swept off her feet by her knight whose name happens to be Sir Hamilton Gardner. Judging by the way you watched her walk away, I think you're equally smitten. Hamilton, when one falls in love, they do tend to fall hard."

"How about we change the subject?"

Mark and Connor laughed at the same time.

"You boys wouldn't be laughing at my expense, would you?"

They all stood as Sienna approached. A lump immediately formed in the pit of Hamilton's stomach, and he gulped hard.

"Are you okay, Mr. Gardner? Am I going to need to get a doctor for you?"

Hamilton blushed, which caused Mark and Connor to laugh again.

"I'm fine."

"That's too bad, Hamilton. I was looking forward to taking care of you."

"Is it alright if I take a rain check on that offer, Ms. Jones?"

"It sure is, as long as you promise to redeem it."

Hamilton offered his arm to Sienna.

"Are you ready to leave, Ms. Jones?"

"If we have to go, then I supposed I am ready as I'll ever be, Mr. Gardner."

Sienna gave her parking ticket to the Valet before turning to Hamilton to hand him a card. Within minutes, her car arrived.

"I don't normally do this. Here's my contact card. I would like to get to know you better, Hamilton."

Another Valet returned with the Audi. Connor opened the rear door and got in. Hamilton got behind the wheel, and Mark Brandt joined him in the front passenger seat. Hamilton drove a hundred feet up the driveway and stopped.

"Why are we stopping, Hamilton?"

"I stopped because someone is following us. I saw two men watching us at the hotel and again at the Pellagio. They came out of there in a hurry."

"What are we going to do?" Mark asked.

Hamilton tossed his cell phone to Connor.

"Connor, find Caleb's phone number. Call him and tell him we're on our way back and that we have a tail. Mark, there is a case between the two front seats. Please open it up and hand me its contents."

Mark opened the case and handed its contents to Hamilton, who slid it over his head.

"I want everybody to strap in tight. I'm going to be driving with the lights off. These night-vision goggles should make it clear enough to see. If they are following us, the situation could get dicey." Hamilton started the car and left the headlights off.

"Here, they come," Hamilton stated.

A set of headlights was moving at a high rate of speed out of the parking lot toward them. Hamilton raced the engine and sped up the driveway with the car containing the two men in pursuit. Hamilton turned the car hard to the right out of the entrance and accelerated. The vehicle rapidly lurched forward as they sped up. The pursuers did so as well. Before long, the speedometer was at 115 miles per hour.

Connor looked frantic as Hamilton made use of the entire road to navigate the twists and turns. Hamilton could sense the fear in the car.

"Don't worry, folks, I've driven the racecourse at Lemans a lot faster than we are doing now. This road will be a piece of cake for me to drive."

"But Hamilton, have you ever driven the Lemans course with two additional people in the car?" Mark asked.

"There is a first time for everything," Hamilton replied.

They were starting to distance themselves from their pursuers when Hamilton spotted a safe place to turn in and hide. He turned in at an auto repair shop and parked in the second row of cars and turned off the engine. In a moment, the car that was following them passed. It was a silver, four-door Lexus.

"I think we'll wait here until it's safe. Connor, were you able to call Caleb?"

"The way I was getting tossed around, it was impossible to make a call of any kind."

"Give me the phone, please. I'll make the call."

"Caleb, this is Hamilton. We just left the Pellagio restaurant and were being pursued at a high rate of speed. I managed to get enough distance in front of our pursuers to hide. The car pursuing us was a silver, four-door, Lexus. That was my intention, Caleb. Mrs. Lane has a secure loft downtown. I'll head there once I think it's safe. I'll text you the address."

"No, Caleb, you don't need to send a squad car. I'm going to use an alternate route in case our pursuers attempt to double back. We'll be fine, but if I hit a snag, I won't hesitate to call back."

After altering their return route back to Seattle, Hamilton eased into the underground parking garage of the building where Gertrude Lane kept a loft. Caleb walked up to the car as they pulled into a parking space and waited.

"I am glad to see you, my friend," Caleb said to Hamilton.

"Trust me, Caleb, I was a little worried."

"How many people were following you?"

"We saw two men follow us out of the restaurant," Hamilton answered.

"I'll have a patrol car keep watch on this building."

"That won't be necessary."

"Last time I checked, I was still in charge so I am going place a watchful eye on this building."

"Post your guys here if you need, but we'll be just fine. This place is almost as impenetrable as Fort Knox."

"In that case, I'll get going."

"Don't worry, if we have any problems, we'll call you."

Caleb gave the men a thumbs-up as he turned and walked away.

Chapter 27

The Seattle Police Department War Room

The Detectives had just finished filling Caleb in on their visit to Hidden Shores.

Caleb sank into one of the chairs in the conference room and drummed nervously on the conference table for a minute or two before he spoke.

"My God, Fish. I know that you and Eric have been over all the evidence multiple times and found nothing out of the ordinary. Isn't that right?"

"Yes, it is. But what if we've been looking at all the evidence the wrong way."

"How do you think we should look at it?"

"Caleb, what if we assume that Hector Gonzales and his accomplice were involved and look through the evidence from that angle and see if we can find the connection? If we look hard enough, we might see something we didn't see before," Hawk interjected.

"I think Hawk is right about this. We have Hector's notebook. Maybe if we can correlate some of the other addresses to known crimes, it will validate that they were involved in the fire that killed my sister."

"I don't intend on loosening your leash on this case very much. But, until we know for sure, I don't think I can give you extra help based on Connor Darke's feelings."

"That's fair enough for us."

"I think I might be able to help in getting proof that Hector Gonzales was involved," came a voice from the door of the conference room.

"Just how do you expect to do that, Connor?" Caleb asked.

"I know people don't put much faith in what I tell them. A lot of what I do and what I've written in my books is from observing the entire picture, taking bits and pieces of what I see, and putting them together to form a hypothesis. I admit that hearing voices is new to me. I think they were always there but got pushed to the forefront with the passing of my grandmother. So, in a nutshell, I wouldn't go off running on anything I say until we have some physical evidence."

"What you're saying is that everything you've told my detectives is questionable?"

"No, I wouldn't say that at all. What I'm trying to say is that I want to back up what I've told the detectives by giving you facts based on my excellent observation skills."

"Where do we go from here?"

"On the way to the Hidden Shores Development yesterday, I noticed that there were cameras at the intersections. Is there any chance they were there at the time of the fire? If so, can we look at the recordings from the time in question."

"If the cameras were there, then we should be able to."

Caleb picked up the phone in the middle and dialed a phone number.

"What do you need now, Fish?"

"I hate to disappoint you, Maxine, but this is Caleb."

"Pardon me, Caleb, what can I do for you?"

"I have an assignment for you."

Within a couple of minutes, Maxine walked into the room.

"What do you need?"

"I want you to pull videos from the traffic cameras from the area leading up to Hidden Shores."

"Not a problem. What time frame would you like?"

"I need you to get me the video for at least forty-eight hours before the fire at the Surley House and a few hours after the fire."

"How soon do you need it?"

Caleb frowned at Maxine.

"I bet you want this done like yesterday, right?"

"You got it, Maxine."

"I'll get it to you as soon as possible,"

"Thanks, Maxine."

Maxine left the conference room. Caleb stood, paused for a moment, and talked to Connor and Hamilton.

"Hamilton, after you called me from the Pellagio last night, I had Maxine come back in and access any available traffic footage from the area. We were also able to get security from the Pellagio. I have the feeds ready to go on screen five."

Screen five flickered to life. Hamilton, Connor, and Mark could be seen exiting the Pellagio and getting into the Audi. The A7 moved out of camera range just as two figures exited the Pellagio on a dead run.

"I'm sure that those two were following us."

"Caleb, why weren't Hawk and I informed that there was an issue?"

"For one thing, I needed to be sure, and secondly, I was sure Hamilton had the situation under control. If I had thought there was a need to call you two, I would have. I think we are going to be putting in some long hours, so I felt that you needed sleep."

Fish looked at Caleb and shook his head.

"I see your point. Unfortunately, the two guys who ran out of the Pellagio never looked up. It's going to make it difficult to get an identification on them."

"You're right, Fish, it will, but I have something that might help."

"What's that?"

"Maxine was able to pull camera footage from the surrounding areas, and we were able to get the license plate from the car that followed them."

"Mr. Darke, yesterday was a most unusual day. I know I may seem very skeptical about your abilities, but regardless of how I feel, please keep doing what you're doing."

The intercom chirped, and Caleb pressed the answer button.

"Hey, Caleb, this is Max. I found the video footage Mr. Darke was looking for. It's ready on screen six. You can review it when you're ready."

Caleb pressed the start button. An image of a black Cadillac Escalade passed in front of two different traffic cameras.

"I believe that's the vehicle in question. Caleb. Is it possible to slow the video down?" Connor asked.

"Sure," Caleb said and replayed the video slower.

The image played in slow motion. A dotted box was around the person in the passenger seat of the vehicle. The resolution of the image sharpened dramatically.

"If it isn't the recently deceased Hector Gonzales. You were right, Connor. Looking at the time and date stamp on the video, it looks like Hector and his accomplice were at my sister and brother-in-law's house twenty-three hours before the explosion. Caleb, we now have a clear connection between our two cases. It's too bad we don't have a clear image of the driver of the car," Fish shared.

Caleb had left the intercom open during the showing of the video.

"Hey, Fish, this is Maxine. I looked at all the feed. I couldn't find anything on the driver. There just isn't a clear image to be had."

"Thanks for looking, Maxine."

"No problem. The two guys were following Hamilton last night when he was most likely heading back to the Alexis Hotel. I was able to catch their images closer to the city. I sent them to screen three; the computer is doing a facial recognition of them as we speak."

"That's great,. As always, you've earned your keep."

Two facial images appeared on the screen, three with names underneath, rapidly flashing. Within a couple of minutes, the box around the facial image on the right had stopped blinking. The name Gregory Cherlenko, with the words' assassin for hire' appeared underneath the image. The image on the left had the name Pierre St. Pierre.

Fish looked at Connor and then at Caleb. "Caleb, this affair has gone way past a simple murder."

"Yes, it has. It is going to take everything we have at our disposal to end it."

"How are we going to protect Mr. Darke and company?" Hawk asked.

"You don't have to protect us," Hamilton spoke up.

"Why do you say that?"

"There is only one way in and out of the apartment building owned by Mrs. Lane. There is absolutely no way anyone is getting past my men."

"Your men? What do you mean by your men, Hamilton?"

"I have to ensure Mrs. Lane's safety, so I oversee her security detail."

"Just how many people do you have on the ground in Seattle?"

"Enough to wage a large-scale war in a small foreign country," Hamilton revealed.

"Why didn't you tell me?"

"That would have spoiled the surprise now, wouldn't it have?"

"You don't seriously have a small army, do you?"

"Relax, Caleb. There are a handful of men in Seattle to protect Mrs. Lane's interest."

"Why wasn't I informed?" Connor asked.

"Mrs. Lane didn't want to burden you unnecessarily."

"What exactly have I gotten myself into, Hamilton?"

"Look, Connor, when we get back to the apartment, I will explain everything."

Caleb walked over to Hamilton. "Based on your background, I am temporarily making you an acting detective."

"What if I don't want to work for you, Caleb?"

"Please, don't push me on this matter. I don't want to arrest you for interfering with an investigation."

"In that case, I acquiesce to your request."

"That's a wise choice. You've put me in a very tough spot. I didn't see any other way to handle this."

"I didn't mean to upset you. I hope that we're still friends," Hamilton said.

"We are as long as you don't do anything stupid."

"I promise we'll be on our best behavior."

"Good. The group that's working for you doesn't respond to a threat unless it is in a defensive mode. Is that understood?"

"I understand it perfectly."

"Can I go home and sleep in my bed tonight?" Mark asked.

"Unfortunately, no, Mark," Caleb answered.

"What am I going to do for a place to sleep tonight?"

"Mark, have you ever slept in a jail cell? The accommodations are a little sparse, but I'm sure you'll manage."

"There is no way I am going to sleep in a jail cell."

"You can always curl up on the couch in our lounge." Fish offered.

"Fine, at least an uncomfortable couch is better than a jail cell," Mark sulked.

"It's not so bad. I've spent the night on that couch more than once," Hawk consoled.

"I'm not sure if I would use that as a testimonial, Mark. Hawk could sleep on a rock and think it was comfortable.

"There is an extra room at Mrs. Lane's flat. You can crash there," Hamilton offered.

"I'd rather do that than sleep on a couch or a cot in a jail cell, so sign me up."

"Good. You'll be safe with Connor and me."

"Caleb, the pot has been stirred. Hopefully, we can get to the bottom of it before too many more lives are lost." Fish said.

"Amen to that, Fish," Caleb replied.

<h1 style="text-align:center">Chapter 28</h1>

The Chase

The light on the intercom flashed rapidly. Caleb pressed the button to answer.

"Caleb, this is Maxine. Turn on screen four. We've located the two guys from last night."

Caleb turned on-screen four. There was an image of the grey Lexus moving at a high rate of speed. Police cars came into view but kept a short distance from the fleeing vehicle. The Lexus came to a sudden and abrupt stop at an empty field. There was nowhere for the car to go.

"Caleb, I'm surprised they didn't try to make a run for it and go through the barrier made by the police cars."

"They might have wanted to, but they couldn't. We used an EMP weapon. It caused a massive electrical short, which is what stopped the car."

"I see," Connor replied.

Just then, the two men in the car got out and started to run. They hadn't run very far when there was a flash like in a small explosion, and one of the two men dropped to the ground.

"What caused that?" Connor asked.

"That was gunfire."

"Does the police department usually shoot first and ask questions later?"

"I think that one of the two suspects shot the other one," Caleb corrected.

The police had moved closer to the stopped car. Four police officers were moving toward the remaining suspect. Suddenly, there were more sudden flashes from both directions. They continued for a couple of minutes and then stopped. The suspect they were pursuing was no longer moving.

"Caleb, can we find out if either of the two men are still alive?" Connor asked.

"I doubt they are, Connor, but we can talk to the lead patrolman directly if you want."

"That would be great."

Caleb removed a radio from a cabinet, turned it on, picked up the microphone, and clicked the talk button.

"This is Captain Clarke calling for Officer Grey."

"Go ahead, Captain Clarke, this is Officer Grey."

"Officer Grey, are all your men okay?"

"Yes, they are, Captain. No one took a direct hit."

"Can you give me a sitrep, please?"

"Captain, per your instruction, we stopped at a safe distance from the Lexus. I was just going to call in and ask if we should approach when the passenger door opened, and one of the two men began to run. Once he started running, the driver opened the door and yelled for the guy to come back. When he continued running, the driver shot the fleeing suspect. It was a kill shot. He got off the shot before we could prevent it. When he saw us coming toward him, he started running. We yelled for him to stop, or we would shoot. He turned toward us and started shooting. We took cover and returned fire. I'm not sure if he's still alive, he doesn't seem to be moving, but we'll approach with caution anyway."

"I would appreciate it if you would check the first body for identification, Officer Grey."

Officer Grey's body camera was on, and one could see a large pool of blood had formed under the dead man's body."

"Captain, what do you want me to do now?"

"Please check the second suspect, Officer."

Grey slowly moved to where the second man had fallen and checked for a pulse.

"This one's also dead, Captain."

"Did you guys find anything in the Lexus?"

"The car was almost clean. The plates on the car came from a stolen Ford Escape. The Lexus was reported stolen from a dealer in Spokane."

"What do you mean, almost clean?" Caleb asked.

"We found papers in the glove compartment of the Lexus."

"What's on them, Officer?"

Grey and unfolded some papers. Their pictures, sir, I'll hold them up so you can see."

The first picture was of Mark Brandt, the second one was a picture of Connor Darke, and the third one was a picture of Hamilton Gardner.

"Let me look to see if there is anything else."

They watched as the officer checked the inside of the car. After finding nothing else, he pulled the handle next to the seat that opened the trunk. The trunk contained an open gun case with two scoped rifles and a bag with cash spilling out of it.

Caleb turned to Connor, Hamilton, and Mark and spoke.

"I think it's safe to say that you three are targets. Even though you have men of your own on the ground here, Hamilton, I'm going to keep my protection duty on the three of you."

"Caleb, would you please ask the officer to scour the area near Cherlenko."

"What would he be looking for, Connor?"

"Something small. I think that Cherlenko threw something away when he ran."

After about thirty minutes of searching, Officer Grey called in on his radio.

"Captain, we didn't find anything small, and quite frankly, I don't think the suspect had time to ditch anything."

"That's good enough for me, Officer Grey. Please have someone on-site until the crime scene unit gets there."

"Will do, Captain."

"Look, Connor, I can replay the video from the bodycam if you would like."

"I would appreciate it."

Caleb rewound the video from the officer's body camera and played it again.

"I'm sorry, Connor. I didn't see anything leave the hand of the suspect as he was running."

"I'd like to go to the crime scene, Captain."

"Sure, Connor, but not until the crime scene unit finishes processing the area."

"Look, Caleb, I am one hundred percent sure that Cherlenko got rid of something, and he wouldn't have done it if it wasn't important. I need to go out there before the area gets trampled."

"Caleb, if Connor says something of importance is out there, then it must be there. We need to be going. I would venture to guess we are not going to be the only ones looking," Hamilton said.

"Caleb, he's right that we won't be the only ones looking. So, let's get a move on," Fish added.

"Fine, Fish, but I'm going to send the crime scene team out there with you guys. I want to make sure that it's processed right."

"However you want to play this, is fine with me, Caleb."

"Fish, I may get to like this new spirit of cooperation."

Fish forced a grin in Caleb's direction. Caleb used a key to open a locked drawer in the wall, pulled out a badge and a gun, and handed them to Hamilton.

"Here, you'd better take this with you."

"That's probably a good idea. Thanks."

"What about me?" Connor asked.

"What about you, Connor?" Caleb asked.

"Aren't you going to give me a gun as well?"

"Connor, have you ever shot a gun?" Fish asked.

"I've been to the shooting range a couple of times."

"You've shot a gun. That doesn't qualify you for action on the front line. Have you ever been through a training exercise, Connor?" Hawk asked.

"What kind of training exercise, Detective Steinbrenner?"

"We have to go through a live training exercise. You have to make a split-second decision. If you make the wrong decision, it could mean your life or the life of an innocent person. Do you want that responsibility?"

"When you put it that way, no, I don't, Detective Steinbrenner."

"Good, that's the right answer. Shall we go then?"

"Hawk, you could have put it a little nicer, you know," Fish teased.

"I'm sorry, Fish, there is no sugar-coating life or deaths," Hawk replied.

"Detective Fisher, Detective Steinbrenner was right. It's probably not a good idea to give me a gun. It would be better if I stick to what I do best. Shall we go? Time is wasting."

"Sure, Connor, let's go."

They walked out to the car, and Fish tossed the keys to Hawk.

"Hawk, why don't you drive?"

"You hardly ever let me drive. What's the occasion?"

"Maybe it's that newfound spirit of cooperation Caleb is talking about. Would it be alright if we go before I change my mind?"

Within thirty-five minutes, Hawk had stopped the car on the side of the road.

"According to my GPS, Connor, this is where the Lexus stopped. If you're right, somewhere in that field is what Cherlenko took the time to hide."

"Can we get started? We need to fan out and start looking."

"Connor, you heard Caleb, we have to wait for the crime scene team."

Connor got out of the car, Hamilton and the Detectives followed suit. Connor started walking out into the field. Fish and Hawk went after Connor; each one grabbed an arm.

"We need to wait."

"That's okay, Detective Steinbrenner, your crime scene team, will be here in less than a minute. A white van with the City of Seattle logo on its door and the words crime scene unit on its side pulled up behind the car they had come in. Three officers got out and walked over to where the group was standing. One was carrying a camera and kept on walking to where Cherlenko's body was.

"Hawk, you cover the left side of the field. I'll take the right side of the field. Hamilton can go with Connor."

Fish pointed to two members of the crime scene team.

"We're not quite sure what we are looking for, but it's most likely small and should look out of place. So, we need to move slowly across the field."

"That works for me, Fish."

Connor turned and looked at the groups.

"No offense, gentlemen, it would be better if you just let me do what I do best."

"What would you like us to do?" Hawk asked.

"It would probably be best if the five of you set up a protective perimeter. I would hate to be surprised by anyone carrying weapons," Connor instructed.

"That's an excellent idea, don't you agree?"

"Whatever you say,."

The men stood guard as Connor walked cautiously through the field. Connor stopped and knelt a few times. After almost an hour of searching, he had found nothing.

"Connor, it's been an hour. I think it's time we help or we get going. They're finished with the bodies, so can we wrap this up?"

Connor turned and put his finger to his mouth as a gesture for Hawk to be silent. He turned and walked ten feet and bent over. He remained bent over for about twenty seconds and then stood and turned to the group.

"Can I get some help over here? I believe I found what Cherlenko hid."

The group trotted over to where Connor was standing over a drainage grate that was a mere ten feet from Cherlenko's body.

"What did you find?"

"I need help removing the grate on this drain."

Hawk walked over to Connor they bent over and grabbed the same side of the grate and lifted it. It fell backward, exposing the drain. Connor bent down, reached in, and retrieved a muddy object from its resting place. Connor stood, wiping the dirt and mud away with his hand, and held it out.

"Detective, I believe I found what Cherlenko was trying to ditch. It's good that I found it when I did; in a couple more minutes, the small stream of water in the drain would have carried it into the main pipe, and I would have never found it."

Connor held out a bronze-colored key he'd retrieved from the drain.

"I can't be one hundred percent sure that this is what Cherlenko got rid of, but it's highly likely it is."

"Can I see the key?"

Connor handed it to Fish, who turned the key over and read the engraving on its back.

"It has the letters PSSL and a special barcode on one side and the number twenty-eight on the other."

"The letters PSSL probably stand for the Puget Sound Savings & Loan," Hawk speculated.

"There is a branch just down the road."

"Don't worry, Fish I'm not a psychic like Connor. I was through here once last summer and stopped at the ATM there for some cash." Hawk clarified when he saw Fish's look of confusion.

Chapter 29

Of Safe Deposit Boxes

In less than five minutes, they pulled in at the bank. Fish walked into the Puget Sound Savings and Loan alone.

"I'm Detective Fisher with the Seattle Police. I need to speak to the manager," Fish announced to the guard, producing his badge.

"Please wait here, I'll be happy to get her for you," the guard said.

After a couple of minutes, a woman approached.

"I'm Wendy Stiles. How can I help you?"

Fish showed her his badge. "Are you the manager of this location?"

"I am. Is there a problem, Detective Fisher?"

"We retrieved this key from a criminal. It has the initials PSSL on it. We were hoping you could confirm if it belongs to your bank."

"May I see the key, Detective?"

Fish handed her the key. "It belongs to our bank. It will only take a moment for me to read the barcode on the back. I have a reader in my office."

Fish followed Wendy Stiles into her office. She walked over to her desk, picked up a barcode scanner, and scanned the key.

"I guess this is your lucky day, Detective. This key belongs to a safe deposit box at this location. I won't be able to let you see its contents without a warrant or permission from the owner, though."

"Ms. Stiles, do you have a name and address for the owner?"

"Our client information is confidential, Detective."

"Ms. Stiles, why don't you save me the time and effort of getting a warrant?"

Wendy Stiles wrote a name and address on a yellow Post-it Note and handed it to Fish.

"Thanks, Mrs. Stiles."

"You're welcome, Detective."

Fish walked back out to the car, where the rest were waiting.

"What did you find, Fish?" Hawk asked.

"The key is for a safe deposit box here."

"We need to get a search warrant."

"We might be able to get permission from Angelica Tiemman."

"Fish, who is Angelica Tiemman?"

"The wife of the person who owns the safe deposit box. She lives nearby."

Within fifteen minutes, Fish and Hawk were standing at the door to 128 Kensington Lane. A woman opened the door.

"Whatever you're selling, I'm not interested."

"I'm sorry, Mrs. Tiemman, we're not here to sell you anything. My partner and I are with the Seattle Police." Both Detectives took out their badges and displayed them. "May we come in?"

"The Seattle Police, are you sure you're at the right house?"

"We believe so, Mrs. Tiemman. We can talk out here if you want, but we would much rather come inside," Fish informed.

Fish and Hawk followed her into the living room.

"Gentlemen, how can I help you?"

"Mrs. Tiemman, can you tell us where your husband is?"

"Tony is away on a business trip."

"When do you expect Tony to be home?"

"I'm not quite sure. His trips usually last one to two weeks. Is Tony in trouble?"

"We're not sure," Hawk answered.

Fish removed his cell phone from his and clicked on a photograph of Cherlenko.

"Mrs. Tiemman..." Fish began but was interrupted by Mrs. Timman.

"You can call me Angel, Detective."

"Angel, do you know the man in this picture?"

"Of course, that's my husband, Tony. Why do you have a picture of my husband on your cell phone?"

"Angel, do you have someone you can call?"

"Oh my God, something happened to him, didn't it?"

"Angel, do you know a man named Gregory Cherlenko?" Fish asked.

"I've never heard of that name before. Why? Did he hurt Tony?" she asked.

"The man in the picture we showed you is Gregory Cherlenko."

"It can't be. I know the picture you showed me is Tony."

"Angel, I'm sorry to tell you this, but your husband was not who you thought he was. His name is Gregory

Cherlenko. Unfortunately, he was not a salesman. Gregory Cherlenko, the man you know as Anthony Tiemman, is a contract killer. He died in a shootout with the police today. The trips he took were paid assignments," Fish told her.

"I'm sure you're wrong, Detectives. Tony wouldn't hurt a flea."

Fish looked at her and sighed. "I wish for your sake that I was wrong, but I'm not Angel."

Angelica Tiemman started to weep. "What am I going to do now?"

Fish handed her a box of tissues.

"Angel, can I call someone for you? You shouldn't be alone."

"My sister, you can call my sister. Just press the number one button on the phone twice, she should still be home."

Within twenty minutes, Angelica's sister Beth walked into the house.

"Angel, what's going on here? What does the Seattle Police want with you?"

Before Mrs. Tiemman could answer, Fish handed Beth his business card.

"Beth, I am Detective Fisher, with the Seattle Police Department. I appreciate you could come right over."

"It no problem. I live close. Our kids all hang out together."

"Beth, do you happen to know where your sister's kids are right now?"

"They are at our mom and dad's for a couple of days. We're supposed to meet them tomorrow and go ice skating."

"Beth, you might want to have your parents keep them for a couple of extra days if they could."

Beth flipped open her cell and called her parents.

"Mom, this is Beth. Can you and Dad keep the kids for a few more days? Something has come up."

"Yes, Mom, I know this is an unusual request, but I wouldn't ask if it wasn't important."

"Thanks, Mom, I'll call as soon as I can. Love you."

Beth shut her cell phone and looked at Fish.

"Detective Fisher, is my sister in trouble?"

"I'm not sure, but probably not."

"Has something happened to Tony?"

Angelica started to cry again.

"Something did happen to Tony, didn't it?" Beth asked.

"Beth, Tony was shot and killed today," Fish answered honestly.

"Oh my God, Angel, I'm so sorry."

Beth sat down on the sofa next to her sister.

"I'm here for you, Angel. I'll stay as long as you need me to."

"Detective Fisher, who shot Tony and why?"

"He died in a gunfire exchange with the police."

"Tony shot at the police?"

Before Fish could say anything more, Angelica Tiemman spoke.

"My marriage, it was all a lie, Beth."

"Why on earth are you saying that? You know Tony loved you."

"Do I Beth? He didn't love me enough to tell me that his name wasn't Anthony Tiemman."

"What are you saying, Angel?"

Angelica buried her face in her sister's shoulder and wept uncontrollably. Beth looked at Detective Fisher.

"Would you tell me what's going on here?" she asked Fish.

"I'm sorry. It's up to your sister to tell you."

"What do you guys need?"

"For right now, we need permission to search the house for evidence, and we also need your sister's permission to open her husband's safe deposit box," Fish replied.

Angelica stopped crying for the moment. She picked up a tissue and wiped her eyes the best she could and then looked at Fish.

"What safe deposit box? Tony didn't own a safe deposit box," Angelica stated.

"He did. It's at the Puget Sound Savings and Loan just down the road. We have the key, and we need your permission to open it. Can you sign a waiver so we can open it."

"That won't be necessary, Detective Fisher. I'll go with you. We can open it together."

"I don't think that's a good idea, Angel."

"Detective Fisher, you're going to have to do it with me whether you think it's a good idea or not."

"Fine, we'll do it your way."

"Beth, I would appreciate it if you would come along for support," Fish asked.

"Sure, Detective, anything you say," Beth responded.

Chapter 30

Puget Sound Savings and Loan

Angelica Tiemman and her sister followed the detectives to the Puget Sound Savings and Loan. Fish and Hawk got out of the car and walked into the building with the two women. As they entered, Wendy Stiles stepped out of her office.

"I was wondering how soon you would be back, Detective Fisher."

"Wendy, this is Mr. Tiemman's wife, Angelica. She would like to open her safe deposit box."

"If you two would follow me, we can take care of it right now."

Fish and Angelica followed Wendy into the safe deposit box viewing area.

"To gain access to the vault, you need to press your thumb on this scanner, Mrs. Tiemman."

Angelica pressed her thumb on the scanner. The door to the safe deposit vault didn't unlock. She tried it a second time.

"Oh, dear," Wendy Stiles said, concerned.

"What's wrong? Why didn't the door unlock?"

"It didn't unlock because you're not Mr. Tiemman's wife."

"Don't be ridiculous, of course; I am."

"Your fingerprint doesn't match the one we have on file for Mrs. Tiemman."

"You can't possibly have my thumbprint on file. I've never set foot in this building before."

"Unless you have a warrant, Detective Fisher, I can't allow access to the safe deposit box."

"I should have one here any minute, Ms. Stiles. I thought this might happen."

Within five minutes, Hawk entered the viewing area.

"Here's the warrant. It just arrived."

"Thanks, Hawk." Fish handed the search warrant to Wendy Stile, who typed in a code and used her thumbprint to open the vault door.

"Please follow me, Detective Fisher."

Fish followed the manager into the vault with safe deposit boxes and quickly found the box marked with the number twenty-eight. He inserted the key Connor had located in the field. Wendy inserted the bank key into the second lock on the door, and the door swung open. Fish pulled out the safe deposit box and carried it into the viewing area. Angelica Tiemman was waiting patiently.

"You might not want to see the contents of the box."

"I can't be hurt any worse than I already am, so go ahead and open it."

Fish flipped open the box to reveal its contents. He then donned a pair of latex gloves that were in his pocket so he wouldn't contaminate the evidence.

Angelica started to reach for one of the items in the box.

"You don't want to do that, Angel. I don't want your fingerprints contaminating anything."

"I'm sorry, Detective, I wasn't thinking." Looking into the box. "My God, why are there so many passports? Who on earth was my husband, Detective?"

"I'm sorry, Angel. Your husband was a cold-blooded killer."

Angelica turned to her sister. "Beth, can I stay at your house? I don't think I can spend another moment in that house. Detective Fisher, was my marriage a matter of convenience?"

"I can't help you with that, Angel. You're going to have to search your heart for the answer."

Fish removed seven different passports from the box. Underneath the passports was a pile of money that had a white piece of paper wrapped around it. Fish opened the piece of paper.

"Detective Fisher, are those one-thousand-dollar bills?" asked Angelica.

Flipping through the stack of money, Fish replied to her question. "Yep, roughly two hundred of them."

"I've never seen that much money in my entire life. That son of a bitch. If I had found out about this money, I might have shot him myself. How am I going to explain this to the kids? What am I going to tell them about the man they thought loved them?"

"I'm sorry, Mrs. Tiemman, but those are some tough questions you're asking me. I think it will take some soul searching before you come up with the answers. Just remember one thing."

"What's that, Detective?"

"Kids are a lot more resilient than we adults give them credit for. Don't be scared to tell them the truth."

"How will I be able to tell them the truth when I don't know what it is?"

"I'm sure you'll figure it out. Besides, you need to remember that truth quite often depends on your point of view."

Angelica Tiemman started to sob uncontrollably.

Fish didn't react to Mrs. Tiemman's crying because he was busy reading the piece of paper from the stack of money.

"What's on the piece of paper you're reading, Detective? Please tell me. There's no protecting me now."

Fish looked at her and put his hand on her shoulder. "It's a payment for a killing he and his partner performed, Angel."

Fish reached into the safe deposit box and removed a leather bag. He loosened the drawstring and looked inside. He closed the bag and set it on the counter.

"Are you going to show me what's in the bag, Detective?"

"I don't think so, Angelica."

"It's a gun in the bag, isn't it?"

"I'm afraid so."

"Do you think he killed anybody with it?"

"There's no way of knowing until we run it through our crime lab."

"I'm going to be sick," Angelica announced, suddenly very pale.

Wendy Stiles quickly handed Angelica Tiemman a trash can.

"Ms. Stiles, this safe deposit box was used to pass information back and forth to Gregory Cherlenko, who you know as Anthony Tiemman.

"You need to understand that we run a background check on all our users. Nothing was out of the ordinary at all," Wendy volunteered.

"I would expect it would have come back clean, Ms. Stiles. I would appreciate it if you would get me the information."

"I can pull it up at the terminal here." Wendy Stiles quickly pulled up the file on the computer screen. A picture of a Hispanic-looking woman appeared on the terminal screen.

"Angelica, have you ever seen this woman before?"

"No, Detective, who is she?"

"According to the bank, this a picture of you."

"That's definitely not me, Detective," Angelica confirmed.

"We know it is not you."

"Who the hell is she?"

"It's the person who passed assignments and money to your husband."

"Please, don't refer to him as my husband. I may have been married to him, but our life together was a lie. Do you think she has been in my bed?"

"I can't answer that."

"I'm sorry, that wasn't fair of me to ask."

"That's okay, Angel, I understand." Fish used his I phone to send a picture of the fake Angelica Tiemman to Caleb.

"Ms. Stiles, do you have a copy of her thumbprint?"

"Sure, it will just take a second."

The image of the thumbprint appeared on the screen. Fish took a copy of it and forwarded it to Caleb as well.

"What do I do now, Detective?"

"Angel," Fish started to talk to Angelica, but she cut him off.

"I don't want to be called Angel anymore. That was his name for me. I don't want it anymore."

"Not a problem. You need to go home with your sister."

"What are you going to do after I leave?"

"I'll go back to the office with my associates. Once we get back, we are going to work on tracking down the woman who impersonated you."

"What about my house? Didn't you say you would have to send a forensics team out?"

"Yes, I did. We'll give you a call so you can be there."

"I don't want to go there ever again. Can I just give you the keys?"

"You should have someone there to witness the search, Angelica."

"Would it be alright if I send my brother-in-law to do it?"

"That would be fine. I don't think we'll have a problem with it. I am going to send a patrol car to your house to sit on it until we can get our team out there."

"What will my neighbors think,"

"It doesn't matter what your neighbors think does it?

"No, I guess it doesn't."

"It won't be easy. I'll see to it you get the support you need."

Fish followed Angelica outside and watched her leave.

"Fish, did you find anything?" Hawk asked.

Fish handed Hawk the contents of the safe deposit box. Hawk donned a pair of latex gloves and looked through the contents of the box.

"Fish, this is unbelievable. Do you think she had any idea at all?"

"Not a clue."

"Damn it, Hawk, sometimes this job just sucks."

"It sure does at that."

Fish opened his cell phone and called Caleb.

"Caleb, this is Fish. I've sent two pictures to your e-mail inbox. I need to get an identification on the fingerprint by the time we get back. I'll fill you in when we get there."

Fish listened to Caleb's talk on the other end of the cell phone.

"Yes, Caleb, Connor was right."

Fish and Hawk got back into the car.

"Well, Connor, unfortunately for Angelica, she was not the Angelica Tiemman registered on the bank account."

"Now we have another piece to the puzzle, don't we, Detective Fisher?"

"I think you're right. I think the person who was accessing the safe deposit box was using it to pass information back and forth with Cherlenko. I was able to get her picture and thumbprint from the bank's computer. I've already forwarded the information to Caleb. Hopefully, he'll have her identified by the time we get back to the office."

"What was in the safe deposit box, Detective Fisher?" Hamilton asked.

"You can look for yourself."

Hamilton pulled on a pair of gloves and started looking through its contents.

"Multiple passports, lots of cash, and a gun. It looks like Gregory Cherlenko was a man from many countries, judging by the different passports. Connor, it looks like you were right about Maggie Blake." Hamilton passed the piece of paper back to Connor.

"What this, Hamilton?"

"Cherlenko's payment for getting rid of Maggie Blake."

"Did Angelica see the contents of the box, Detective Fisher?"

"Yes, unfortunately, she did."

"I bet she didn't take it very well."

"She didn't. She feels betrayed."

"That's understandable. Is someone going to stay with her, Detective Fisher?"

"She is going to stay with her sister. She doesn't want to set foot in her house again."

"I can't say that I blame her. Is there anything the Seattle Police Department can do for her?"

"I gave her my card and told her we could get somebody to talk to her."

Chapter 31

Return to Seattle

Fish eased the Ford Crown Victoria into a designated space in the Police Department lot. Within a couple of minutes, they were inside the war room. Caleb walked in behind the group as Hawk placed the box of evidence on one of the tables. He pulled out the piece of paper that had been wrapped around the cash and handed it to Caleb. Caleb read it and then looked at the group standing before him.

"Connor was right, someone murdered Maggie Blake," he confirmed.

"Caleb, it seems to me that two hundred thousand dollars is a lot of money to pay to have someone killed," Connor said.

"Whoever is behind all of this has deep, very, very deep pockets. Who is going to give me the summary of your excursion today?"

"I thought I would do it, Caleb," Fish said.

"Hawk, would you please take the box upstairs and put it into the evidence locker."

"I'm on the way."

Hawk left the Operations Center carrying the box of evidence. Fish began to replay the events that led to its retrieval.

"Connor was right about the victim, Gregory Cherlenko. He hid something in the field where their car stopped. Connor found a key to a safe deposit box at Puget Sound Savings and Loan. We went to the nearest branch office to locate the box that belonged to the key. Lucky for us, we were at the right branch, but the key didn't belong to Gregory Cherlenko."

"Who did the box belong to if it wasn't Cherlenko's?"

"The box belonged to an Anthony Tiemman."

"Who the hell is Anthony Tiemman?"

"Anthony Tiemman and Gregory Cherlenko are the same person. The branch manager told me we needed to get a warrant or Anthony Tiemman's wife to open the safe deposit box. We went to Anthony Tiemman's address, where we met his wife, Angelica."

"Did she confirm Gregory Cherlenko was her husband, Anthony Tiemman?"

"Yes, she did. Angelica agreed to go with us to the bank. When we got there, we discovered she was not the person on the account. Someone used her name to access the account. I served the warrant you sent to gain access to the box, where we found the evidence Hawk took to the locker. The picture and the thumbprint are listed as being Angelica Tiemman."

"I'll send a team out to the Tiemman house to gather evidence if there is anything there. Did you explain that to Mrs. Tiemman?" Caleb said when Fish was finished.

"I did. She doesn't want to be at her house anymore. She is going to send her brother-in-law over when our team gets out there."

"Fish, you and Hawk did great work today."

"It wouldn't have happened without Connor." Fish advised.

Caleb looked at Connor.

"I admit that you are continuing to amaze me. Would you consider being a full-time consultant?"

"Maybe, part-time, I would," Connor said.

"At this point, I'll take whatever you can give us."

"Did you get any feedback from the thumbprint and the picture I sent?" Fish asked.

"I have it on screen one."

Caleb picked up the remote and turned it on. The image that Fish had sent to Caleb appeared on the center screen. To the right of the picture was an arrest sheet for Louisa Sanchez.

Hawk returned to the war room and looked at the image on the screen as he walked in. Fish read the contents of the screen out loud.

"Louisa Sanchez. She lives at 1555 Crescent Moon Way in Olympia and has a list of priors: theft, prostitution, drugs, etc."

"Fish, she's got a tattoo of a baseball on her arm with the initials RJ inside."

"What's important about that, Hawk?"

Hawk opened up a small pocket notepad and started flipping through its contents.

"It's here in my notes," Hawk yelled out excitedly.

"What exactly do you have?" Caleb asked.

"Captain, when Fish and I were at the hospital visiting with Chris Felton, we asked him questions about Hector Gonzales. He had talked about Hector's brother mostly, but right before he passed out, he said that Hector had a tattoo on his arm that contained the letters RJ. I asked Chris who RJ was, but he had passed out. As we were leaving, I distinctly heard him mutter, 'Reggie, RJ is for Reggie Jackson. Louisa Sanchez has the same tattoo."

Fish looked at Hawk curiously.

"Hawk, are you sure he said the name Reggie?"

"Yes, I am sure, Fish. I distinctly heard it."

"I didn't hear it, Hawk. I don't remember him saying, Reggie."

"Fish, I guess sometimes you need a younger set of ears."

"Just rememberthat you were the one badly in need of oxygen after the morning run we took."

Caleb cleared his throat to get everyone's attention.

"If you detectives have finished stroking your egos, can we get back to business here?"

They replied with a resounding, "Yes, Captain."

Fish flipped open his cell phone, placed it in hands-free speaker mode and dialed a phone number. It rang almost instantly. The ringing stopped as the call was completed a female voice answered Fixorium.

"This is Detective Fisher with the Seattle Police Department can I speak with Ricardo Gonzales?"

"Sure, you can, Detective Fisher, as long as you let me talk with Detective Hottie."

"Kaylene, I need to speak to Ricardo. I will pass your request on to Detective Steinbrenner, but I wouldn't stay up nights waiting for him to call."

"Please hold for a moment, Detective. I'll go get Ricky."

After a five-minute wait, the voice of Ricardo Gonzales.

"This is Ricardo Gonzales, how I can help you?

"Ricardo, this is Detective Fisher. I would like to ask you if your brother Hector knew someone named Louisa Sanchez?"

"Sure, we both did, Detective. Louisa is our cousin, but we called her RJ because she was a big fan of Reggie Jackson."

"Did your brother have the initials RJ tattooed on his arm?"

There was a long moment of silence before the answer came.

"Yes, he did, Detective, in a baseball on his right arm. Growing up, Hector and Louisa were always getting in trouble together. They had the same tattoos. I believe they might have had a kid together. Wow, Detective, this is the first time I have heard her name mentioned in years. Is there anything else I can answer for you, Detective Fisher?"

"No, not at the moment, Ricky. Thanks."

"Sure thing, Detective."

Fish exhaled loudly and then spoke.

"That's not what I thought Ricardo was going to say at all. My best guess is that the romance between Hector and Louisa Sanchez never ended. Caleb, I think we need to get her under surveillance."

"I think Fish is right, Caleb. She has to be getting her marching orders from someone. If we sit on her, maybe she will lead us to them. What do you think?"

"Sounds like a good idea to me, Detectives. We need to get on it today."

"I have a feeling she is going to lead us to Hector Gonzales's associate. We also need to be on the lookout for a tall man with a jagged scar down his cheek."

"Keep that in mind. Connor, I thought you might want to know that the onboard computer was removed from Maggie Blake's car. I'll let you know if they find anything. I expect we're going to find that someone tampered with the car's computer just like you thought."

"Where do we go from here?" Connor asked.

The first task is to set up surveillance on Louisa Sanchez. The second task is someone needs to go to Spokane to interview the driver of the dump truck that killed Maggie Blake. I'm open to suggestions on who goes where."

"Can I offer my two cents?" Hamilton spoke up.

"Sure, you have the floor."

"Since I am a pilot and have a plane at my disposal, I think Connor and I should go to Spokane. Either Detective Fisher or Steinbrenner can accompany us. We can leave first thing in the morning."

"I think it's a good plan with one exception. I am going to accompany you and Connor to Spokane. Detectives Fisher and Steinbrenner can go to Olympia tomorrow and get the surveillance set up on Louisa Sanchez."

"What about Mark, Caleb?"

"Hamilton, I guess we better bring him along. I will grant him an exclusive report on the murder of Maggie Blake. That should soothe Mark's bruised ego."

"I doubt Mark will complain about the offer. I'll make it happen."

"Good, I want to keep Mark on our side as much as possible."

"Caleb, how long do you want Hawk and I to sit on the surveillance?"

"Just long enough to get it set up, Fish."

"If we aren't going to sit on the surveillance, who is?"

"I was thinking of sending Ben and Jenny Silver in to do the surveillance."

"You can't be serious. Ben and Jenny Silver, is that a good idea?"

"No, it's a great idea."

"I don't understand why you think so."

"Ben and Jenny Silver have been working special assignments under my direction ever since they left our service. In my opinion, they are the perfect people for the job. Let's call it a wrap for today."

"That sounds good to me. I'm sure Hawk and I wouldn't mind a night at home," Fish replied.

"Connor, you had yourself quite a day today."

"I was just doing what needed to be done."

Hamilton patted Connor on the back.

"If you're ready to go to the apartment, our friend Mark has graciously offered to cook for us, and since cooking is not my forte, I accepted his offer wholeheartedly."

"Gee, Hamilton, I'm surprised."

"About what?"

"I just figured that there wasn't anything you couldn't do."

"There are very few things I can't do. One is cooking, and the other is singing."

"Is it alright if I take your word on the singing part?"

Hamilton looked at Connor and uttered the word coward.

Chapter 32

SPD War Room

Caleb was looking over Connor's shoulder. The two men were staring at a computer screen when Fish and Hawk walked in.

"Caleb, you know if you get here a little bit earlier, you can start kicking the rooster in the ass on your way into work. Better yet, maybe we should just set up a cot in one corner, and we can all take turns power napping here until we solve the case."

Caleb looked up at the two detectives and rubbed his bald head.

"I like that idea, Detective Steinbrenner—a cot in the corner would work. But there will be no overtime pay or conjugal visits allowed."

"I was just kidding. What are you and Connor watching?"

Caleb pushed his hand on the remote. Screen number three flickered to life with the image that was on the laptop. Two officers were approaching the front door of a house. One of them pressed the doorbell. As soon as he did, the house exploded shrapnel hit both of the officers. The officer nearest the door took the brunt of the blast.

"What is the condition of the two officers?"

They are both gone. Nothing much left of either one.

"I assume that it's tied to our case? Where did this happen, and why?"

"Based on Connor's suspicions, it wasn't a coincidence. It was bad timing that Maggie Smith hit a dump truck pulling out of a construction site. The Tacoma Police Department pulled the onboard computer from her car and analyzed it. Someone hacked into the car's onboard computer through the OnStar system, disabled her brakes, and sent the engine racing out of control."

"Doctor Blake's wife probably didn't know anything about what her husband was involved in. She didn't stand a chance, did she?"

"No, she didn't, Hawk. Back to your question, Fish. The house in the video is in Spokane. It belongs to the dump truck driver. The Tacoma Police were there to bring him in for a second round of questioning." Caleb paused for a second and then cleared his throat before he began again. "We all saw that didn't go very well. The truck driver, his family, and two of Tacoma's finest were killed."

"Gentlemen, from this moment forward, all information goes through me before it gets made public. We are going to put our heads together to figure out the next step."

As Caleb finished speaking, Detective Fisher's cell phone rang. Pressing the answer button, he talked to the caller.

"This is Detective Fisher."

"I didn't know it was you on the phone, Hailey. What happened to your phone?" Fish listened to his daughter more and spoke.

"Hailey, I need you to start from the beginning and try to do it calmly, and please give me a second so I can put my phone in hands-free mode. When I say go, I want you to do your best to talk a little slower."

Hailey Fisher's voice was full of emotion as she began to talk. Her breathing was shallow and extremely rapid.

"They're gone, Dad, all my friends are gone. Why did they do it?"

"Listen, Hailey, I need you to back up as best you can and tell me what happened."

"Jennifer, my roommate, called me yesterday afternoon to tell me that two guys from the FBI were looking for me. Jen told them I was playing blind man's bluff with my friends and where I could be found and what I was wearing."

"Hailey, what the hell is Blind Man's Bluff?" he asked tersely.

"I can't believe that you need to know what blind man's bluff is right now. I wish you could stop being my dad, the super cop, for a minute."

Hailey's voice sounded hurt and defeated.

"It's a game that my friends and I play that's all about trust. One person puts on a blindfold and moves very slowly toward the edge of the building. His partner gives him instructions that send the player close to the edge of the building. The player that gets closest to the edge without losing their nerve is the winner."

Detective Fisher's voice suddenly became soft and sullen.

"I'm sorry, Hailey. I have no intention of lecturing you right now so please, continue."

"I was running late, so one of my other friends took me to where we were playing. As we approached the building where my friends were, I could see Stacy on the building near the edge. She was wearing my Seahawks jacket and cap. As we started to slow down to stop and get out, there was a massive explosion. The building fell into a pile of dust."

There was a long, eerie silence, and then Hailey spoke in a very emotional but barely audible whisper.

"They are all dead, Dad. I heard Stacy scream at the moment of the explosion. It's a sound that will haunt me for the rest of my life."

Hailey began weeping slowly.

"I promise you, I'll protect you."

"You'll protect me, Dad? Really? That's just great. Why don't you peddle what you can't sell to me, to one of my friend's parents? I'm sure they all know by now. It made national news headlines today. I don't think they will find any comfort in your words either."

"Listen, Hailey, I am sorry. I don't know what else I can say."

"Maybe you can promise to keep me from scratching Caleb Clarke's eyes out when I see him next."

"Why do you want to do that, Hailey."

"I was researching that guy he wanted me to find. It all went south in a hurry when I started digging into the dark web."

"Look, Hailey, I need to know where you are."

"I'd rather not say, Dad. I don't know if this communication is safe. One of my friends saw a tall, sinister-looking man carrying out my computer equipment."

"Did they say what he looked like, Hailey?"

"My friend said his face was long and had a jagged scar. She said he reminded her of death."

Hailey began crying uncontrollably.

"I know you're scared, honey, but I need you to listen to me closely, Hailey."

There was a very meek and timid reply of yes.

'I want you to go to where the Pufferbellies are all in a row. Do you understand?"

"Yes," she replied.

"I know you're using a burner phone at the moment. Lose it when we finish talking. If I'm not there when you get there, you know what to do, don't you?"

There was a long moment of silence.

"I do, Dad."

The phone went dead as the call ended. Fish closed his cell phone and looked at Caleb and sneered at him.

"Hailey is in trouble. I'm going to go get her."

"If Hailey is on the run, how are you going to be able to find her?" Caleb asked.

"I already know where she will be and when she will be there."

"I'm surprised you haven't already left,."

"I just have one question for you, Detective Fisher."

"What would that be, Hamilton?"

"Pittsburgh is a long way from Seattle. I was just wondering if you had formulated a plan on how you are going to get her?"

"Not exactly. I was going to do my planning on the move. So, if you don't mind, I'm going. I'll call you when I have a plan."

"I can help move your plan along. You see, I have Mrs. Lane's private jet at my disposal, and I am quite sure you will not get there any faster."

"I appreciate your offer, but this is my mess. I can handle it."

Hamilton glared at Detective Fisher as he spoke to him.

"You know, Detective Fisher, what do you say you suck up your pride for a minute so I can help you save your daughter."

"Hamilton is right, Fish. Pull your head out of your ass for once and get, the out of here."

Fish threw his hands up in the air, admitting defeat.

"Fine, I'll do it your way."

Hamilton slapped Fish on the back and raced out of the conference room. Fish was hot on his heels. Connor let out a heavy sigh and turned his gaze to the ceiling. Caleb looked at Connor, who was silently moving his lips as the two left the room.

"How about you say a prayer for me while you're at it, Connor."

Connor's frown turned into an ear-to-ear grin.

Chapter 33

Caleb looked at Connor. "Connor, I thought you would go with Hamilton. I'm surprised you didn't."

"I have a feeling there is a bigger need for me here."

"Connor, I'm glad you stayed. I believe you're right."

The phone on the conference room table buzzed. Caleb answered.

"This is Caleb Clarke."

"Caleb, this is Ben Silver calling in. I just wanted to tell you that we're at Louisa Sanchez's house. I think you'd better get out here. You're going to want to see this."

"Ben, we'll be there as quickly as possible. Make sure nothing is disturbed until we get there."

"I'll make sure of it, Captain."

Caleb turned and looked at Connor.

"You're coming along, aren't you, Mr. Darke?"

"I wasn't sure I was invited."

"Connor, I thought it went without saying you're going."

Within ten minutes, they were on their way to the house in Olympia, Washington, to meet Ben Silver. Ben was standing on the curb, looking very impatient as Caleb pulled up. Ben stared at Connor as he exited the vehicle and watched him walk up onto the sidewalk.

"Who did you bring with you, Caleb?"

"Ben, this is Connor Darke. He is consulting for us."

"Connor Darke, that name seems familiar. You're the Love Doctor, aren't you?"

"I prefer to be called a marriage psychologist, Mr. Silver."

"I'll call you whatever the hell you want me to, Mr. Darke. Caleb, why did you bring this guy along?"

"For one thing, who I bring along is my concern and no one else's. Shall we go in?"

They entered the house together. It was a two-story, square, brick building and looked exactly like every other house on the street.

"Caleb, let's go upstairs first."

The second floor contained three bedrooms. The door to the middle bedroom was open. The three men peered into the room as they reached the top level. It had a queen-size bed, a nightstand with a lamp on it, and nothing else. The sheets and blankets were in a heap at the end of the bed.

"Caleb, the room at the street end of the hall is pretty much the same as this one. The room to our right is what I want you to see."

The group walked down the hallway and entered the third bedroom, which had once held computers and servers. Caleb looked around the room and then spoke.

"Why the hell did someone need to have a server in a house like this? What the hell was Louisa Sanchez up to?"

"If we go to the basement, Caleb, it might help explain what the equipment was for."

"Lead the way, Ben. Connor and I will follow."

Connor was still standing in the middle of the room as the men walked toward the door.

"Are you coming with us, Connor, or do you want to meet us in the basement?" Caleb asked

Connor walked over to where the computer racks were, knelt, and swept his hand along the floor underneath the right rack. A gold cufflink skipped across the floor. Connor grabbed the cufflink, stood, and studied it.

"What did you find, Connor?"

Connor turned toward the trio, who were still standing in the doorway.

"I found a cufflink with the initials TJI engraved on it. There is a small diamond dotting the I."

"Can I see it if you don't mind?"

"Sure, Caleb."

Connor handed the cufflink to Caleb, who studied it intently. A worried look formed on his face. Connor studied the change in Caleb's face.

"Is something wrong, Caleb?"

"I'm not sure. If I'm right and this belongs to who I think it does, how the hell did it end up here?"

The three men were standing in the basement two minutes later, a lone light bulb hanging from a wire dimly lit the hallway. In total, there were nine closed doors in the basement. The group opened up the first door they came to, as the door swung open, they let out a collective gasp. The small room contained an iron-framed cot that had a heavy chain and a metal ankle bracelet welded to it. Over in one corner was a chamber pot.

"Caleb, I've looked in all the rooms; each one has the same furnishings as this one. I think this house is used for human trafficking."

"I hope not. This might not be related to the case we are working, but one thing is for sure: we won't stop until we have answers."

Ben glanced around the small room.

"Caleb, where did Mr. Darke go?"

"I don't know. I didn't even realize he left the room."

Caleb walked out into the hallway and called Connor's name.

"I'm down the hallway in the room on the left, Caleb. Can you come in here and help me?"

The group walked down the hallway to the room where Connor was. He was attempting to turn one of the beds on its side. Ben looked at Connor, who was struggling to flip it up.

"You can save your strength, Mr. Darke. We've already searched all the rooms."

Connor continued trying to turn the bed on its side.

"Fine, Mr. Darke, you can have it your way."

Ben Silver walked to the other end of the bed and grabbed the frame. Together, they were able to get it on its side, exposing a hole that had been crudely cut into the plywood attached to the metal-framed bed. Connor knelt on one knee and managed to barely squeeze his hand through the hole. After a few seconds, he pulled out a small spiral notebook. He flipped it open and began to read. After a few moments, he handed the notebook to Caleb.

"I'm sorry, Caleb, I can't read this out loud."

Caleb began reading the first page out loud.

"There's no time. They expect me to be ready. I've tried to get out, but all the exits are blocked. Mom, I pray that someone finds this notebook. Mom, I'm sorry for everything. I wish I had tried harder to get along with you. I don't know if we will ever see each other again. I know they plan to move me soon. I hope you can find it in your heart to forgive me. Mom, I will always love you. It's signed by Jasmine Lee."

"Caleb, the name Jasmine Lee, was on the list that Mark had run off the missing person database. I am willing to bet that some of the rest of them are on there, too."

Caleb continued flipping through the pages. He looked at Connor and Hamilton.

"There has got to be at least thirty different names in here. What the hell are we going to do?"

"I don't quite know how, but we are going to find them."

"What makes you think we will, Connor?"

"Because, Caleb, I don't think I would have been sent on this path if it wasn't worth going down."

"I certainly hope you're right."

"So do I."

Two Olympia police officers were standing in the doorway.

"Captain Clarke, none of the neighbors are home right now. Did you find anything of significance?"

"Yes, I did, Officer King. We found a notebook with names of girls that were being held against their will."

"Captain Clarke, are you telling me the owner of this house kept young women prisoners here."

"Unfortunately, yes, I am, Officer King."

"Do you happen to know where she is now?"

"Unfortunately, I don't."

Caleb turned to Ben Silver.

"Ben, can you sit on this house until a crime scene unit can get here?"

"Sure, Caleb, it won't be a problem. I doubt anyone will be coming back, but I will let you know if they do."

"Good, Ben, I appreciate it. Connor and I are going to head back then."

Caleb and Connor left the basement, headed upstairs, and then out. As they walked down the stairs from the front porch, an older lady approached them.

"It's about damn time the police got here. I've been waiting all morning for you guys to get here."

"I am truly sorry to Miss... ?"

"Tisdale. I'm Mrs. Elaine Tisdale. I have been waiting all morning for someone to take my statement."

"What do you want to report?"

"I'm hard of hearing could you ask me again but speak up this time?"

Caleb raised his voice and asked her again.

"You should already know what the problem is, Officer. I called hours ago."

"Mrs. Tisdale, you're going have to tell your story again anyway, so why don't you tell me what the problem is?"

"I need you to catch the guy who hit my car. He got out to look at the damage, then he just got in his car and left. Isn't there a law against that?"

"Yes, there is, but we will need a description of the car and a license plate number if you got it."

"I can give you a description of the car. It was a green foreign job. It should be easy to find. It had a white front left fender."

"I'll need something a little more specific than a green foreign job, Mrs. Tisdale. What make was it?"

"How would I know? Those foreign cars all look the same to me."

"Did you get the license plate number by any chance?"

"I'm sorry, but I couldn't read the plates on the car. It should have a dent in its rear left bumper from hitting my car."

"Mrs. Tisdale, it may be hard to find a car without the license plate number."

"You might have been able to find them had you gotten here when I called."

"Again, I'm sorry, but it's doubtful we'll find the car."

"What about the driver, can't he be arrested?"

"Well, Mam, his picture might be in a database, but that won't work unless you got a good look at his face."

"Would his picture work for you? Could you catch him with it?"

"You took his picture?"

"Yep, I sure did. I like to birdwatch. I had one here on my feeder that I hadn't seen before, so I went to get my camera. When I did, I heard a noise. When I looked through my front window, I saw the green car had backed into mine. When he stopped to look at the damage, I took his picture. I can go get my camera if you want."

"That would be fantastic, Mrs. Tisdale."

Within ten minutes, Mrs. Tisdale was handing her camera to Caleb.

"Here's his picture, Officer. If you need to take it, I understand. Just make sure I get it back."

"I would like to take it with me if you don't mind. We'll get back as quickly as we can. Did you ever see this man here before?"

"I've seen the car before, but never the driver. When you looked at my camera screen, you looked like you'd seen a ghost. Do you know the man who hit my car?

"Maybe. It reminds me of someone I used to know."

"If you know who he is, Officer, won't it make it easy to find him?"

"Not necessarily, Mrs. Tisdale, but we'll do our best. Did you call this into your insurance agency yet?"

"No, I was waiting for you fellas to get here before I did."

Caleb removed a business card from his wallet and handed it to her.

"Here's my card. Make sure you call your insurance company. If they give you any problem, call me."

Mrs. Tisdale looked at the card and then looked at Caleb and smiled.

"You'll have to forgive me for my coarse language. I didn't know the police would send a captain to talk with me."

"Not a problem, Mrs. Tisdale. Just remember, it's never a problem to expect the best. Like I said, call if you need me."

"I will, Captain. I promise."

Chapter 34

West Seattle

Caleb stopped the car in front of a three-story brownstone in West Seattle.

"Connor, the cufflink you found belongs to a dead detective. This is where his widow lives. You're welcome to stay in the car, but I prefer you come in with me."

"Sounds good to me, Captain."

They got out of the car and walked to the front door of the brownstone. Caleb rang the doorbell. Footsteps could be heard coming closer to the door. The door opened.

"Caleb, what a surprise. I didn't expect to see you."

"Can I come in, Barbara?"

"Of course, you can."

Barbara Ingles smiled at Caleb as she brushed away a loose hair that had fallen on her face.

"It's too bad the kids aren't home. They will be disappointed they didn't get to see you."

"I promise I'll come back when they're home."

"Great, Caleb. The kids will be excited to know that you might come to visit."

"Barbara, this is Connor Darke. He is assisting the department with a case."

"Mr. Darke, you're even nicer to look at in person."

"Thank you, Mrs. Ingles, you're too kind."

"So, Caleb, to what do I owe this unexpected honor?"

"I found something I think belongs to TJ, and I thought that you might want to have it."

"After all this time, you found something of TJ's. What did you find?"

"We found a cufflink."

Caleb handed the cufflink to Barbara, who looked at it. Tears began to well up in the corner of her eyes. She sniffed and wiped her eyes as she spoke.

"It's his. I would recognize it anywhere. Adam is going to be so excited to know that it's been found. He wanted to have them for his wedding next May. I can't wait to give it to him. I can't believe you went out of your way just for this."

"I was happy to do it. There is something I would like to ask you, Barbara."

"Ask away. I'll answer it if I can."

"I vaguely remember TJ mentioned he owned a camp somewhere. Can you tell me if he did and where it is?

"TJ's family owned a camp on Lake Moses. What's your interest in it?"

"I couldn't remember the name of the lake for the life of me. I've been thinking about renting a place on a lake next summer, so I thought I could check it out."

"If you wait a minute, I'll get you the address."

"I would appreciate that."

Barbara walked into the den and came back carrying a piece of paper and handed it to Caleb.

"Barbara, I can't thank you enough."

"Are you kidding? You've helped me out so much with the kids, it's the least I can do."

"We have to go, Barbara. I'll come and see the kids soon. Maybe we can go bowling."

"I'm sure they would love it."

Caleb smiled, turned, opened the door, and walked out with Connor in tow.

"I'm glad you didn't say anything about her husband."

"Just because we found his cufflink, doesn't mean TJ is still alive. Barbara and her kids took his death hard. Telling her where we found the cufflink would have opened old wounds."

"What do we do now?"

"I'm going to call Ben and ask him to go out to Lake Moses on the outside possibility TJ Ingles is still alive. He might be there. This car is equipped with hands-free calling, so let's contact Ben."

"Caleb, I didn't expect to hear from you so soon."

"Is the crime scene team there yet, Ben?"

"They arrived about fifteen minutes ago. Why?"

"Ben, I need you to do some surveillance for me."

"Sure, not a problem. Just tell me who I'm looking for, and where and when you want me to go."

"The time would be now. I am sending you to Lake Moses. TJ Ingles's family owned a house there. If he's still alive, he might be there."

"What if he's not?"

"Then he's not. It's as simple as that. I will text you the address as soon as we hang up."

"I'll get there as quickly as I can. Luckily, I have all my surveillance gear with me. I'll call you when I get set up out there."

Caleb ended the call and then sent a text message with the address. He immediately called Hawk to fill him in about the visit to TJ Ingles's wife.

"You know, Caleb, if that son of a bitch is still alive, I want first dibs. The cheap bastard borrowed five thousand dollars from me. I doubt Barbara even knows about it," Hawk said.

"Hawk, if he is still alive, you're going to have to take a number. There might not be much left of him by the time I get done with him."

"I still want my time in the barrel, Caleb."

Erie Bound

Hamilton had the Dassault Falcon at 20,000 feet and still climbing. Fish was sitting in the co-pilot's seat, scanning the horizon.

"If Hailey's luck holds out, she'll be in Erie, Pennsylvania, waiting for us. Is that going to be a problem, Hamilton?"

"Detective Fisher, it couldn't be more perfect."

"Did you file a flight plan?"

"Sort of. It was difficult to file one when I didn't know where we were going. On top of it all, we're probably being monitored right now."

"I'm sorry, Hamilton. I guess I wasn't thinking too clearly."

"You don't need to beat yourself up about it. I hadn't intended to file an accurate one anyway. I assumed we were being followed. Why don't you sit back, relax, and enjoy the ride?"

Three and a half hours later, Hamilton rousted a sleeping Detective Fisher.

"Wake up, Detective. It's time to land."

"I don't see an airport ahead of us," Fisher said.

"We're not landing at an airport. Trust me, Detective, you're in good hands."

Within a few minutes, Hamilton lowered the landing gear and continued his descent onto a small patch of asphalt in front of them.

"Please, don't tell me we're landing there. It barely looks like a runway."

"Don't fret, Detective. I can land this thing on a postage stamp."

Within less than ten minutes, the plane was touching down on the small runway.

"How on earth are we going to get to Erie from here, Hamilton? This looks like the middle of nowhere."

Hamilton turned and smiled at Fish.

"Did you happen to notice the long ridge just off to the north side of the runway as I turned to line up with the landing strip?"

"I did. What does that matter?"

"You'll know why it matters in a minute."

Hamilton turned the plane to the right. As he did, two grass-covered doors slid open to reveal a spacious hangar.

"Why go to so much trouble to hide a hangar?"

"This property was used back in the nineteen forties for special operations. I acquired it for Mrs. Lane. I have a handful of places strategically placed around the country to make her traveling less noticeable."

"Where the hell are we?" Fish asked as they walked out of the hangar.

"Edinboro, Pennsylvania."

Fish scanned the immediate area.

"How are we getting to Erie? I don't think running there and back is a good idea."

"Would you prefer an exhilarating walk?"

"If that's the only choice, I'm ready. I prefer that we get going as quickly as possible."

"Our ride will be here momentarily."

"How long is it going to take us to get to Erie?"

"Twenty to twenty-five minutes, depending on traffic. Everything has been taken care of."

Hamilton began looking at his watch. "We'll be on our way in two minutes or less."

Within seconds, a panel truck was speeding toward them. Fish started to reach for his gun.

"Relax Detective Fisher. Our ride is here."

The truck slowed. There was a black Aberdeen Farms logo trimmed in gold on both sides.

"You can't be serious."

"What's wrong with our ride?"

"You couldn't find something a little less conspicuous?"

"Detective, this truck is always at the farmer's market in Erie. Since today is a market day, no one will think about it. We'll be able to slip in and out of downtown. Besides, where are you going to find a bulletproof vehicle?"

A young woman jumped out of the truck, ran over to Hamilton, jumped into his arms, and kissed him on his left cheek.

"Hello, kitten," Hamilton said.

"Detective Fisher, this is my Goddaughter, Karen Christians. Kitten, this is Detective Ken Fisher of the Seattle Police."

Karen gave the keys to Hamilton. "Promise me you'll bring my baby back unharmed."

"I'll do my best, Kitten." Hamilton looked at Fish. "Shall we go?"

The two men climbed into the truck. Fish was in the driver's seat.

"Why is this truck bulletproof?"

"Do you really want to know?"

"I probably don't."

"This truck was originally built for the Brinks Armored Car Company."

Within thirty minutes, they pulled the truck into the parking lot for the farmer's market in downtown Erie.

"Why don't you stay with the truck while I go get Hailey. I wouldn't want anything to happen to it. I should be able to get her and get back within fifteen minutes."

"Are you sure she'll be there?"

"I sure hope so."

Twenty minutes later, Fish was heading back toward the truck with his daughter alongside him. When he had reached the edge of the farmer's market, Hamilton jumped into the driver's seat and backed it out of the parking spot. He gunned the engine, spun the rear tires, and shot through the parking lot. Fish looked toward the parking lot and saw the truck shooting toward them with Hamilton behind the wheel. He grabbed Hailey's arm, drew his gun from its holster, and started running into the street. Hamilton spun the steering wheel, turning it toward Fish and Hailey, who were running. He stopped fast so Fish and

Hailey could get in. Fish slid the side door open and pushed Hailey in.

"Go, go!" Fish yelled out as he dove into the truck and rolled over on his back. Three shots flew over his head and slammed into the left inside wall. They sped forward in a hurry. Hamilton spun the wheel hard to the right and continued accelerating.

"Where are we going? This sure as hell isn't the way we came."

"Don't worry about it. I planned an escape route."

Hamilton made a hard left and then a quick right.

"Is that a drainage culvert we're headed toward?"

"Are you worried about getting a little wet, Detective Fisher?"

"Not all. I trust that you know what you're doing."

"Isn't improvisation fun, Detective?" Hamilton let out a deep-throated laugh.

"You may notice I'm not laughing."

"Relax, I was joking."

Hamilton was driving in a large drainage tunnel with just the running lights on. Within a short minute, they were at the end of the tunnel and on a severely rutted dirt road.

"Hold on back there. The ride is going to be quite rough."

"We'll do our best to hold on if you do your best to get us there in one piece," Fish replied.

"I'm working on it."

They pulled out of the rutted dirt road and onto a blacktop surface.

Within a couple of minutes, the hangar containing the Dassault Falcon was in sight. The plane had been backed out and was sitting in place with its engines running.

"That's my girl," Hamilton shouted loudly.

"I hope you all are in the mood to make a run for the plane. We have company."

Hamilton pushed the accelerator to the floor. It shook and leaped forward like a cheetah being let out of its cage.

"Jesus, Hamilton, what does this truck have under the hood?"

"The engine is stroking six hundred and fifty horsepower. I built it myself for moments just like this."

"Why did you think you had to prepare for moments like this?"

"That is a question I will answer at another time. I hope you're ready to run."

Hamilton slammed on the brakes and turned the steering wheel hard. The rear end spun around and slid to a stop within ten feet of the plane. Everyone exited and made a mad dash to the plane. When everyone was aboard, Hamilton pulled up the stairs and locked the door.

"Find a seat; we're going out hot."

Hamilton jumped into the pilot's seat. He turned to Seth Martin, who was now sitting in the co-pilot seat.

"Let's roll, Seth."

The plane lurched forward and rapidly accelerated. In less than fifteen seconds, it started lifting off the ground. Fish looked out the window and saw vehicles coming down the runway toward them.

"It looks like we barely made it, Hamilton."

"We're not out of the woods yet, Detective Fisher."

“Why? What's wrong, Hamilton?”

“I'm picking up inbound aircraft coming after us.”

“What does that mean?”

“It means that someone has other plans for us. Do you have a queasy stomach, Detective?”

“I don't like roller coaster rides if that's what you're asking.”

“You and your daughter might want to locate an air sickness bag and keep it close at hand.”

“Do you expect rough weather, Hamilton?”

“Not exactly, Detective. We are going to turn and burn as close to the deck as possible. The longer we can stay under the radar, the better off we'll be. The air closer to water is more turbulent, so hold on tight.”

Hailey looked at her father. He had never seen that look in her eyes before. He knew it was a combination of fear and sheer exhaustion.

Chapter 35

The Next Day

The sun hadn't even begun to show on the horizon when Caleb turned on the lights in the war room. He rolled a portable whiteboard into the room and started writing.

"Caleb, I wanted to thank you for giving me the exclusive to the story on Maggie Blake."

Caleb turned from the board to face Mark and offered him a handshake.

"You deserved it, Mark. I read the article you wrote about her death. It was good."

Hawk had quietly walked in behind Mark and slapped him on his left shoulder. Mark jumped.

"Jesus, Detective Steinbrenner, you almost gave me a heart attack."

"I didn't mean to startle you. I agree with Caleb about your article."

Caleb looked at Detective Steinbrenner and raised his left eyebrow.

"So, Detective, where is your partner this morning?"

"Fish will be in with Hamilton and Connor in a few minutes. Hailey didn't want to be left alone, so Hamilton is taking the time to show her how well protected she is."

"Hopefully, they will get here soon. I'm expecting a report from Ben. He is at the Ingles camp on Moses Lake."

Five minutes later, Fish, Hamilton, and Connor entered the room.

Fish slid a computer thumb drive across the conference table to Caleb.

"The information you wanted Hailey to find is on that drive, Caleb. Whatever is on it must have been worth killing her friends for." Caleb looked at Fish.

"Is Hailey alright?"

Fish shot an 'I might just have to kill you rather than answer the question look' at Caleb.

"Caleb, shall we take a look at what Hailey found?"

"In a little while, Fish. We have a chat with Ben coming up on-screen one."

"What's Ben up to now?"

"He's on a stakeout at Moses Lake."

"Moses Lake, what the hell is going on out there?"

"It's not what, it's all about who. We suspect TJ Ingles has risen like the proverbial phoenix from the ashes of the dead. We'll know in a couple of seconds."

Ben's image appeared on the screen. He was in front of the camera on his laptop in a small lakeside hotel.

"Good morning, Caleb. Who's there with you?"

"Ben, I have Detectives Fisher and Steinbrenner, along with two consultants who are assisting with our case. Is there anybody at the Lake Moses location?"

"Yes. There are two people at the lake house, one female and one male. I'm uploading a video I shot from long range. I would tell you who they are, but it's self-explanatory. An image of a woman of Hispanic descent came clearly into view. She was wearing a black one-piece bathing suit and was standing on a dock.

"Son of a bitch, if it isn't Louisa Sanchez," Fish exclaimed.

Before Louisa Sanchez could dive into the lake, a man walked up behind her. He kissed her neck and put his arms around the waist.

"You've got to be fucking kidding me. It's TJ Ingles. I was a pallbearer at his funeral," Hawk exclaimed.

"You're right, Hawk, it is TJ. He must be involved in this mess."

"Ben, this is Caleb. Do you think they suspect they are being watched?"

"I highly doubt it, Caleb. They have been moving in and out of the house like they don't have a care in the world."

"Ben, is there anyone else with them?"

"I don't think so. My thermal imaging system is only picking up two people."

"I am sending a group led by Detective Fisher your way. They should be there in about three hours. Please wait until they get there."

"Sure thing. Jenny and I are at the Sage and Sand Motel at 1110 S. Pioneer Way in Lakes Moses. We'll sit tight until they get here. I have remote surveillance set up on the Ingles property. I'll only move if they do."

"Great, Ben. Help is on the way."

"Fish, I want Hamilton and Connor to go along, but please keep them away from the property until the scene is secure," Caleb instructed.

"Not a problem, Caleb."

2015 North East Lake Road

Ben Silver stopped down the street from the Ingles family property. He got out of the car and took out a bulletproof vest.

"Where's my vest?" Jenny Silver asked.

"I think you should sit this one out, Jen."

"I don't want to sit this one out, Ben."

From behind Jenny, a voice spoke out.

"Ben is right, Jenny. You should sit this one out. The Moses Lake Police Department is backing us up." Fish agreed.

"Fine, Fish. I don't like it at all, but I will sit this one out. Only as long as you guys promise to protect Ben. Our baby is going to need a father."

"We'll do our best, Jenny," Hawk said.

"Ben, how many are in the house?"

"I believe there are still just two people."

"I can't believe TJ Ingles is still alive. I went to the funeral for that son of a bitch."

"We all did, Fish."

"It sucks to be you right now, doesn't it, Fish?"

"Why do you say that, Ben?"

"You're going to have to break the news to Barbara."

"We'll see about that. Are you ready to go?"

"I'm ready."

"Ben, you and I are going in through the front door while Hawk covers the back with the locals."

Fish and Ben approached the front door. Fish turned the handle. The door was unlocked. They opened the door quietly and entered the living room. Noises were coming from one of the bedrooms down the hall. They crept toward the sounds. A woman was on her knees between the legs of a man. His eyes were closed.

"Hello, TJ. You look pretty good for a dead guy," Fish said.

The girl started to lift her head to look. TJ pushed her head back down.

"Don't stop now, Louisa," TJ uttered.

Fish walked over, grabbed Louisa Sanchez, and placed a gun at her side.

"Get up, Ms. Sanchez. You're done whether TJ wants you to be or not."

Louisa Sanchez stood. Ben handed her the clothes that were on the bed. "Get dressed." Ben began reading Louisa Sanchez her rights. Fish pulled TJ Ingles to his feet, pulled his hands behind his back, and handcuffed him.

"Come on, Fish, aren't you going to read me my rights?"

"As far as I know, TJ, you don't have any rights." Fish placed his gun under TJ's chin.

"In fact, TJ, I don't think I would even get in trouble for killing you since you're already dead. Would I?"

"I know you, Fish, you won't shoot me."

Fish pressed his gun a little deeper into TJ's chin.

"It would be nothing less than what you deserve, you bastard. I went to your funeral. I don't have any more tears to shed for you."

"You have to understand the position I was in, Fish. I was gone undercover so much that I lost who I was. When I was home, I felt so out of place. I didn't know my family anymore. I didn't mean to hurt them."

"I'm sorry, TJ, I don't understand it—not in the least. All I see before me is someone who is half the man I thought he was. So, tell me who the hell is behind all of this?"

"I'm sorry, Fish, I can't."

"You can't or won't?"

"I can't because I don't know who is at the top."

"How do you get your orders, TJ?"

"I have a locker at the Seattle train station. Once a week, I go there and pick up information."

"What kind of information are they supplying you with, TJ?"

"Who the next target is, and where they are."

"TJ, how are you getting paid?"

"I have a Swiss bank account. Money is deposited into it every month."

"Who was your next target?"

"Your girl, Fish."

"My girl?"

"Yeah, your girl Hailey. She's on the run. They'll get to her before you do."

"I doubt it."

"Fish, you have no idea what these people are capable of. Trust me, they will keep trying until they succeed. Fish, can I ask you a question."

"You can ask, but I'm not sure I'll answer."

"That Hailey is a sweet young thing. Is she as good in bed as she looks like she would be?"

Fish hit TJ in the solar plexus harder than he had ever hit anyone in his life. TJ was struggling to breathe.

"You know she's my daughter, dickhead."

"Doesn't mean you haven't tapped into it, Fish."

Fish hit TJ in the jaw, knocking him over.

"TJ, you're an asshole."

TJ struggled to get back on his feet. Fish helped pull him to a standing position.

"Gee Fish, I thought we were friends."

"Barbara was the best part of you. Give me something to help our investigation."

Before TJ could answer, the window in the room exploded. Glass shards flew everywhere. Some of the shards ripped into Fish. Fish grabbed TJ to pull him down to safety. He was too late. Blood was already gushing from a bullet wound in his chest. Fish pressed his hand down over the hole in TJ's chest.

"Hold on, TJ. Help is on the way."

TJ whispered into Fish's ear.

"You need to find Trinity."

"What's Trinity TJ?"

He received no answer. TJ had already bled to death. Ben had pulled Louisa Sanchez to the floor and was using his body to protect her. Multiple shots rang out. Ben and Fish waited for them to end. After a few minutes, they could hear footsteps and then a familiar voice.

"Are you guys okay?"

"We're in here, Jenny. We're alright, but Ingles is dead. Did you see the shooter?" asked Ben.

"Ben, I saw the flash from the gun. It was a long way off."

"Jen, do you know where Hawk is?"

"He and the two police officers went after the shooter. Fish, you need medical attention."

"Why is that?"

"You're bleeding. You should get it looked at. I'll call an ambulance."

Within twenty minutes, the paramedics arrived and patched Fish up. Hawk came bounding into the room where they were working on his partner.

"Wow, Fish, you look like shit."

"Thanks for the vote of confidence, Hawk."

"Not a problem." Hawk looked over at TJ's lifeless body. "Is he dead or just mostly dead?"

"He's dead this time, Hawk."

"What do we do from here?"

"Caleb wanted these two brought in. At least we can bring Louisa in."

Hawk walked over to Louisa Sanchez.

"Louisa, what about the girls you were keeping locked up in your house?"

"I don't know anything about any girls," she replied.

"We found a notebook with the names of girls in it. They all claimed they were held against their will."

"I have no idea what you're talking about."

"Look, if you help us locate them, we might be able to get your sentence reduced," Hawk offered.

"I've got nothing to say except I want a lawyer."

"Hawk, there is no use in trying to get her to talk."

Hawk and Fish opened the front door of the house and stepped outside with their prisoner in tow.

"Detective Fisher, is it alright if I go in? I would like to take a look around."

"Go ahead, Connor, but you should wear these."

Detective Fisher handed Connor a pair of latex gloves.

"Hawk, did you guys find anything on the shooter?" Fish asked.

"No. We found where we thought the shooter was, but there was no physical evidence. I'm sure the shooter was a professional," Hawk answered.

"What now?" Jenny asked

"I spoke with Caleb. Hawk and I will head back to the office as soon as Connor is done inside. He recommended you guys be available."

"I bet Caleb isn't happy about our dead suspect."

"I wouldn't expect him to be. I think he's more concerned about how the people behind this are on top of our every move."

"Fish, what does Caleb want us to do?" Jenny asked.

"I'm not sure how he wants to utilize you two at the moment."

"Ben and I will head home until someone tells us where we're needed."

After twenty minutes, Connor and Hamilton came out. Fish was drinking bottled water as the two approached the car. He stopped drinking and looked at Connor.

"Detectives, for some reason, I'm not drawing any feelings from being here. I don't know what to think at this point."

"Connor, it's been a long day. I suggest we head back to Seattle and get a good night's sleep. It may be the last one we're able to get for a while."

Chapter 36

SPD War Room Next Day

Fish escorted his daughter into the war room, followed by Connor and Hamilton. Caleb was stirring a cup of coffee as the group walked on. He walked over to where Hailey Fisher was standing with her father.

"I'm happy you're safely back in Seattle, Hailey."

Hailey slapped Caleb across his face. The blow sent half of the coffee from Caleb's cup onto the floor and the large table in the war room.

"You son of a bitch, Captain Clarke. My friends and everything I've worked for are gone," Hailey said through tears. "I should have been one of them. I should have died on that roof. I'll have to live with that for the rest of my life."

Caleb looked at Hailey. His heart sank into the pit of his stomach as he tried to search for something to say.

"Hailey, you need to understand that if I thought the task I gave you was going to end up in such a senseless tragedy, I would never have asked you to do it. Please, don't let the deaths of your friends be in vain."

Hailey removed a memory stick from her pocket and slid it across the table to Caleb.

"What's on this, Hailey?"

"It's the information you wanted, Caleb. It's what I found on John Pierce and a supposedly dead special officer named Gary Danzig. But I will save you the trouble of even looking at the information. I know it like the back of my hand."

"If you know it so well, Hailey, go ahead and enlighten us."

"Captain Clarke, John Pierce owned Imagine Electronics, but more importantly, I was able to trace where his money came from. It took some time, but his funding was routed through a bunch of shell companies that all led to Albertus Magnusson."

"Albertus Magnusson, the reclusive billionaire?"

"That would be the one. Captain, it seems that he is a silent shareholder in a lot of biotechnical companies involved in leading-edge research."

"Hailey, I don't believe there is anything wrong with a rich person investing in the future of technology."

"You're right, Captain Clarke. There isn't anything wrong with investing your money in future technologies. But what if I told you the reason he's investing is that his son has a rare but undisclosed genetic disorder that will take his life within the next five years? If I were in his shoes, and money was no object, I would be exhausting every effort to find a cure for him as well."

"It still doesn't tie him to the case we're trying to solve. It just makes him a desperate father."

"Maybe what I'm going to tell you next will help tie the noose around his neck. Gary Danzig is still alive and on a project funded by Albertus Magnusson with the code name Trinity."

"Are you sure about that, Hailey?"

"I'm positive, Dad. I owe it all to you. Remember when I was young, you would make special treasure hunts for me?"

"I remember those hunts were fun, weren't they?"

"When I think about those hunts now, Dad, I realize you were trying to help me. You would work with me to look at the clues as a picture rather than separate events. When I looked at all the clues in total, it led me to Project Trinity. Dad, what is important about Project Trinity?"

"Hailey, everyone in this room is here for one thing. We're trying to solve a series of murders that may lead us to some missing girls, including your cousin Cassie. That's why we have to be one hundred percent sure of your analysis."

"I'm sure about my analysis. I am my father's daughter, after all."

"Hailey, it is my humble opinion you are exactly like your father. If you say you're sure that's good enough for me," Caleb interjected.

"Thanks, Caleb. It means a lot to me that you said that. I will, however, always hold you responsible for the death of my friends."

"I wish I could rewind the clock for you, Hailey, but I can't. With this new information, we need to put a full court press on finding out the what, where, and when about Project Trinity."

Caleb reached over, wrapped his arms around Hailey and hugged her.

"Fish, I know you and Hawk have been over all the evidence in your sister's case multiple times. Since Albertus Magnusson is seeking a genetic solution for his son, maybe it's time you two revisit Gentec."

Mark loudly cleared his throat. Caleb's attention turned to Mark.

"Is there something you would like to add to this conversation, Mark?"

"Yes, Caleb, there is. If you do what you have always done, you're going to get the same results."

"What's your point?"

"How many times have Detectives Fisher and Steinbrenner visited Gentec?"

"Fish and I have made three visits to Gentec to date, Mark. What would you have us do differently?"

"I'm an investigative reporter, Detective Steinbrenner. Why not let me do what I do best and go interview them. If the company is involved, maybe we can trip them up."

"I know Connor and I are consultants, Caleb, but I think Mark has a point. If you send detectives in, they are going to be tight-lipped. We might get farther with Mark asking the questions. Connor and I can go in with him and act as his camera crew."

"Hamilton, I can see you going in with Mark, but I'm not so sure about Connor. I'm sure someone at Gentec will recognize him."

"Caleb, we have a great makeup artist at the paper. I'm sure my editor won't have a problem lending assistance. I don't think that when we're done, anyone will recognize either Hamilton or Connor. With Connor there, maybe he will pick up something that will help the investigation."

"Fish, what do you and Hawk think about Mark's proposal?"

"Caleb, it's worth a shot. What do you think, Hawk?"

"I say, let's go."

Caleb turned to Mark and studied his face for a moment.

"Alright, Mark, we'll try it your way. How soon can we get ready to go?"

Mark looked at his watch and answered Caleb.

"It's nine-thirty right now. How about we shoot for one o'clock this afternoon."

"Good, Mark. I can have our tech guys set them up with listening devices. I can have the surveillance truck in place ahead of time. I'm sure there must be some road work in order."

"Caleb, can I ask you a question?"

"Sure."

"Can I go along in the van with my dad?"

"I know that you feel safer with your dad, Hailey, but I'm sure you would be safer here."

"I want to go along so I can help."

"Just how do you think going along will help?

"Caleb, the van is going to be parked fairly close to Gentec, won't it?"

"As close as we can get it without being too obvious. What are you thinking?"

"If we get close enough and Mark gives me enough time, I could hack Gentec's computers, looking for any information that would help your case."

"I'm sorry, Hailey. I'm not going to let Caleb put you in harm's way again."

"Dad, like it or not, I'm already in this mess up to my eyeballs. So please, for once, trust me."

"I do trust you. I just want to protect you the best way I know how."

"You're going to be with me in the van, aren't you, Dad?"

"Of course I will."

"I won't need much time to get in and get out. So, we can give Mark as much time as he needs before I start to hack their intranet. You just have to be ready to go if I say we need to go."

"I guess we can do it your way, Hailey."

"Thanks, Dad. I love you."

"I love you too, Hailey."

Two and a half hours later, Mark, Hamilton, and Connor were standing at Mark's desk. Mark was showing them how to run the equipment they would be using when Sienna stopped by.

"Mark, when you get to Gentec, ask for Karen Upshaw. She's their public relations person."

Sienna looked at Mark's aides.

"Mark, these guys aren't your regular crew. Would you care to introduce me?"

Hamilton clutched his heart and pretended to swoon. A look of shock came across Sienna's face.

"Oh my god, are you alright?"

"Yes, Ms. Jones. It's just my heart you've crushed."

"I'm sorry, I don't understand."

"I was sure that it was love at first sight. Now I'm not so sure."

Siena studied the man in front of her. After a moment, she laughed and placed her hand on Hamilton's arm.

"Oh my god, Hamilton, I'm so sorry. Please accept my apologies."

Siena then turned to Connor, who was completely bald, cleanly shaven, and wearing dark sunglasses.

"Mr. Darke, if it wasn't for the fact that you're here with Mr. Gardner."

"I'm sorry to disappoint you, Sienna, but that's not Connor Darke," Mark replied.

"It's not? Well, I guess I'm just hell-bent on making a complete fool of myself."

"If you're a fool, Sienna, then you happen to be the most beautiful fool I've ever seen," Hamilton wooed.

Connor, Hamilton, and Mark laughed at Sienna.

"Gotcha.," they chimed in unison.

Chapter 37

The Stakeout

The State of Washington, Department of Public Works, van pulled over and parked within a quarter mile of the Gentec facility. Two workers in dark gray overalls got out, took out four traffic cones, and placed them in the back and the front of the van. Inside the van, Fish and Hawk were turning on surveillance equipment. They sat down at the console and donned earphones that were equipped with microphones. A car driven by Mark passed the Department of Public Works van and turned into the Gentec parking lot. The strap of the camera bag that Hamilton Gardner carried over his shoulder contained a built-in camera.

"Hamilton's camera is working fine, Fish. Do you want to go ahead with the audio check?"

Fish spoke into his microphone as the trio approached the entrance to the building.

"Mark, if you can hear me, I want you to pat Hamilton on the back as he opens the door for you."

Hamilton grabbed the handle and pulled the door open. Mark patted him on the back.

"We've got visual confirmation from Mark. He can hear us."

Hawk turned and looked at Fish and chuckled lightly.

"Hey, Fish, did you get a good look at Hamilton? He looks like he's part of a motorcycle gang."

The two detectives watched as the trio disappeared inside the building. They listened to Mark as he entered.

"Good afternoon, Shelley. I'm Mark Brandt from the Seattle Times."

The receptionist studied Mark's face and then looked at Hamilton and Connor.

"I know you don't remember me, Mr. Brandt, but you and I have met before."

Mark ran his hand through his hair and smiled at her.

"Your name is Shelley Cook, if I remember correctly."

"That's right, Mr. Brandt, it is."

"Shelley, I have a one o'clock appointment with Karen Upshaw. Is she available?"

"Karen is expecting you and will be here momentarily. You can have a seat if you want."

"I prefer to stand."

While he was waiting, Mark started reading one of the multiple patent plaques hung on the wall. A door opened, and a woman in her early fifties approached.

"Mr. Brandt, I'm Karen Upshawthe public affairs officer for Gentec. At Gentec, we pride ourselves on doing the impossible. So, where would you like to start?"

"Perhaps we can start my interview here, Ms. Upshaw."

Mark pointed to the patent plaques adorning the walls.

"Ms. Upshaw, the business here is genetic engineering, isn't it?"

"Yes, it is, Mark. How about I give you a quick tour of our facility first, and then I'll answer your questions."

Karen Upshaw looked at the equipment bags that Hamilton and Connor were carrying.

"Mark, you won't be able to take any pictures or video. Your crew is welcome to come along, but their equipment stays here. I will provide you a DVD with a company profile when you are through. Shall we?"

"Please lead the way, Ms. Upshaw."

Karen Upshaw passed her badge over a card reader next to the door that allowed access to the bowels of the building.

"The hallway to the left is where the offices are located, and the hallway to the right is where our laboratory does all our testing. Because of the nature of the work done here, you will only be able to see the lab through the glass."

The group, led by Karen Upshaw, walked down the hallway and stopped in front of the lab window.

"These labs, gentlemen, are the heart and soul of Gentec. You can see by the signs the lab is divided into three main areas. The area to the right is dedicated to working on genetically improving crops such as per acre yield and nutrient content. We strive to make it drought and blight-resistant. The center part is used for work on animal genetics, and the area to the left is where our genetic sequencing areas are."

"Does Gentec have a direct partnership with outside labs, or is your business a dog-eat-dog kind of world?"

"Mark, some projects we get are divided among different labs because the complexity of the task can't be handled by one lab."

Detective Fisher spoke to Mark Brandt through his earbud.

"Mark, please take your time."

Hailey, who was now watching the video feed from inside Gentec, grabbed her dad's shoulder.

"Dad, those hidden cameras were a great idea. Can you back up the video?"

"I can, Hailey, but what are you looking for?"

Fish reversed the recording.

"Dad, pause the video, please."

"Oh, my God, Dad, it's him."

"It's who, Hailey?"

"Dad, I saw him in the lobby of the computer technology building at Carnegie Mellon."

"Fish, I'm going to capture his image and run it against the database."

The computer in the van started crunching the man's image against the national database. After fifteen minutes, it stopped and flashed wanted with a name.

"Fish, this guy used to be an enforcer for the Russian mob. This guy must be onboard to protect Gentec. Do you think we should call this into Caleb and have him picked up?"

"Hawk, if we have him picked up now, it might spook the people at Gentec. We need to get them to show us their hand. Let's call Caleb and get him to set up a routine traffic stop to check licenses and registration. Instead of arresting him now, we can use the traffic stop to tag the vehicle he's driving. He might lead us to who and what we're looking for."

"Hailey, are you positive this is the guy you saw in Pittsburgh?" Fish asked.

Hailey shook her head yes in acknowledgment.

"Hawk, I'm going to call Caleb and advise him of the situation."

Fish called Caleb about finding a wanted fugitive.

"Hawk, Caleb agrees with setting up the traffic stop. He also wants to put a tail on Karen Upshaw. I'm going to let Mark know he needs to wrap it up."

Fish spoke through his headset to Mark.

"Mark, you need to move this interview along and wrap it up."

"Shall we move back up front and continue the interview out in the lobby."

In less than two minutes, the group was standing in the lobby. Mark pointed to the patent plaques hanging on the wall.

"Do you mind if I take a couple of minutes and read some more of these patents?"

"You can read as many as you like, Mr. Brandt."

Mark read the next six patent plaques and stopped and looked at Karen Upshaw."

"I'm not an engineer, Ms. Upshaw, so some of the terminology on these plaques is above my level of comprehension. I get the distinct impression your company uses genetics to improve things. Is that right?"

"Mark, the aim at Gentec is to improve things through genetics."

"I happen to see that most of your patents were awarded to Charles Surley. I see that a few of them were awarded to Mika Pence. I would like to interview Mr. Pence if possible."

"Mr. Pence is at a Genetics conference, so you will have to settle for me."

"Is Mr. Pence your lead engineer?"

"Since the death of Mr. Surley, yes. Mr. Pence and Mr. Surley formed Gentec while they were in college together at Harvard."

Hailey started typing feverishly on her computer keyboard. After a minute or so, she yelled out an aha.

"Do you have something for us, Hailey?"

"Dad, she's lying about Mika Pence. There is no record of a Mika Pence ever attending Harvard."

"Hailey, you hacked Harvard that quickly?"

"My search was above board, Dad. I just chatted with a guy I know in admissions there."

"How on earth do you know a guy in admissions at Harvard?"

"Dad, now is not the time to discuss who I know and why."

Hailey went back to typing on her computer. Fish spoke into the microphone.

"Mark, she's lying about Mika Pence ever attending Harvard. Use the information if you need to."

Mark smiled at Karen Upshaw.

"Ms. Upshaw, how has the death of Charles Surley affected the growth of Gentec?"

"Although the death of Charles Surley couldn't have come at a worse time, we have been able to expand our business by finding clients who wanted to take advantage of his work. Our growth has been steady."

"Ms. Upshaw, does your company perform Gentec engineering on anything other than animals or plants?"

"Mr. Brandt, if you're asking if we perform genetic engineering on humans, the answer would be a resounding no. The only aspect of human engineering we do is to provide validations for universities that are doing DNA research."

"Mark, here is a DVD that will give you some insight into what we do."

Karen Upshaw handed Mark the DVD.

"Mark, I have a tight schedule. Is there anything else I can answer for you quickly?"

Karen glanced at her watch and then shot a very frustrated look at Mark.

"Ms. Upshaw? Do you know who Albertus Magnusson is?"

"Doesn't everybody, Mark? The man has more money than God."

"Ms. Upshaw, is he one of Gentec's investors?"

Karen looked at a message on her phone.

"Dad, we've got to go and go now!"

"What's wrong, Hailey?"

"Don't ask, just go."

Fish banged on the side of the van, and the two maintenance workers who were attending to the pothole put away their tools, got in, and prepared to head back to headquarters. Karen Upshaw closed her phone and looked at Mark.

"My apologies, Mark. what was your question?"

"I asked you if Albertus Magnusson is one of Gentec's investors?"

Karen paused for a long moment before she answered.

"I am not at liberty to discuss any of our investors with you, Mark."

"Are you going to deny that Gentec is performing research to save Albertus Magnusson's son?

"As I have said before, we don't experiment on human subjects."

"Come on Karen, we all know for the right price that anyone or any company can be bought."

"This interview is over, Mark."

"Why, what's wrong?"

"This interview is beginning to sound like an inquisition to me. You and your crew can see yourselves out."

Mark left the building, followed by Hamilton and Connor.

"Mark, why don't you give me your car keys?"

"What on earth for, Hamilton?"

"Because we have to make a fast exit. I bet you didn't realize the cameras in the lobby were following our every move."

Mark handed him the keys.

"You won't get any arguments from me, Hamilton."

The car was pulling out of the Gentec parking lot. Mark, who was now sitting in the passenger seat, turned and looked at Connor, who was sitting in the backseat.

"I certainly hit a sore spot with Karen Upshaw when I started asking about Albertus Magnusson, didn't I?"

"You certainly did, Mark. Based on the look on Karen Upshaw's face, Mr. Magnusson has his fingers into Gentec."

"Mark, Ms. Upshaw was also lying about Mike Pence."

"I know she was, Connor. Fish told me through my earbud she was lying about him."

Chapter 38

The Department of Public Works van turned around and shot past Gentec in the direction that Hamilton was going.

"Why did you want us to leave in such a hurry, Hailey?"

"Dad, I was in the middle of downloading some files from Gentec."

"Who the hell told you to hack Gentec's computer?"

"I'm sorry, Dad, I had to."

Fish began yelling at his daughter.

"Why did you think you had to, Hailey? The problem becomes that we can't use any information that you might find against Gentec in a court of law because of how it was obtained."

"I said, I'm sorry, Dad."

Hawk took off his headset and looked at his partner.

"Ken, I know this isn't any of my business, but maybe you should lighten up a little."

"You're right, Eric, it isn't any of your business, so butt out."

Ken looked at his partner and then looked at his daughter.

"I guess I didn't handle things very well, Hailey. I'll try harder to temper my emotions.

"Dad, I just wanted to find out if there is a connection between what happened to my friends and

Gentec. Somebody is responsible, and I want you to make them pay, Dad."

"Did you at least get something useful?"

"It wasn't easy for me to get through Gentec's firewall. I was shocked at how quickly they started chewing through my routing. Whoever is watching their system is smart. I didn't even get a chance to download the folder completely. I shut off my router before I was discovered."

"That's not what I asked you. Did you find anything important?"

"I'm not sure. I have to find a way to unlock the folders I copied."

"Start working on unlocking files while I call Caleb and get the traffic stop set up."

Fish called Caleb and spent ten minutes updating him on the situation at Gentec. Hailey looked at her father with an inquisitive look on her face.

"What's next, Dad?"

"We're going back to the office so we can all regroup with Caleb. Please keep working on breaking the encryption on those files."

Within forty minutes, they were walking into the war room. Caleb was wringing his hands as they walked in.

"Is everything alright, Caleb?"

"No, not exactly. Fish, Mark is on his way to the hospital for surgery at the moment."

"What happened?"

"Mark and company were pursued by two men in a black BMW when they left Gentec. Their pursuers were intent on not letting them get away, so they started shooting. Mark took a bullet through his shoulder. Luckily for them, Hamilton was driving."

"Have we caught the shooters yet?"

"Not yet, Fish, but thanks to Hamilton, we were able to get a good description of the shooters and the car. We'll catch them."

"Caleb, which hospital did they head for?"

"Northwest Medical Center. Hamilton and Connor are on their way and will be here shortly."

"You know, doesn't it seem odd that someone seems to be on top of our every move?"

"I've been thinking the same, Hawk, so I have been watching anyone TJ was close to."

"TJ was so abrasive that I don't believe he had any close friends, Caleb."

"It would take a lot of time to look at everyone. So, where do you suggest we start?"

"Maybe we should start with his partner. If he was hopping into bed with Louisa Sanchez, he might have been in her bed as well."

Caleb typed the extension for the duty officer into the hands-free phone. A male voice answered.

"This is Officer Wentz."

"This is Captain Clarke. I would like you to find Detective Janet Larkin for me."

"Caleb, we haven't heard from her since she asked for time off three days ago. Your guess is as good as mine where she might be."

"I would appreciate it if you would get her back in."

"I'll give it a try, Captain. What reason should I give for cutting her time off short?"

"Tell her whatever you want to, just get her here."

"I'll do my best, sir."

Hamilton and Connor were standing in the doorway. Caleb looked over at Hamilton and Connor.

"Which one of you is going to tell me about Mark's condition?"

Hamilton spoke up.

"The bullet went clean through Mark's shoulder, Caleb. Luckily, the bullet missed anything vital on its way through. I used the car as a battering ram to drive our pursuers off the road. Did we have any luck picking them up?"

"The car was empty. I have patrols out sweeping the area."

"What's going on here?"

"We were just discussing the possibility that we might have a mole inside our ranks. It seems to me that we have been one step behind throughout this investigation," Caleb explained to Hamilton.

"Do you have any idea where the leak is coming from?"

"We are looking at his ex-partner as possibly being the leak. She called in to get a day off three days ago, but we haven't heard from her since."

Caleb looked over at Connor, who seemed to be genuinely disturbed.

"Are you alright, Connor?"

Connor remained motionless for two minutes before he finally answered Caleb.

"I'm sorry, Captain. What did you ask me?"

"I asked if you are okay?"

"I'm fine, Captain. Do you have a picture of your missing detective?"

"I can pull one from her file. It will take a second or two for me to put it on screen one."

Screen one sprang to life with an image of a woman in uniform.

Connor stared at the image for a long time.

"Have you seen her before, Connor?"

Connor, who was still deep in thought, nodded to Captain Clarke.

"Where have you seen her, Connor? I need to know."

"In my head, Captain. She was with one of the girls I've seen in my head. You can call back the car you sent to pick her up.; It won't be necessary."

"Why, Connor, is she on her way here?"

"No, she isn't. Detective Larkin is already dead."

"Are you sure?"

"Detective Larkin says to tell you that she's sorry."

"Shit, our leads are disappearing faster than we can find them."

The phone in the conference room started ringing. Caleb pressed the answer button.

"Go for Captain Clarke."

"Captain Clarke, this is Officer Davis. Per your request, we have set up the traffic stops on either end of the road in front of Gentec."

"Do you have something to report, Officer Davis?"

"Vladimir Petrovich passed through the checkpoint about fifteen minutes ago. We were able to tag the car he was driving. It's working well. You should have no problems picking up the signal."

"That's great, Officer. Hang on a second. I'll open the program. I am picking up a strong signal, Officer Davis. Thank you for a job well done."

"No problem, Captain. The suspect was carrying a valid State of Washington driver's license. I've sent a

copy of it to your inbox along with the vehicle description."

"That's great, Officer Davis."

"Captain, Karen Upshaw is with him."

"So noted, Officer."

"Hopefully, if all goes well, our two birds of flight will lead us to enough information that the stuff Hailey picked up in her foray into Gentec's mainframe won't matter," Caleb said to the group after hanging up.

"It could also be a dead-end, Caleb."

"Let's hope not. We need a break."

Hawk pointed at the on-screen image one.

"Captain, the blip isn't moving."

A pointer appeared next to the stationary pulsing blip on-screen one. The words 309 Cloverdale St Building E were next to the arrow. Caleb pressed a button on the phone; it began to ring and was answered on the third one.

"This is dispatch, Officer Schultz."

"Officer Schultz, this Captain Clarke. I need patrol cars sent to the Cloverdale Business Park. I want all of the entrances and exits blocked until Detectives Fisher and Steinbrenner get there. I want no one allowed in or out. Do you understand?"

"Perfectly, sir. I'll get cars dispatched immediately."

"Thank you, Officer Shultz."

Caleb turned off the phone and looked at Fish and Hawk and pointed a finger at them.

"Alright, gentlemen, let's get a move on it.

"Caleb, what about Hamilton and Connor?"

"Hawk, they are going to come with me. We'll keep a safe distance until the area is secure."

Within thirty minutes, two cars pulled up to the Cloverdale Street entrance of the business park. An officer got out of his car as they pulled up. Fish rolled down the window and held out his badge as the officer approached.

"What's the situation, Detective Fisher?"

"Gentlemen, we have a suspect in a murder investigation somewhere near office number 4 in the E row."

Fish pointed to the position on the map of office E4.

"My partner and I will move in from the far end of the E office row. I want you and your partner to position yourselves behind the E row in case they try to exit through the back door. This is a dangerous situation, so everyone needs to approach with caution. Is that understood?'

The officer uttered a resounding yes.

"Detective Fisher, what about back up in case things go south on us?"

"Hopefully, things won't go badly, Officer. We are going to proceed on a silent count, so I want everyone in position within ten minutes. Please approach silently and with caution. Let's move, gentlemen."

Ten minutes later, the two detectives were slowly approaching the car that Vladimir Petrovich was driving. Within fifteen feet of the vehicle, the door to E4 opened, and Petrovich was carrying a stack of boxes to the car. He placed them in the trunk. Fish called out to him.

"Vladimir Petrovich, I am with the Seattle Police Department, and I would like to ask you a question or two."

Petrovich glanced around and saw the two officers behind him and the two detectives in front of him. He started to raise his hands but stopped and retrieved a gun from a holster inside his vest. One of the two officers yelled for Petrovich to drop the weapon, but instead, he aimed it at Hawk as he approached. Four shots rang out in succession. The last two shots fatally struck Petrovich. One of the two officers yelled the suspect is done. The detectives moved to where the suspect had fallen. Hawk knelt and checked the fallen suspect for a pulse.

"Fish, he's gone."

"Damn it. I wanted to get this guy alive."

Fish looked over at the wide open front door of the office. He glanced at the two officers who were standing next to the body.

"I have no idea of how many people are inside but expect that we will encounter another suspect. So, please remain alert, gentlemen," Fish instructed.

They moved into the office. There was a wall with a door in it. A loud, whirring sound could be heard from where they stood. They approached the door wall and opened it slowly. A man was standing next to a woman, who were standing in front of a shredder feverishly feeding documents into it.

"This is the Seattle Police Department. Stop what you're doing, and slowly turn around."

The two stopped shredding documents and slowly turned around to face the officers. Fish recognized Karen Upshaw. He studied the face of the man standing next to her, and then turned to Karen Upshaw and proceeded to read her rights. When he was done, he handcuffed her and spoke as he turned towards the officer.

"Officer, would you take Ms. Upshaw to your patrol car and stay with her until we're finished here?"

"No problem, Detective."

The officer led Karen Upshaw from the building. Fish moved over and again stared at the man and let out a long string of expletives.

"You're the last person I expected to see standing in front of me, Charles."

"My name is Pence, Mika Pence."

"You can cut the crap, Charles. I know for a fact you're not Mika Pence."

The man stood motionless and utterly silent as Fish continued to look at him.

"I've got to hand it to you, Charles. I almost didn't recognize you. The plastic surgery and the hair color change almost had me fooled."

The man in front of Fish remained silent and unmoving.

"I'm sure you're wondering how I knew it was you aren't you, Charles? It 's amost impossible to pick up the tell of a great poker player. Do you want to know what I picked up on?"

Fish moved within a few inches of the man and spoke.

"It was your eyes, Charles. There is nothing you can do or say to convince me that you're not Charles Surley."

Charles moved his eyes rapidly back and forth and then gulped.

"Hello. Ken. I'm surprised to see you here."

"Not as surprised as I am to see you, Charles. You look pretty good for a dead guy."

"I wish I could say the same about you, Ken. You look tired. Aren't you sleeping well?"

Fish threw an uppercut, catching Charles in the jaw, dragged him to his feet and was about to strike a third blow when Hawk intervened.

"Fish, you can't beat him to death."

"Leave me alone, Hawk. I can beat the crap out of him if I want to."

"Look, Fish, you're skating on thin ice with anger management issues as it is. We need your brother-in-law alive so we can close this case. You won't give Caleb a choice if you don't stop beating him."

"Choice? What about my sister Hawk? Do you think she had a choice? I need to do this for her."

"Killing Charles isn't going to bring her back, Fish."

"You're right. It won't bring her back, but it will sure make me feel a lot better."

"It will only make you feel better for a little while. After the euphoria over killing Charles is over, the pain of her death will still be there."

"I'm willing to take that risk, Hawk."

A voice then came from behind the detectives.

"You don't want to kill him, Detective Fisher."

Fish spun around and looked at Connor Darke, who was standing in the doorway.

"Stay out of this, Mr. Darke. The way I see it, he's already dead. If you're going to tell me something like I don't have it in me to kill him, you can save your breath because I'm not interested."

"Detective Fisher, I was going to tell you that she doesn't want you to kill him."

"Who doesn't want me to kill him?"

"Your sister is begging you not to. She says he may be your best hope for finding Cassie.

"I just want to know one thing, Charles."

"What's would that be, Ken?"

"Why did you have her killed? She wouldn't have hurt anyone."

Charles looked at him and spoke without emotions.

"She would have ruined everything. What I did, I did to better all of humanity."

"You are a bastard, Charles."

"If I had to do it over again, I wouldn't change a thing."

"It's too bad you aren't going to have a chance to do it over again, Charles."

"Sure, I will, Ken. I have a mission to complete, and you won't be able to stop me."

"We'll see about that, Charles. You're under arrest."

Fish forcefully spun his brother-in-law around and handcuffed him.

"Did that hurt, Charles? Well, if it did, that's just too bad."

"What about my rights? You haven't read them to me yet."

"The way I look at is that you don't have any rights."

"Of course I do."

"Well, Charles, being that you're already dead, I'll give you the same rights you gave my sister. Which are exactly none? Trust me, before I'm done with you, you're going to beg me to kill you."

Chapter 39

Gertrude Lane's Penthouse, Downtown Seattle

The door opened to the room Charles Surley was in. An entourage led by Caleb Clarke walked in and sat down at the table, flanking either side of him. Charles Surley gazed slowly at each man. His gaze lingered for a long time on Connor Darke, trying to place where he knew him from.

Fish was the last to sit down. He was carrying a large box that he set on the table. He then sat down across from Charles and removed a file folder from the box.

"How many more hours do you intend on keeping me here?" Charles asked.

"Mr. Surley, you will be kept here until we are good and ready."

Charles looked at Caleb, who was speaking.

"Who the hell are you, and where am I?"

"I am Captain Caleb Clarke of the Seattle Police, Mr. Surley. As to where you are, that is entirely unimportant to you."

"I've been here for hours without any food or drink. Can I please have something to drink?"

Hamilton left the room. He returned carrying a bottle of water. He twisted off the cap and placed it in front of Charles, who looked at him and spoke.

"Would you mind taking the cuffs off so I can drink the water?"

Hamilton reached into his pocket and pulled out a long straw and placed it in the bottle of water. Caleb looked at Charles and spoke.

"This will have to do, Mr. Surley. The cuffs are staying on."

"You still haven't read me my rights, Captain Clarke. I have rights, you know."

"You're in a truly unique situation, Charles. You see, the body in your grave would have to be exhumed by your next of kin to confirm that Charles Surley is still alive before rights can be read to him. Seeing that Detective Fisher is your only next of kin, you know that's not going to happen. The bottom line is, you don't have any rights."

"You can't get away with this. It's against the law."

"We will get away with violating whatever rights you think you have."

"Karen Upshaw knows that you have me, and so will others, Captain Clarke."

"Since you brought her up, let's discuss Karen Upshaw for a moment, Charles. You see, Karen was all too willing to save her bacon, which included the fact that Charles Surley, the founder of Gentec, was, in fact, deceased. She is standing pat on the fact that we have Mika Pence, which we know not to be true. Officially, you're a non-existent person with exactly zero rights."

Charles screamed at the group of men gathered around the table.

"You can't do this. I have a mission to finish."

"Charles, Operation Trinity is going to be over soon."

Charles sneered as he spoke out.

"Like you think you can shut it down. I highly doubt it."

"Operation Trinity is going to be shut down with or without you."

"You can't shut it down. The government won't allow it."

"What makes you think they won't allow it to be shut down, Charles?"

"The work I'm doing is important to the government. They are the ones that funded it for Christ's sake."

"That's where you're wrong, Charles. There's an arrest warrant already out for Albertus Magnusson, your main supporter. The people in the government who authorized your funding didn't route your project through the proper channels. They hid the project in a bunch of different slush funds. I do have to admit that your ideas of being able to repair defective genes and using that technology to engineer a super soldier are quite impressive."

"But you see, Captain Clarke, that's why I have to be allowed to continue my research."

"There are at least fifty reasons why you won't be allowed to continue your research, Charles."

Caleb stood up, opened a manila folder, placed a picture on the table in front of Charles, and called out a name as he did.

"Benjamin Blake, the dentist who changed all the dental records. Charles, we found documents where you agreed to everything which makes you equally guilty of murder."

Charles looked at Caleb for a moment.

"He's dead?"

"So are his wife, daughter and next-door neighbor, and the hit parade goes on. The ones in front of you are just the tip of the iceberg."

Caleb placed more photos on the table in front of Charles, who stared at them for a long time. Charles looked up when he was done and spoke.

"I had no idea."

"Well, Charles, when you make a pact with the devil himself, this is what happens. You're an accessory to every murder that occurred. When we finish with the murder charges, we can add kidnapping, abuse, unlawful imprisonment, and a host of other charges dealing with the girls that you deprived of their innocence."

Caleb began placing pictures of girls in front of Charles and calling out names.

"Penny Harrington, Gabriela Smith, Dawn Fairbanks, Salina Green...."

Caleb stopped for a moment as Charles shouted out.

"They're all runaways who would never be missed."

Fish walked over with the last picture, which was a computer-generated picture of his niece and Charles's daughter. He grabbed Charles by the arm and spoke to him.

"Take a good look at this picture of your daughter, Charles. It will most likely be the last one you ever see of her."

Fish slammed the picture of his niece down on the table.

"You're her father, damn it! It was your duty to protect her, not take advantage of her."

Charles looked at his brother-in-law. There was no emotion on his face when he spoke.

"I needed her to prove my theories. It was the only way I could get the funding I needed."

Fish grabbed Charles by the throat and started to squeeze it. Charles began to choke and spoke in short, staccato breaths.

"Go ahead, Ken, get it over with. Don't stop now. You've always had trouble with finishing tasks."

Fish relaxed his grip on his brother-in-law's throat.

"No, Charles, I'm not going to kill you."

"See, it's just like I said, you don't like to finish things."

Fish lunged for his brother-in-law but was grabbed by Hawk and Hamilton.

"You guys need to let go of me."

"We're not letting go of you until you calm down."

Fish took a deep breath and relaxed.

"Fine, you two can have it your way."

"I might not be able to carry through with killing you, Charles, but I have a much better idea in store."

Fish walked over to where Charles sat and patted him on the back.

"You see, Charles, I do have something worthy of such a fine upstanding person like you."

Fish leaned in as close as he could to his brother-in-law's ear.

"I'm going to put you in Kandahar Prison and forget my family ever heard your name. You've heard of it, haven't you, Charles?"

Fish patted his brother-in-law on the back.

"After a week, you'll be begging for them to kill you. I'll make sure they keep you alive for their amusement."

"I'm an American citizen, you can't do that."

"Oh, really, are you sure about that, Charles?"

"I know you, Ken, your sister used to tell me you didn't have a mean bone in your body. You won't do this to me. You can't."

"I can't? That is why you're wrong, Charles. You see, I have anger management issues. I was always able to hide it from my family, and thanks to you, I don't have to."

"What about my rights as a human being?

Fish picked up the pile of the pictures and shook them at Charles.

"Rights, you think you have rights? The fact is, Charles, you violated the rights of all these young women, and I guess their rights trump yours. I like the fact that you're worried about what's going to happen to you. When and if the inmates grow tired of you, they will make sure to take care of your dead body and send it out with the trash."

"You won't do that. You need me to lead you to Cassie."

"That's where you're wrong. In the last few hours, we've been putting together a plan to raid the lab where you've been doing all your research."

"Ken, things are in motion that even the great Detective Ken Fisher can't stop."

Fish let out a laugh.

"You know Charles, you are a comedian."

"Do you want to tell him or shall I?

"You can tell him, Fish."

Fish grabbed Charles by the shoulder and squeezed.

"The man I pointed to Charles is Sir Hamilton Gardner. He despises people who prey on innocent children, and so do his friends at MI-6 in London. MI-6 has been watching your company with great interest. We know there isn't much time. We are planning a quick strike on your facility. You're going to see your life's work all unravel right before your eyes."

"The work I was doing was important. It has to go on."

Caleb moved in and looked at Charles, leaned over, and spoke to him.

"Charles, I have no doubt your research will go on in some form. As far as the government is concerned, they are washing their hands of everyone involved in your project."

There was a look of terror on Charles's face. Beads of sweat were forming on his brow. His voice was now quite shaky as he spoke.

"There must be some deal we can make. You want to make a deal, Charles?"

Charles nodded his head at Caleb.

"I doubt there is anything you can offer us that we can't get?"

"I can connect all the players and put them in one neat package for you, Captain Clarke."

Fish grabbed his brother-in-law by the chin and lifted it, sneering at him as he spoke.

"What's the matter, Charles? Don't you like the idea of being bent over and abused?"

"I was hoping to avoid that, Ken."

"I'll tell you what, Charles. Instead of me dropping you in jail in some third world toilet, how about I let every girl you kidnapped and used have their shot at you, and then I'll let them decide what do with you. If I were you, I would pick option A; it will probably be less painful."

There was no reply from Charles.

"Time to go, Charles."

Chapter 40

Operation Free Bird

Caleb stood in front of a group of about forty people in a hangar at the airport in Boise, Idaho. He looked around at the faces of the people in the crowd who were anxiously awaiting information.

"I would like to introduce General Rip Turner, who is going to lead this effort."

General Turner stood up and walked to the podium.

"Ladies and gentlemen, we are gathered here for an unprecedented operation on American soil. From this point forward, everything you hear, say, or do is classified as top secret. Does anyone have any problems with that?"

Not one responded.

"Good, I'm glad you are all on board. This is a rescue mission. We are going to free thirty-one young girls who are being held against their will. This has been designed as a quick strike mission. Once we reach the target, I expect to be in and out in less than thirty minutes. If you would please look at the screen behind me, I will show you our target."

A picture of the hospital and outbuildings in Trinity, Idaho, were displayed on the large screen.

"Ladies and gentlemen, our job is to go in neutralize the guards and staff, and then remove the girls. By the time we have stabilized the situation, buses will be there to bring the girls to a makeshift triage center that has been set up in the next hangar. The strike team has been divided into three groups— Alpha, Bravo, and Charley. The main purpose of the alpha group is to take out the guards in each one of the four-guard towers using tranquilizing rounds. Bravo group will lock down the two staff dormitories to keep the staff from being harmed or doing anything stupid. Charley group will go in and release the girls and escort them to safety. If you all do your jobs as you've been trained to do, this operation should go smoothly and as planned. Does anyone have any questions?"

A female soldier raised her hand. "General Turner, do you expect any shots will be fired?"

"I'm not going to lie to you. The people behind this project may go to great lengths to keep us out. If you're shot at, you have my permission to return fire. The reason we are going in at such a late hour is to minimize the risk because most of the staff will be asleep."

Another soldier raised his hand.

"General Turner, won't they know we're coming?"

"We're going to approach using new Stealth Helicopters. We intend on coming up this river gorge (pointing to a large map) and then rising over the mountains behind the facility. It's time to go. Alpha and Bravo groups will depart five minutes ahead of Charley group. I will land with Charley group and enter the main building."

The group started exiting the hangar to the waiting helicopters. Caleb walked over to Connor, who was walking toward the exit.

"I'm sorry, Mr. Darke, you have to sit this one out."

"Caleb, I have every right to go."

"You're right, Connor; you do deserve to go."

"So, why can't I go?"

"Connor, you're not trained for combat. I think you're going to be very busy after the retrieval."

"Can't I go and stay in the helicopter?"

"You can watch and listen to the entire operation from the mobile command center outside. I'm sorry, Connor, I have to go."

Caleb ran to the awaiting helicopter while Connor walked up and into the command center.

"Connor, dear boy, I'm so happy to see you."

Connor turned to his right and was staring directly at the face of Gertrude Lane.

"Gert, what on earth are you doing here?"

"Connor, all the king's men couldn't keep me away from this show."

Connor nervously looked around the room.

"Don't worry, dear boy; she's here. I'm sure she'll be back any minute."

The command center had a bank of eight monitors set up. A tall, lanky soldier with a headset motioned to Connor to sit down.

"Mr. Darke, you can watch and listen from here.," the young marine advised.

Connor sat down and watched the monitor. He felt a hand on his right arm. Julie was standing next to him. There was a tear in the corner of both her eyes.

"Julie, are you alright?"

"I'm fine, Connor."

"What are you crying about then?"

"For being a psychic, I swear you can still react like a man, Connor. I'm crying because I'm happy to see you and because I care about the safety of the girls."

Connor swept Julie up in his arms. He was having trouble finding the words he wanted to say. Julie could sense his bewilderment.

"It's going to be okay, Connor. It has to be okay."

"I know it will, Julie. Thanks for being here."

"Wild horses couldn't keep me away from this."

"Julie, I know this isn't how I imagined it would happen, but could I ask you a question?"

"Sure, you can, Connor. I don't have anything to hide."

"I never thought you did."

"What do you want to know then?"

"Julie, would you do me the honor of becoming Mrs. Darke?"

"I don't know, Connor."

"Why, I thought...."

Julie cut Connor off in mid-sentence. "It's just that I thought you would become Mr. Strand."

"I'll take the name of mud if you want. I can't live another moment without you."

"Don't be silly, Connor. I don't want to be Julie Mud. Julie Darke works just fine for me."

"So, it's a yes, then?"

"Connor, it's been yes ever since I first met you when I was fifteen."

"Me too."

Gertrude Lane, who had been watching, walked up and punched Connor."

"Ow! What the hell was that for, Gert?"

"For taking so long to ask her, you goof."

The head marine for the command center shouted out, "Five minutes and counting. Bring up the visual."

The lead helicopters were now over the hospital compound. When the countdown clock reached one minute, two voices were heard.

"Alpha team deploying. Bravo team is deploying."

The Charlie team's helicopter hovered in place while the Alpha and Bravo teams secured the hospital site. Within five minutes, the Charley team helicopter landed. General Turner led the group into the hospital. One of the Charley team members had a helmet video camera to enable viewing of the operation by people in the command center. The sentry on guard stood up and saluted General Turner.

"Open the doors, son."

"I'm sorry, General. I have explicit instructions that no one can enter without authorization."

General Turner removed a paper from his pocket and handed it to the sentry.

"Son, that is direct authorization from the President, who just happens to be the Commander in Chief of the combined Armed Services. I suggest you get these doors open immediately."

The sentry looked at the Executive order and then at the general and saluted.

"Yes, sir."

"One more thing, son. Where are the keys to all the rooms kept?"

"Keys?"

"I need all the interior doors unlocked."

"I can do it from here, sir."

"What are you waiting for, son? Get all the doors unlocked now! One more thing, son, until I get to the bottom of who is behind this mess, I'm restricting you to the barracks here. Do you understand?"

The sentry saluted General Turner.

"Yes, sir."

Fifteen minutes later, Connor, Julie, and Gertrude Lane watched as the last of the girls were loaded into the buses. Tears of joy were flowing freely down their faces.

Chapter 41

The Return

Four hours later, Caleb walked into the command center, followed by Fish and Hawk. Fish walked over to Connor. Without saying a word, he grabbed Connor and gave him a bear hug.

"Thank you, Connor. This wouldn't have been possible without you." Fish's voice was choppy and emotional as he tried to choke back tears of relief.

"How's your niece, Detective?"

Tears began welling up in the corner of Fish's eyes.

"She's confused, bewildered, and tired. She will need a lot of time to heal."

"I can't think of a better person to help her get through it, Detective."

Tears were now streaming uncontrollably down Fish's face.

"Fish, you're not crying, are you?" Hawk asked.

Fish turned to his partner, wiping his eyes.

"No, the helicopter kicked up a lot of dust."

"Sure, Fish, whatever you say." Hawk reached out his hand to Connor. "It's been an honor."

Caleb walked over to Connor.

"It's going to take some time to round up everyone involved, Connor, but I'm sure we'll get it done. The computer that was in Charles's office is a treasure trove of information about the entire project."

"That's great, Caleb."

"Are you sure you won't consider being a permanent consultant, Mr. Darke? You would be an asset to our team."

Caleb realized that Connor hadn't heard a single word he'd said. Connor turned and walked out of the door of the command center. Gertrude leaned over to Julie and spoke.

"Go after him, dear. You need to be with him."

Julie followed Connor at a brisk walking pace. She caught up, reached out her hand, and entwined her fingers with his. Connor looked at her and smiled. They walked together without saying a word. They entered the hangar that had been set up as a temporary triage center. Teams of doctors and nurses were moving in and out of the cordoned-off areas. Connor walked down the aisle and stopped. He drew back the curtain in front of him and entered with Julie, still holding his hand. There was a young teenager in the bed with thick, curly blonde hair. He walked over to the bed and stood quietly, looking at her. After a few moments, her eyes fluttered and opened. She looked at Connor and smiled.

"Thank you for listening."

"No thanks are needed."

"I wasn't sure anyone would hear me."

Connor Darke bent down and hugged the girl and began to sob. After a couple of minutes, he released her and stood up.

"I'm sorry that it took me so long to hear you."

"It's okay, Mr. Darke. I had faith in you."

Connor turned to Julie. "Julie, this is Cassandra Surley, the first girl and one of many who asked for my help."

"It's a pleasure to meet you, Cassandra," Julie said.

"You can call me Cassie, Doctor Strand."

"It is most certainly a pleasure to meet you, Cassie. I feel that I know so much about you."

"The pleasure is mine, Doctor Strand."

"Connor, why did my father do this to me?"

"I'm sorry I can't answer that."

"Is he here?"

"Yes"

"Can I see him?"

"I'm sure your uncle can arrange that."

"What will happen to him? Will he go to jail?"

"I can't honestly say, Cassie. I would expect he will endure some form of punishment."

"He has to Connor. He let my mother die. How could he do that? Didn't he know that we loved him?" Cassie began to cry.

Julie walked over to Cassie, pulled her close to her chest, and held her while she cried.

"I know it seems impossible at the moment, Cassie, but everything will be alright," Julie soothed.

After a few minutes, Cassie stopped crying and fell fast asleep. Julie eased Cassie's head back down on the pillow. Connor and Julie turned around and were staring straight at Gertrude Lane.

"Connor, it was a job well done."

"I never thought of it as a job, Gertrude. I think I've finally learned how to listen."

"Indeed, you did, Connor. You listened well." Gertrude looked in at the sleeping girl. "Poor thing, she will have a rough time of it."

"Thankfully, she's young and resilient. With help, she'll be able to get through it."

"I'm sure that she will, Connor."

"Julie, can I ask you something?"

"Of course you can, Mrs. Lane."

"Call me Gert, dear. I kind of like it."

"Gert it is. What do you want to know?"

"Can I host your wedding at my estate?"

Connor started to reply to Gert, but Julie pressed a finger to his lips.

"You know, Connor, it doesn't matter where I say yes since I already gave my heart to you. So, how about we make Gert happy?"

"I'm not going to win, am I?"

Just then, he could hear Cassie's voice in his head saying. "No, you're not."

Connor looked at Julie and smiled.

"Cassie agrees with you, Julie."

"It's settled, isn't it?"

"Yes, it is. It's time to start the next chapter of our life," Connor replied.

The End